# THE BLACK PHOENIX

# THE BLACK PHOENIX

## SELAH CHRONICLES

JEFF GRAHAM

**ARPress**
45 Dan Road Suite 5
Canton MA 02021

Hotline: 1(888) 821-0229
Fax:      1(508) 545-7580

Ordering Information:
Quantity sales. Special discounts are available on quantity purchases by corporations, associations, and others. For details, contact the publisher at the address above.

Printed in the United States of America.

| ISBN-13: | Softcover | 979-8-89356-105-0 |
| --- | --- | --- |
| | Hardcover | 979-8-89356-106-7 |
| | eBook | 979-8-89356-107-4 |

Library of Congress Control Number: 2024907145

# Table of Contents


**Chapter One:** "The story so far.".................................................................1

**Chapter Two:** Max and John Henry Watson are on patrol .......................8

**Chapter Three:** Waking up at Pete's .......................................................15

**Chapter Four:** Max goes to Reed's Church. .........................................22

**Chapter Five:** "We got a dead body in the dead cow compost pile.".........28

**Chapter Six:** "Home Sweet Home".........................................................38

**Chapter Seven:** "Treasure found in the Chicken coop." .......................45

**Chapter Eight:** Doctor Churchill has a car accident ............................49

**Chapter Nine:** "I just had the longest night."........................................56

**Chapter Ten:** Summer Vacation Seventy-Nine....................................61

**Chapter Eleven:** Mad dash and put on my Sunday best!......................64

**Chapter Twelve:** I wake up another time jump?....................................74

**Chapter Thirteen:** "Cow Poo is a natural skin moisturizer."..................76

**Chapter Fourteen:** "UFO Aliens are here, they ain't going anywhere. Get used to it."................................................................................................89

**Chapter Fifteen:** "The Gospel according to Paul" ................................91

**Chapter Sixteen:** "I am a Mystery wrapped in an Enigma. Something a conundrum?" ..............................................................................................97

**Chapter Seventeen:** Confessions at The Compost Pile.......................103

**Chapter Eighteen:** Personal Revelations .............................................105

**Chapter Nineteen:** One Big Dysfunctional Family.............................120

**Chapter Twenty:** "Who is your Daddy?".............................................122

**Chapter Twenty-one:** Family Drama ...................................................125

**Chapter Twenty-two:** Even Heroes get sick .......................................131

**Chapter Twenty-Three:** Then Came Suddenly........................137

**Chapter Twenty-four:** "OK I know who my Daddy is now what?" .......142

**Chapter Twenty-five:** "The Voices in my head are getting louder" .........147

**Chapter Twenty-Six:** "Choices" .....................................165

**Chapter Twenty-seven:** "This was your life" ........................175

**Chapter Twenty-eight:** Reality Check Praise The Lord ......................184

**Chapter Twenty-nine:** "Making the crooked path straight." ..................186

**Chapter Thirty:** "Nineteen Eighty-two" Jack purposes to Ruth Leann" .204

**Chapter Thirty-one:** "The Long Night"................................223

**Chapter Thirty-two:** Nineteen Ninety-Three ........................229

**Chapter Thirty-three:** WE ARE STILL HERE................................231

**Chapter Thirty-four:** SHOCK AND AWE................................237

**Chapter Thirty-five:** Here we go again ................................241


Black Phoenix Chronicles is the 2nd part of the series.
Please check my first book "The Max Faraday Chronicles"
if you haven't done so already.

# CHAPTER ONE
## "The story so far."

Who am I and why should you read my story? My name is Max Faraday. Nobody is going to believe me but here I am putting it all down on paper. I am a man of two presents or time periods. Forgive me this Sci-Fi stuff is new to me. A week or more ago I came home for my 1982 High School Reunion in July 2002. I was staying with my friend Jamie Scott and his family. They hate guns. On the way home from the Reunion we picked up his kids at the babysitters. The little girl gets out and bounces a ball and it fumbles out of her hands and rolls into the street.

Just as I was getting out, a car speeds up my instincts take over and I get her picked up and out of the way! I was then hit by the speeding car! Paralyzed or stunned, I then wake up in September of 1978! I am a Thirty-eight year old man in a fourteen year old body! I can't tell anyone, or they would lock me up that kid is crazy! I know I would.

So here I am Thirteen- Fourteen in the eighth grade all over again. I went to bed in 1978 and woke up in a coma in 2002.

I had friends come and visit me, but I could not move, they thought I was a vegetable.

My mind went back to 1978 and I learn to deal with my situation. Eventually I get out of the coma in 2002 and become a local County Police Officer. Getting the job was not that hard, I was an up-and-coming Detective in Chicago. Did I mention I did Black Ops in the CIA? Can't tell you much more than that, then I would have to kill you.

I am a Marine Core Mechanic to boot. Semper Fi. I may even be a Genetically Mutated Sleeper Agent for the CIA named Black Phoenix. I am still trying to figure that one out. "Stay tuned."

I have heard it said, "You show me your friends and I'll show you your future."

My Friends Paul Chapel and his wife Marcy are with me in both timelines. You can judge for yourself if Paul has grown up any. Paul is an Air Force Reservist and a full-time cartoonist for Wildtale Comics. He helps run the Chapel Family Farm on the side.

In 1978 he is just a kid like me trying to figure out life in general.

Steve Pearson Doctor of Psychiatry Stephen Pearson I should say is a genius know it all. He taught at The FBI for a while and now has multiple Best Seller self-help and do it yourself books and that damned biography. Home Hearth is his multimillion-dollar company. Amazing he started out as a foster kid who knew?

Kathy Chapel Pearson, his wife had Scoliosis as a kid. She had braces on everything we called her Lightning rod. She grew up and now she is District Attorney Lightning rod. No braces now she grew out of it I still call her lightning rod though.

Jason Cooper got in trouble and his dad had enough. Took down all his posters and painted his bedroom walls white and marked down every day till his son's eighteenth birthday. You are out of the house! Scared the crap out of him! By the time he graduated high school he had joined the Air Force and learned to use computers. He created a video game called Deer Crossing Alley Valley Highway. It becomes a hit! Jason enjoys the good life and comes back to our hometown to raise his kids and becomes a gym teacher.

Adam is a silent modest kid who never gets into trouble. So, we help him get in trouble. It is what friends do. Adam becomes a Detective in Seattle Washington how he ended up there I think he likes the coffee. He gets caught up as a bad cop and comes home with his tail between his legs. Steve helps him and hires him. Now he is Home Hearth's Decorator and head carpenter. He likes to shoot Bow and Arrow trick shooting as a hobby.

Dr. Dan Cottager my God he is such a klutz two left feet. How he became a doctor I don't know. I am thankful because he stays sober.

Dr. Churchill Smith on the other hand not so much. I shouldn't be so hard on Churchill because we are both going to a Twelve Step program in 2002.

Reed Jackson Redneck Fireman Country Music singer he sees UFO's Nuff said.

Peter Cortez in 1978, he is eight years old in the eighth grade a genius by any standards and me and Paul are his bodyguards. In 2002 he was the head Tech guy at Ice Works Industries. He owes me a few favors.

As a kid Jack Hammer was screwed up by his big brother Jake. It took some time but me and Jack have become good friends. Jack's wife Ruth died of cancer leaving him to raise three kids on his own. Sadly, Jack got lost in the bottle now he is trying to get his kids back. Getting his life together he leads The Twelve Step Program that me and Churchill go to.

Karl Ray Chambers K. Ray C. for short. I just found out he died of cancer. I never knew. Actually, maybe I didn't care. He was the kid that had a death wish. Jerk of a kid always getting into trouble. Was that his way of asking for help?

I have had to kill in my line of my work God and country and all. I accidentally killed a little girl who was a hostage I wish I could take that back. Maybe I can, I don't know?

Me and the guys are planning to hog tie K. Ray C. make him get a checkup. We are hoping they might find the cancer before it kills him. I hope so. He is, was a funny annoying guy. I miss him. My Mom is taking care of an old lady, Mrs. Horton. She has a Bad heart so while she is gone, I am staying with friends. I come from a big family I am the youngest. My mom Maxine Faraday loved me. My mom's husband Marcus Faraday, who may or may not be my father was an abusive alcoholic. Don't you even say, "Like father like son!" My Parents divorced when I was eleven. So, for the most part I have been raised by a single mother. She remarried after I joined The Marines. She died a few years later. She smoked died of lung cancer she would have been Seventy-five.

Officer John Henry Watson is my partner in my investigation. Whoever tried to run over Jamie's little girl has a bad history and a drug smuggling ring. Their Nitro rocket cars leave dead deer all over the highway. That is how we found our first piece of evidence.

Jamie and his family are in a safe house now. Me and John Henry Watson are looking for a Mystery Man. My old CIA partner Agent Badger has helped me in my investigation.

I don't think I can trust him.

Top it all off every now and again I have this guy in a black robe that looks like Moses "Bridge." He is all powerful He may be all seeing he can go Forward and back in time! Funny thing is he is a fictional Character in Wildtale Comics.

Friday October 13th, 1978, I wake up at Churchill's "I feel lucky." At lunch time we go over the check list. After lunch Reed comes up to me and asks, "Hey, would you like to go to my church?" The question makes me pause because I have been to his church as a child before and I hated it. Reed's Tact hasn't changed much as he has gotten older. Don't you want to go to Heaven? Before I know it, I say Sure I'll go with you to your church on Sunday. Reed says Sure we'll pick you up, I ride the church bus with my Dad we will be there to pick you up 8:30-9:00.

After School "Me and The Guys hog tie K. Ray C. and take him to the hospital."

There he is walking home from school. The nice thing is K. Ray C. is a loner so we can get him all by himself quite nicely. Slowly we creep behind him into Paul's pickup truck just waiting for the right moment. Just then the truck backfires and it sets everyone off like a starters pistol! K. Ray turns around to see what all the noise is and that is all he sees. A pillowcase covers most of his face! What is happening?! Tie his legs and arms down! He yells "Help stop!" This is crazy! Shut him up! I got Duct tape! Damn something smells! Paul yells K. Ray did you shit your pants! AH! We didn't plan for this. I don't think I have enough Duct tape for that. Paul yells back There ain't enough Duct tape in the world to cover up that! Just tie him down and load him in the truck Lets GO! We are off to the Hospital!

When we get there the doctors and nurses are ready for K. Ray. And sedate him.

Paul says as they are taking him away If you need a stool or urine samples you can get it from his underwear. He let it rip on the way here!

Elsewhere Dr. Sam sits Dale and his wife Faith Chapel down in his office, he has some bad news to give. Faith the test results have come back you have Bone Cancer.

Oh, dear Jesus she prays! Dale pleads to Sam, "what can we do?" Sam assures me I have already set up appointments. We fight this for all we have in us. We start on our knees. We do the tests we do the research. And we ask The Good Lord Jesus Christ for a miracle. Sam, Dale, and Faith come together in one accord uniting in prayer. Outside Sam's office Dr. Churchill Smith watches and then walks away.

We wait in the waiting room as they begin tests. Dr. Churchill Smith Sr. comes out and says Hey I would just like to let you know guys I am proud of you for what you did. It takes a lot of love to do what you just did. Churchill jr. asks How long till we know? A while son. We can take it from here thanks again guys. Reed says Love. All I wanted to do was be part of tying him up, and now He thinks I love the guy?

Tests are done and Dr. Smith talks with K. Ray's mother. It will take a while before the tests come back. Mrs. Chambers asks Doctor what should I do for my son? Dr. Smith notices a tiny gold cross around her neck saying I am not a man of faith, but if I was prayer might help. If you would like to pray with someone. With tears she agrees, and Dr. Smith leaves and comes back with Dr. Sam. Mrs. Chambers is livid Get him out of my sight you get him out of my sight! Dr. Smith says Your son could be dying of Cancer I suggested you could pray for him, and would you like to have someone pray with you? So, I get Dr. Sam. I will not have a Buddhist or whatever Vietnamese pray for my son!

Sam exclaims I am a Christian! Mrs. Chambers yells My brother died in Vietnam killed by The VC I will not let that touch my boy! Dr. Sam exclaims The VC killed my family too! Mrs. Chambers replies, "You are all the same!" Dr. Smith shouts Silence and stares at Dr. Sam and he leaves. With clinched teeth Dr. Smith tries to get a hold of the situation I am sorry I did not know please forgive me. Mrs. Chambers replies I will not let my son be touched by that man. Dr. Smith confirms Then you have already signed your son's death certificate. Because one of his specialties is cancer treatment and the prevention of it. When I and other doctors are out playing golf, he is looking researching studying looking for doctors who are experts in the field of medicine. Do you know Dale Chapel? Yes, He was an Air Force Pilot in The Vietnam war? His wife has bone cancer, and he is their doctor. You think you are the only one who lost someone to the Vietcong? Dale lost his brother. We left a lot of good people back there! Sam lost his whole family because they would not join the VC! We left a lot of good people back there.

Mrs. Chambers takes her son home and Dr. Smith and Dr. Sam talk. How can Mrs. Chambers call herself a Christian and hate you because you are Vietnamese? Dr. Sam answers Because she is ignorant and right now still full of hate. How it is an agnostic is such an expert on Christianity? Dr. Smith answers, "I just don't know sometimes." Jesus Christ, I like at times. But it is his so-called people that tick me off. Max and my son, Paul, and the boys coming together to help that boy. I love those boys, Sam, I really do. Dr. Sam smiles saying God is not looking for perfection he is looking for those who are willing.

I go to Mrs. Horton's, and I see her sitting in her chair. She wakes up as I enter. She asks, "How is Dr. Smith? I answer He thinks the world of you. She smiles saying Well I think the world of him, he is a good doctor he cares so much for people he just does not always know how to show it. How could he be around you for so long and not be touched by God through you? Mrs. Horton lets tears flow as she speaks. I would like to think he was touched by God through me. I guess it is like there is a vacuum when I was in the house, he is thankful for everything, but he never thanked God for it. She adds I tried in the beginning to say prayers with the children but Churchill Sr.'s father was bound to separate himself from God. Why did God let this happen I suppose. The children needed a mother figure and for the most part my children were grown. I would like to say I set a good example for them; in the end they have to make their own choices in life Max. You are such a good friend and example to Churchill he is a little bit slow. I pray he will make Jesus his choice. I gave Mrs. Horton a hug and say goodbye.

I spend the night at Pete's His parents speak only Spanish in the house as a rule. He is a gifted little guy so I will give him that. He reads college textbooks and speaks in three and is working on for languages already. His father studied in the States with Mr. Cooper. When Dr. Churchill and Mr. Cooper had the crazy idea of setting up a Local radio FM station in our little town Pete's dad was the first guy Mr. Cooper called. Pete's Dad runs it now and in the 80's they will work on setting up a Cable TV network. A part of me can't wait for MTV and CNN.

# CHAPTER TWO
## "Max and John Henry Watson are on patrol"

Monday July 29, 2002, I wake up not knowing what happened to K. Ray C. So, I get dressed and head to the police station early, yet I have a feeling there is something I have to check out at the High School. A History Rewrite at The High school library, it is now called The K. Ray C. & Wendy Pearson Memorial library. I ask in a whisper, "What was it all worth? Bridge stops time around me and says What was it worth? What is one's life worth? Yeah, that is my question What was it worth? We hogtied him so he could get to the hospital and get a checkup. It would be nice to see him alive and well annoying us like he used to. Bridge reminds Perhaps you have forgotten the song "Thanks for the gift." Thanks for The Gift? I know you will give me strength to carry on. There have been good and bad times in all it's been fun. Although I miss Him already, and He hasn't been gone long. I'll miss holding His hands, giving him a hug, and the day will come I will see him in Eternity. Thanks for The Gift. That little three-year-old child did more in teaching love than a healthy person can do living to one hundred.

Bridge asks Why was it so hard to get him to the hospital? Max Sheepishly replies Because he didn't care if he lived or died. Bridge says Then give him a reason so next time you won't have to hogtie him.

But the Memorial? Does not have the date that he died. I look at it and if you look at it is blurry? What does it mean? Bridge puts his hand on my shoulder saying Could mean many things child.

You are not meant to know. He could still survive the Cancer. The future, the past in this case is in a flux to your eyes.

Let me ask you, would you treat K. Ray C. any less or more if you knew he was going to live or die? I don't know. Then let time pass as you have a child and pray for guidance.

Now go to work, you are a protector of the innocent.

As I walk to the parking lot, I see The Cavanaugh City Sheriff drop off his son at the High School. That guy could be the one who tipped off The Mystery Man where Jamie and his family were? As I pass him, I nod my head and say I'll be seeing you, Sheriff.

He just smiles as I walk by and waves back at me. It just burns me! That guy could have tipped off the Mystery Man that almost got Jamie killed and I can't do anything about it till he slips up again and I catch him. He has a son going to the school that he helps supplies drugs too. As I enter the Carter County Police Station Chief Tom says "You are a little late this morning? I replied I was Remembering an old friend and felt nostalgic. It was not my intension to be late, I was asking myself and God What was it worth at the time?

"Morning Briefing" I come into the briefing room with mixed feelings, and I see my partner John Henry Watson and I sit down next to him. Police Chief Tom starts talking and I kinda drift off in thought. I put on my Carter County Police uniform this morning and it feels different, I guess. I wore the uniform of a U.S. Marine and then the suit and dark sunglasses of a CIA agent and the black jumpsuit of my Black Ops and I still don't know about Black Phoenix? My ears perk up with We have a new "Rookie" in our midst "Wink" stand up Officer Max Faraday. I stand up. Say a little about yourself.

Well, I joined the Marines after High school. Someone yells Semper Fi! I joined the CIA did sometime in The New York P.D. Went back to the CIA then Joined the Chicago P.D.

Ah somewhere in there I ran security for Counting Tornadoes and here I am with you.

Dead silence so I sat down. Chief Tom Finishes his briefing with You be careful out there.

They laugh at the car as John Henry gets in the so-called old Police cruiser. Hey, you laugh now, but this old! I pat him on the back whispering Down boy, remember we are here to keep secrets. He gets in the driver's seat. "Max and John Henry Watson are on patrol." As we leave the station John reaches into his CD collection and puts in a CD of Hank Williams Jr. I comment You like Hank? John says Paul got me on him. Those farmers love their country music. You come in their yard with Rap or Motown, and they will shoot you on sight. Hank Williams Jr. I am one of the boys who really got a good suntan.

"Music If you don't like Hank Williams, you can Kiss our Ass." comes out of the speakers. The car has a good sound system, I think we will keep it.

Bank robbery comes over the radio. Let's move it! Another car calls in and identifies that it will intercept. John Henry calls Backup and is on the way and turns on the siren! Without stealth mode the cruiser handles just like an ordinary car. John says Push the button. I reply It is tempting, but we have to wait for the right time. He looks at me Time my ass we have too intercept! Over the radio the officer describes shots being fired from the Bank robbers! The Officer calls Where is that backup?! So, I open the glove box and push the damn button!

Everything goes quietly except for the blaring siren, and we accelerate at speed!

The pursuing police cruiser is taking fire. We can now see bullet hole through the windshield and radiator steam and smoke begins to shoot out of the engine.

A few seconds later we can see a fire coming out of the hood! John Yells over the radio Larry get that car off the road and get out NOW! Larry pulls over. I turn around to see him get out, as I turn forward, I see in the rear view mirror the car explodes!

After the explosion we slowed down, The Bank robbers are almost a half mile ahead and John realizes this ramming the accelerator to the floor! Causing the car to rise in the front! "Can you justify a high-speed car chase?" The robbers swerve in and out of lanes trying to cause accidents to slow us down God only knows about stray bullets and that is not counting the police car on fire that we left behind. We are getting close, and it is a straight road ahead and no oncoming traffic. Thank God! I see a passenger get out of the window and start shooting! The bullets strike the windshield, and it takes a second to realize we are bullet proof! John Henry yells, "We are bullet proof!"

The shock does not register as we continue to increase speed and ram the back of the bank robber's car! The Passenger with the gun loses his balance and falls rolling ass over teakettle! John puts on the breaks and we skid doing a donut on the highway!

The robber's car swerves from side to side, and we see a tire blow! Causing it to lose control and hit the ditch on the left then flip and comes upside down in a hay field! More Carter County Police arrive, and the scene is under control. I go to the Passenger with the gun he is dead, twisted body with a head that kissed the pavement. John goes for the driver. His body was out of the car it flew out when the car hit the ditch and went out the sunroof like a rocket with the rubber gasket of the sunroof as proof around his waist!

Chief Tom comes by bringing coffee and says to me This was just your first day, just wait for tomorrow. John comes to us and asks How is Larry? Tom replies Shook up but, ok, how are you? About the same. And you Max? I nod in agreement. Tom looks at our car. Bent up your fender a bit. No bullet holes? Write it up they lost control in your pursuit. Oh and one thing since you are not going to be buying gas at the "Quick Gas and Save" you can buy the donuts with the gas card. Officially it will be on the books as a gas purchase, but who has to know. Good work you two. I look at John and wonder How does he know about the car?

After we made our reports and done our paperwork, we decided to checkout Deer Crossing Alley Valley Highway. John is too quiet on our patrol. Having a car chase can do that, I guess. I see an Amish horse and buggy and remember I brought my own CD's To get the mood to change I put my Weird Al CD in and Amish Paradise comes out the speakers. I point out Right there is where we picked up the car's glass and paint chips.

John shakes his head. The first thing I did when I went on patrol in this county was hit a deer just down the road from here. I replied, "Yeah I get that a lot."

Lunch with Sheriff Tom, Tom is sitting at a booth with a paper in one hand and a coffee and donut in the other. How did you know about the car? Tom replies "Your friend is Ralph Shurlow." Yeah. Paul showed me Big Bertha. The retired Sheriff of Lincoln County and I sometimes play golf. It might be a good idea to park the car at The Chapel's farm. At some point some of the officers were wondering how you got to the chase in such quick time. John says I was driving I got carried away, that car can move. Tom comments Yeah after you got Fire chief Jackson's truck shot up you needed wheels of your own.

After lunch we drive around the countryside, I can really see the difference the years can make. Family farms that have gone out and the mega farms that have taken their place.

Off in the distance I can see parachutes dropping and say Someday I have got to do that.

John says You would never get me to do that I am keeping my feet on the ground.

We get out and the kids are playing cowboys and Indians or something and hay harvest is going on. The Semi Big Bertha comes in with a load and I wave the driver down. Mind if I pop the hood? The driver looks around and Paul is nearby, and he nods his head, and the driver pulls the lever that pops the hood. John's eyes go wide as he looks at the perpetual motion device. Paul adds Yeah, I'm going to give the old girl a new paint job when the harvest is over. When she is not running the fields, she is plugged in and helping on the electric bill. Paul asks us, "What are you kids doing?" Oh, I thought I would show John Big Bertha. The hood goes back down and the truck rumbles on. Paul continues Yeah, the trick is to get the sound and shake just right so you don't think there is anything funny about it. You don't want to draw attention to yourself. Paul points to one of his kids quoting the T-shirt.

"Just because you can glow in the dark does not necessarily mean you should."

John scratches his head Yeah, we know that any chance we could park the cruiser here?

Paul says Oh sure I can always plug in another vehicle in. We both look at Paul Another Vehicle?

Heck yeah My farm is hooked up to Ice Works Power line at Pete's place down the road.

I have Big Bertha My John Deere four-wheel drive and my pickup. Dusty is working on making a Combine for The Shurlow farm and after he makes them one, he'll make one for me. Dope smoking tree huggers think they know it all.

I wave goodbye saying Thanks Paul we will be in touch.

Dinner at John Henry's Connie has dinner made for us when we arrive.

Their children are still at summer camp, and it hits me when I see the pictures on the refrigerator that if me and Kate Dent were married and able to have kids our kids would be about the same age. Connie asks, "Is there any chance you could do a special for this Sunday at my church? At The Cavanaugh City Baptist? Yeah. I am in charge of Specials this month and I just had a cancellation. Seams their family is in witness protection or something. "Jamie and Ellen." By the way how are they? I have not heard to tell you the truth, we are not taking any chances. Connie puts her hands on her hips stating I understand the problem, what I have is I need a special,

I would do it myself, but I was asked to be in the nursery and help keep an eye on Junior church. Does it matter what I play? Not God gave Rock and Roll to you please. No. Too many little old ladies would have a heart attack. I was thinking You could sing and I could play for you. Can you sing "There is more woman than anyone can take away?" I guess we are progressive enough to let it slip by at our church. Ok I'll put us down.

# CHAPTER THREE
## "Waking up at Pete's"

SATURDAY October 14th, 1978, As I wake up at Pete's I put on my clothes and head for home the grass has got to be mowed. Mr. McGraw has moved more of his Mr. Smith's Lawn Care Perfection equipment into our garage. I find my old lawnmower and I check the gas and oil and start it up and start cutting grass. I missed it last week with all that has been going on in my life between this life and the one I have in the future or is it the present, I don't know any more?

Before Noon a police car pulls up and Mr. McGraw gets out and looks at the lawn.

I shut off the lawn mower to be polite and listen. I was going to mow your lawn today for you, but you already have it done. I replied back Yeah, I hated to let it go, I have been staying with friends while mom is taking care of Mrs. Horton. Mr. McGraw states, "You did a fine job too you sure I can't hire you fulltime?"

I would have done it myself, but I have been getting so many jobs I have had to turn some away.

I reply Well Saturdays and Sundays are my usual days off?

Mr. McGraw agrees "Me too I would never work on a Sunday."

Any chance you would like to work for me today?

Well, I was supposed to meet with my mom for lunch, let me talk to her and I'll find you and let you know.

I find Mom making lunch at Mrs. Horton's Max be quiet Mrs. Horton is resting. I lower my head and whisper "It is not going to be much longer is it, Mom?"

Mom whispers back No honey, I took her to the doctor's office and Dr. Smith wants to have an operation, he thinks he can do some procedure. Oh mom, I got up early and mowed the lawn at home and Mr. McGraw asked me if I could work for him.

That was so good of you honey, Could you do Mrs. Horton's I mean it has been almost three weeks. The last time she had it done it was what's his name's lawn care it was not a very good job. I can ask. OK I'll make you some lunch and you can go to work for Mr. McGraw.

After lunch as I run to catch up with Mr. McGraw, I find him a couple blocks from Mrs. Horton's. He is about to start mowing and he sees me and asks, "Well can I offer you a job?"

I guess for Saturdays at least. Any Chance I can do Mrs. Horton's?

Sure, I have the spare already to go. Here is a list of places to go.

They are all new for me. I ask, "Is this place new for you? Yeah Why? It is not on the list. See look at the house number, it is the house next door.

Mr. McGraw puts his head down, I hate to say it Max, you just saved me some embarrassment.

Sometimes my eyes, I can't see straight even with my thick glasses.

Numbers and letters get blurry my wife does the books and. She usually shows me around, so I know which house to go to. She got the call last night and wrote it down.

Sympathetic to the situation I say Listen I'll go get the other lawnmower and I'll be around.

He lifts his head, tries to smile and asks, "You know where these houses are right?"

Yeah, I had a paper rout years ago, so I know pretty much where everybody used to live.

Mr. McGraw asks Years ago used to live?

I don't know how to answer that, so I just head home to get the other lawnmower.

As I am about to finish with Mrs. Horton's yard, she comes out I turn the mower off to hear her and she says you have done a fine job Max it looks wonderful.

Thanks. She asks, "Did I ever tell you why I chose to live next to a funeral home?"

No, I don't think you did. It is because in my day my father said it was not proper for a lady to drive herself. You see I am the youngest in my family and they have all died. I did not want to be a bother to ask anyone for a ride to the funeral parlor so when this house came up for sale, I bought it. Max ponders I don't know what to say so I say, "That was very practical."

Really, if I could do it over again, I would rather drive a car than be so lady-like.

I respond So what are you saying Blame everything that is wrong in the world on our fathers?

No child, it is amazing how God can use people for his will. How?

He allows us to go through things so we can share what God has brought us through so we can show God's love to others. As your friend says it Sometimes, we are the only Bible people will ever read. Our life's experiences are gospels unto themselves.

I admit Yeah right, your father kept you from driving, and my father called me bastard we are really relating. She shakes her head stating the pain you suffered has helped you touch others with God's love with your testimony. Well, that testimony came at a cost.

A cost none greater that what Christ paid at the Cross. I pray that you and Marcus will be Father and son someday, maybe not today but someday. I say Don't hold your breath.

She reminds me Max I am not long for this world, but you are, and I hope you will find love for your father because there is no real life with hate in you, you just exist. God wants you to have life more abundant. I could not deal with the life you have lived; I am so thankful Jesus has been there for you through the hard times and has carried you.

Thank you, Max! There are lives you touch every day that I could not touch.

We are made different and special because he loves and wants us to show his love through us, even through our pain.

I don't know what to say, I hate the way she is so right.

I have been there and seen children that have been abused and shared my history.

I would rather have a nice family with a white picket fence and a little dog. But that is not what I had is it. She looks at me then asks, "Do you think I could drive your lawnmower?" It takes a few minutes to give her the pointers and I set her in the right direction, and she is off. I walk beside her and keep a close eye on her. My mom comes out and nearly has another heart attack.

"Max get her off that thing!" I reach in to slow it down and take it out of gear.

Mrs. Horton is so cute explaining Oh Maxine I was just having a little fun.

Mom says Max. What am I going to do with the both of you?

Mrs. Horton puts her hands on her hips and says Well as for me I won't be around much longer, I would kiss Max and keep him, he is an angel.

Dusk comes and we put the lawnmowers away Mr. McGraw hands me a Fifty and says good work. I respond, "Oh Mr. McGraw that is not a twenty, this is too much." You earned it, Any chance I could get you to work for me after school? No, I have a job at the C. Connection. If I don't lose it for taking another night off that is. But if you are looking for help, I may be able to help you find some.

I have dinner at Mrs. Horton's and spend the night there.

I call Reed Jackson and tell him to pick me up here.

TUESDAY July 30, 2002 Deer Crossing Alley Valley Highway.

We travel up and down Deer Crossing Alley Highway Carter County covers a good part of it, I doubt if the sum of our investigation begins and ends here.

We start canvassing house to house from the South to the North.

People who are home have little if anything to say.

A few might Yeah late at night here they come whoosh out of nowhere.

Any particular day? Fridays and Wednesdays usually but sometimes they skip a day I think? But everyone had to say "Well Somebody should do something, they leave dead deer all over on the highway."

Along the way we pulled over several speeders I mean we are police officers we have to do our job. Going over forty five is a bit dangerous in these woods.

The Final Stop of the day is The last house that is on the border of Carter County and James County line. Someone is home and We go through the questions this time we get a lead. What date did you say? Friday July 12, 2002?

Well didn't you know there was a hit and run earlier that night in James County?

That happened North of here about ten miles. Do you know if there was any witnesses?

Lightning fast car hit that damn Stealth jogger. Wearing nothing but black jogging suit at night some damn people. Thanks for your help We'll look into it.

"Well Somebody should do something, they leave dead deer all over on the highway."

As we drive back I say to John I think we should switch to nights.

Yeah right. You and me doing nights. "I think he is being sarcastic."

Oh look there is a good place to park where we can wait for them to drive by and catch them running drugs.

"Yep sarcastic."

When I get home Max the dog is waiting for me along with notes in my mailbox of people telling me my dog should be tied up or put in a chain link fence kennel.

I check my voice mail. Hey Max this is Jason me and my Dad have been drawing up plans for turning the barn into a bed and breakfast. Give me a call when we can get in touch.

Then it hit me, I remember our conversation when we were looking for the deer.

Big Paul mutters Ah damn that had to be a ten point or at least a twelve-point buck!

Churchill declares "You are crying because there is a dead dear."

Paul yells back, "Well if the Midnight Stealth jogger that wears nothing but a black sweat suit you would say he was stupid son of a-."

The good doctor stops him by saying "Only if I was drinking, I try not to swear when I am sober. "

I gotta call Paul.

Hi Paul, remember our conversation when we were looking for the deer?

Word for word or in general? The Stealth Jogger! Yeah, what about it?

Where did you hear or read about it?

Oh it was in the paper I think the 13th. Hit and run. Why?

I wonder if our guy hit him before he hit the deer.

Paul replies, "Damn, that boy was busy that night."

Do you still have the paper? Somewhere? Can I have it?

Sure. But you can check it out on the Paper's web site. Thanks Paul.

# CHAPTER FOUR
## "Max goes to Reed's Church."

SUNDAY October 15th, 1978, I wake up early and get dressed and the bus picks me up to go to Reed's church. It is filled with poor kids and some of their mothers. And a few Holier than thou people who think they are doing God's will by not driving a car on Sunday. Reed smiles and says I have saved a seat just for you.

I don't say it out loud Oh Kay Lord what have you gotten me into now?

The bus is near full the kids somewhat happy to be going. I think it is because they are getting out of the house.

We pick up The Thomson family little Jimmy is somewhat cleaned up. His father is staggering over a hangover and his mother is wearing sunglasses.

They sit near the front. Reed asks Is it wrong to hate Max and be a Christian? I ask What or Who do you hate? Reed explains How can a person let their kid go to school or church and not take good care of them? How can an adult who sees what we see continue and not say anything? I nod in agreement saying I know what you mean Reed, If I knew Jimmy was going to be riding the bus I might have brought a sandwich for him. Wendy and I sometimes do that when his mom doesn't make him breakfast. Reed agrees Yeah I ride the bus and I might only see him here on the church bus but still something ain't right. Thank God my Dad has been off the bottle for almost a year. I don't say it, I look at him in the back of the bus and I think to myself that you know of. We arrive at the Church and we are herded in like cattle with a few God bless you for coming.

"Sunday School Class" I want a lobotomy I will spare you the details. After Sunday School We are driven to the front of the church. Where we sing from the hymnal book led by a quire that sings off key. Reed tries to sing along and for his sake I'll go along with it I mean this is Reed Jackson for him this is him really trying. We used to be enemies and here we are in church. The Lord works in mysterious ways. Someday he will know better right now instead of being washed and bathed in The Blood of The Lamb he is Washed in Vinegar and bathed in Formaldehyde is what all he knows. God Help him.

This and shoving me and other Catholics Why is Marry crying? Tracts is keeping him out of trouble? If I were him I would be asking for my offering money back, but that is just me. The sermon is, I don't know because I am too busy looking for exits signs and I am stuck in the middle and I can't get out. Would God consider it a sin to say I had to go to the bathroom and I didn't really have to go in this church? The Preacher is preaching fire and brimstone and the guy who really needs to hear it Jimmy's dad who is fast asleep two rows back and I can hear him snore.

"John the Baptist" now he could preach. I open my Bible to Matthew 3:1 ¶ In those days came John the Baptist, preaching in the wilderness of Judaea,

2 And saying, Repent ye: for the kingdom of heaven is at hand.

3 For this is he that was spoken of by the prophet Esaias, saying, the voice of one crying in the wilderness, prepare ye the way of the Lord, make his paths straight.

4 And the same John had his raiment of camel's hair, and a leathern girdle about his loins; and his meat was locusts and wild honey.

"Wow That is like a biker with a leather jacket."

5 Then went out to him Jerusalem, and all Judaea, and all the region round about Jordan.

6 And were baptized of him in Jordan, confessing their sins.

7 ¶ But when he saw many of the Pharisees and Sadducees-

"Like the guy in font of me preaching fire and brimstone."

-come to his baptism, he said unto them, O generation of vipers, who hath warned you to flee from the wrath to come?

8 Bring forth therefore fruits meet for repentance:

9 And think not to say within yourselves, we have Abraham to our father: for I say unto you, that God is able of these stones to raise up children unto Abraham.

10 And now also the axe is laid unto the root of the trees: therefore, every tree which bringeth not forth good fruit is hewn down and cast into the fire.

11 I indeed baptize you with water unto repentance: but he that cometh after me is mightier than I, whose shoes I am not worthy to bear: he shall baptize you with the Holy Ghost, and with fire:

12 Whose fan is in his hand, and he will throughly purge his floor, and gather his wheat into the garner; but he will burn up the chaff with unquenchable fire.

13 ¶ Then cometh Jesus from Galilee to Jordan unto John, to be baptized of him.

14 But John forbad him, saying, I have need to be baptized of thee, and comest thou to me?

15 And Jesus answering said unto him, Suffer it to be so now: for thus it becometh us to fulfil all righteousness. Then he suffered him.

16 And Jesus, when he was baptized, went up straightway out of the water: and, lo, the heavens were opened unto him, and he saw the Spirit of God descending like a dove, and lighting upon him:

17 And lo a voice from heaven, saying, this is my beloved Son, in whom I am well pleased.

Reed's dad is an usher and taps Jimmy's dad on the shoulder to wake him up. He and another usher asked him to get up please. Mr. Thomson gets up and they go outside.

After the service I look out the window and I look outside in the parking lot Mr. Thomson is banged up My guess an attitude adjustment. Little Jimmy has filled up cookies and juice and is sporting a grape juice mustache. He is happy singing Jesus loves the little children. I see Reed's Dad rubbing his knuckles looking out at Mr. Thomson. I wonder if he is reflecting on the reality, he used to be Mr. Thomson, the only difference is his wife Mrs. Jackson had enough and left.

I get this feeling. Go to the pastor's office now. I really don't know what it is, I have had similar feelings like this before, I have found it is good to trust them. As I go to the pastor's office, I find the door is locked, I turn the knob anyway and it opens for me. I walk in and I feel the need to open a drawer? I do, what I find is Filth of pornography! This guy is sick. I open a closet; I find a box I pick it up and put it on the desk more of the same. I feel the need to leave, and I do, it is like nobody sees me?

The hallway is full, yet I walk out of there and nobody notices me.

I look back and see one of the deacons saying I need to get something in the Pastor's office. He gets a key out and he unlocks the door, and he goes in. He yells Holy SHIT! The talking and the conversations that were going on in the hallways became silent. The Pastor leaves his post where he was shaking hands to see what is going on? I head out the door I am tempted to stay, yet I feel it is necessary for me to put some distance between me and there. A bunch of us are back at the bus waiting for the driver. I wonder what is going on? People start asking aloud.

The Thomson family gets on Mr. Thomson is quietly muttering We are never coming back to this church again. This makes Jimmy start to cry thinking, "What did I do wrong?"

I see Mr. Thomson get out of his seat just about to strike Jimmy. Reed's dad says Sit down and shut up. He sits down. Reed asks, "What happened Dad?" The father says We will talk about it when we get home. The stern look makes

Reed sit down face front and I don't think he said anything the whole ride home.

After the poor kids get off the bus the holier than thou talk amongst themselves.

I know my little girl wants to invite them all over to the house to play, I just don't know. And I don't want that in my house.

"The Phrase When Bad Christians happen to good people repeats in my head."

When I get to Mrs. Horton's Mom is there to greet me when I get off the bus How was church? After lunch I tell my sorted details leaving out the preacher with the porno problem. Mom says Well it was nice of you to be good enough to go to his church when he asked. Mom leaves and Mrs. Horton says You didn't tell your mom everything.

I admit I am a little bit perplexed about it myself. Mrs. Horton smiles You listened to The Holy Spirit child. Yeah, but why didn't anybody else listen and do what I did? She explains I am sure some were called, but few of you, my child listened. Some would have taken the moment to show others how holy they are. Some who knew looked the other way thinking He isn't doing anything I have not already done. Some who knew might have thought it is not my business what he does in privet. Some would say I don't know, and I don't want to know. Some might have thought He is the Pastor I have no authority to question him. Some may have even said to themselves it is not very polite to go in to the pastor's office like that.

One who cares not what others might think, who has ears to hear, oh the Devil be warned what God can do with those who are willing. Be warned Max the Devil is angered by what you have done and the stand you have taken.

I say, "Bring it on."

This warning makes her take notice at me Max Satan will bring down all Hell around you.

Hell, I say, "Been there, done that, and it didn't impress me much and I kicked his ass on the way out."

I leave Mrs. Horton and go for a walk. I come back to Mrs. Horton's and My mom says Connie called and asked if you wanted to come over and spend the night and practice piano and basketball? So, I gather my things and I spend the night at Connie's. Mrs. Mack calls to us and says, "Come on kids it is time to go to church."

They are Baptists.

When we get to their church I sit with Mr. Mack and Connie, Mrs. Mack is up front playing the piano. After a couple of the Hymns are sung, she begins playing the piano as she worships God in music. The beauty that comes from the music begins to wash over us and I can just imagine the filth that I had witnessed today floating away because it cannot be in His presence.. I just soaked it in. As she finishes and they take up the offering I lean over and ask Connie. Do you think you or me will ever be able to play like that?

Connie does not answer me back and maybe I should not have asked the question and just let it all soak in.

After the service. "Ice Cream"

The Macks do not watch TV very much, and if they do it is usually sports like Basketball. And since there is no "Basketball" tonight we are playing it out on their driveway court. Later We come in the home and Connie begins to practice her piano performance for the upcoming recital. I never made it to the Recital. Originally, I was still pretty beat up by Jack's brother's gang. So here I am getting a second chance.

Mrs. Mack asks, "Have you prepared a piece?" I say, "Oh sure I am just figuring out if it is the one I want to use or not."

"Well, why don't you play it." Connie says with a big smile, "Yes, let's hear it. She gets off the bench. I opened my big mouth now I have to perform, And I sit down and play "Ebony and Ivory." When I finish Mrs. Mack says It is not a classic, but I like it. Do you have anything more original?

# CHAPTER FIVE

## "We got a dead body in the dead cow compost pile."

WEDNESDAY 31, 2002

The more me and John go over the evidence we find the Dirty Little Secret is Cavanaugh City and Deer Crossing Alley Highway is the Crossroads of drugs traffic. John gets a call on his cell phone while we are on morning patrol. Hello? Duke what is happening? Off the record? Yeah, I can come by your place I guess "off the record." Be there in five. I asked, "Who was that?" Oh, Paul set me up with him, Duke has a dairy farm and I buy some of my meat from him. Organically grown no artificial nothing, good milk too. So, what is the problem? I don't know he didn't say.

We see Duke on his Four-wheeler and he motions us to follow him. Back into the fields.

John carries on Yeah Duke lets me hunt in his woods snowmobile in the winter I can go anywhere on a snowmobile. Duke gets off the bike and says, "You gotta see this."

We get out. What we see is a human body half buried in the compost pile..

I open the trunk getting out the kit and put on the gloves the body is a bit decomposed, my guess is this is our missing man. John says Ah Max you think this is who I think it is?

I get tweezers pulling a piece of bandanna out of his nose and I say I think we have a match. John asks Duke, "what is this?" Duke answers Compost, I put my dead cows and old feed when it goes bad out here. John mutters Ah damn Duke there are dead cows in here? Duke replies Hate to see them die but they make good compost. Jokingly John asks, "You didn't put this guy in here, did you?"

Duke jokingly replies No this is three-year-old shit, this poor son of a bitch is too fresh. If I was to bury him, I would have put him over there, where the fresh is.

John asks me, "Who do we call on this? I mean if this got out, we would stir up something."

I agree Yeah, I would like to keep the Mystery Man thinking we are just spinning our wheels if we can? Duke asks What is going on? We give Duke the long and short of it.

Elsewhere Churchill goes back to The Hospital It has been the time allowed off prescribed by "Dr. Sam." Dan says Great to have you back. Churchill replies I have gone almost a week without having a drink and Candy and I might actually have a chance. Dan encourages. Hey that is great. Over the intercom Dr. Smith, you are wanted on the telephone. Who could that be? He is handed a phone at the front desk. Hello? Max, what's up? You're kidding right? Can I get time off to see the body? Dan's eyes go big when he hears the word body. Give me a minute. Churchill whispers Dan they think they have the body of the guy who hit that deer? Dan asks, "Can't they call a coroner?" Dr. Smith gives a dumb look. Just Go I'll cover for you.

After explaining the situation Duke says Damn. "Well, somebody should do something; they leave dead deer all over on the highway." I call Paul and Marcy next Marcy comes out to Paul's garage yelling! Max & John Henry found a dead body in Duke's dead cow composting pile! Paul mutters I told him not to put hitchhikers in his compost pile, that is the first place they will look. Marcy slaps him upside his back because she is too short to reach his head, Paul Stop that, this is no place for such foolishness. By the time they get to Duke's Chief Tom is here in plain clothes.

Holding his nose Churchill says We have to get the body stored in a cold place now!

As we look at the body, I see something familiar from the file that we have on the suspect.

I recognize the tattoo I really think this is him. Paul waves the stinky air away and says Bag him up and you can store him at my place I have a walk-in freezer. I am going to have to get a case of Arm & Hammer for the freezer though for the damn smell.

I ask Where did you get a walk-in freezer? Paul answers, "I got it from the school before they tore it down, I got it out in the shed." On the really hot days I have gone in there to cool off.

Tom says I hate to say it, but I agree, let's take it there if we bring a body anyplace else, we will raise suspicion. Churchill adds I'll go back to the hospital if anyone asks, I'll say I took an early lunch break. Then it is agreed none of us says a thing about the body. Churchill you pass the word to Dan and Paul you tell Jason. Keep our group in the loop of things but that is all. We'll meet at Paul's later tonight. I have dental records and other identification. To make sure this is our guy. Churchill says an autopsy tonight would be my guess. Paul adds You don't need an autopsy we know what killed him that big hole in his chest. I reply, "The bullet is still in there we need to get it out to see if we can get a match to the killer's gun."

Paul says, "Well let me get my metal detector and you can use my jack knife and you can get it out." Everyone says, Paul stop it! Marcy slaps him on the back, and I slap him on the head because I am taller. With a big smile he says Ouch!

We go about our separate ways and we meet back at Paul's. Later in the day Dan and Churchill do the autopsy. Paul and Marcy have dinner for us this time and we all chip in with all the meals Paul and Marcy have put on for us, they shouldn't feel bad when they pass the hat. Benjamin is home from the hospital he comes by me and asks Will you sign my cast? Sure, little guy.

Pete Jr. Paul's second oldest son asks Dad, is that dead guy one of the ones responsible for all the misfortune in our town? Paul says to his son kinda looks that way son.

Pete Jr. replies I hope Max gets whoever is responsible and they end up dead like that guy. Paul looks at his son and shakes his head and says Lord be willing. The rest of Paul's kids come out after chores. What is going on Daddy? Paul gets down to their level and explains, "Well kids there is some bad people in the world, and for a little while we have to help our friends keep a secret." "What kind of secret Daddy?" The people who hurt Max, Jamie and little Benjamin. They killed one of their own and we found the body. And Dr. Dan and Dr. Churchill are looking for the body over to make sure who it is.

A child asks Is it a really bad man that died.

Paul replies Yeah, I think so. Might have even killed that silly Stealth Jogger by accident too.

Where is the body? In the freezer. What food is it near?

I have to smile because they are like "little Pauls" when they ask the question. Paul smiles, "The ice cream the French fries the frozen desert." One of the kids mumbles Ah why couldn't you put him near the frozen vegetables? Paul chuckles, "Well everything will be alright." Yeah, but the ice cream.

Churchill comes out of the makeshift operating room and has heard the conversation and asks Well what about the dead bad man? One of Paul's kids says He is going to Hell because he doesn't know Jesus, and to be dead is to be absent from the body and to be present with The Lord. Where are you going when you die Dr. Churchill?

I ponder Out of the mouths of babes.

Paul smiles and says Ok Kids get to the house now. As they leave Churchill says It's our guy alright. So, what now?

I ask, "The body can stay here right Paul?" Paul says Sure it may be a new way to get my kids to eat their vegetables.

Everybody chuckles then says Oh Paul.

Jason and Mr. Cooper come into the garage and ask Is this a bad time to show you some of the designs for the Bed and Breakfast? I am tired yawning I say, "No go right ahead."

They start rolling out designs and ideas. Adam gets a glimpse and says Oh I love this.

Steve adds this will make a great meeting hall. Paul shakes his head and adds I hated the idea at first, but heck that is pretty nice work. Wildtale Publishing has been after me to set up a Comic Book theme restaurant maybe I should break down and do it if you are doing a B & B. We all say Hey you should Paul that would be great!

I ask Paul Ah I wonder if it would be possible to purchase the farmhouse that we used as a safe house for Jamie? Paul smiles Move out of suburbia. As fast as possible yes.

Why? Neighbors don't like dogs and other things. Paul comments, 'You are going to have to patch up the bullet holes. I chuckle stating Well Adam is going to redecorate anyway."

Adam says with glee I can't wait. I still haven't had time to get furniture so I can really move out at any time, right Paul? What about my hunting buddies? If they are friends of yours I am sure we can figure something out.. Burney says I am sure we can figure something out at a fair price. Paul sputters Heck you can move in tonight if you want.

I love the idea of having Mr. McGraw's old farmhouse and it will be interesting to see what Jason and Adam will do with it all. But with bullet holes and all I think this place is home. Max has been running around the yard since I got here, and she is at the door as I unpack. Bang! I am coming, Max! Bang! I hear you just a minute! Bang and the door opens. I am going to have to fix the door and put in a doggie door too. I put my head down and I am fast asleep.

October MONDAY 16th 1978 I wake up at Connie's and I get dressed and head to school.

As I walk to school, I find the guys. Jimmy for once had a breakfast. Jason Cooper says My Dad was going to take me to school with him, I told him no way, I mean I love him and all, but I need my space too. Churchill adds "Yeah, my dad is getting all needy and all wants to know what I am doing how are my grades." I say you should enjoy him while you have him you never know. Dan replies Yeah you never know when someone you love might die.

Any news on K. Ray C.? Churchill murmurs I can't ask and my Dad, he can't really tell any way.

That is why it is called Patient Doctor Confidentiality. Hey there is K. Ray C. He won't know whether the tests will take a while and he might not want to tell us anyway. I tell them, "You guys go ahead I'll go and check on him."

Hi K. Ray how you doing? He looks at me and says, "You told." Yes, I did. He looks both ways to make sure no one is listening in. Thanks, but don't tell anyone I said that Ok. Why the big fuss then? I don't care if I live or die, but it is nice to know someone cares. Your mom cares. She has to, that is her job. I think there is more to it than that. Well, she is tired of it if I live or die by the cancer, she watched my dad die with it. Maybe she is ready to watch you live and get over the cancer? Yeah, well maybe. If I am clear of cancer this year, you wanna tie me up again and drag me to the hospital for a checkup next year? Only if you don't poop and pee your pants. He smiles I make no promises. Same time next year.

He has been the top of his field for years. For a stand he has taken Mr. Cooper was fired and let go. He has started a fledgling construction company making doll houses and mailboxes. To keep his family above water and to keep an added income he has been asked to come back to teaching Art and possibly drafting. "I'll just stay till I find something better." Hello students, I am Mr. Cooper, The first kid to say my name rhymes with pooper is going to stick their noses against the chalk board for the rest of class. K. Ray C. I know you; you were thinking it just try it. K. Ray whispers to Jason your dad is good. Since this is our first time together, I would like to see what you like to draw there will time to assign your work and art is the works of the soul. So right now, the art supplies are here draw what you like, and I'll come by and talk to you.

I can barely draw a stick figure and I sit next to Paul who can draw everything and anything. Mr. Cooper says Come on Max, you can do better than that. I can honestly say Mr. Cooper it does not get much better than this.

He glances over at Paul, and he says it is Paul right, can I see your work? Paul asks You're not going to hold it up and say I am not doing anything wrong, in one breath and then in the next you say to the class, Class This is not what I want you to do? I might be in Special Ed. But I ain't that stupid, that I can't tell you are screwing with my head.

Mr. Cooper sighs. She was your last art teacher too? Paul replies to Miss. Bug up her butt. That's the one. Yes sir. She had a bad heart and had to retire The Lord works in mysterious ways Mr. Cooper. Mr. Cooper asks, can I look at your sketchbook? Sure. Nice, very structured I see you want to be a comic book artist. Paul agrees Someday I want to work for Wildtale Comics.

You have talent, but you had better practice and practice some more. I wish I could say you got the road paved before you but there are a lot of kids your age and adults who are going to try and get there too. Make this a hobby and outlast them. They will give up and find a nine to five job and hate themselves or have a decent life. But only you can make your dream come true. If you want it. In any case have a career to fall back on when the dream job fires your butt, and you have a wife and kids and car and house payments and….

Paul mutters I'll be farming on the side till the day I die, won't I? If you are lucky. Well, I'll have that career in comics to fall back on. Mr. Cooper smiles and pats Paul on the back.

I smile thinking if he only knew.

At lunchtime Mr. Cooper goes to the Principal Gates' office. I can't believe you let that old hag teach art class as long as you did Gates. Watch it Cooper, you are showing severe disrespect.

Paul Chapel is a good student have you seen his stuff and she ripped him apart.

Hey maybe he needs to be ripped apart a little, Paul is in Special Ed. He could be in the regular class, he slacks off. Being in dreamland thinking about Wildtale Comics does not help the situation. Stop babying him Cooper. Next year he is going to be a freshman.

I have the high school coach drooling over this boy, if he can't get his grades up, he won't be playing football.

Cooper continues If you spent any time with Paul, you would find out he does not like football anyway. Maybe, but if he wants a job off the farm college would be his way out.

Science and History are his strong points when he puts his mind to it he can do just about anything. But to do that he is going to have to get out of Special Ed. Mr. Cooper takes a deep breath. I am sorry Gates it is just Paul who reminds me of me and well. I remember that old hag and you didn't get along so well. Hey, you are a teacher now, making this personal is what we do. Art is not a top priority, and she filled the space I needed. I wouldn't be surprised if they cut art out altogether. You have to be kidding? Well, that is a discussion for another time let's get some lunch.

Lunch time recess.

I see Reed and ask Why are you so quiet? Reed sheepishly responds My Pastor got caught yesterday and I guess I am still in a bit of shock Max. I ask, "What happened?" "As if I had to ask?" Reed continues Someone walked into his office to get something and found pornography all over the place. I guess he tried to deny it at first, somebody went to looking around some more and found another stash of the stuff. I whisper, "There was more than what I found?" What? That is terrible.

Yeah. And that ain't the worst of it. When we got home my dad decided he would go back to the church to see what was going on. That Son of a Bitch was gone with the church treasury. I don't know what we are going to do? Reed goes off to sit by himself. He believed in that man, didn't he?

I see the guys and I say Hey guys anybody want a job after school and Saturdays?

Steve asks, "What kind of job?" Working for Mr. McGraw's Mr. Smith's Lawn care Perfection business. Steve says I have tried to get a job with him before. Why does he need help now?

I explain His eyes are bad and he can only go where he can drive a lawnmower.

I helped him last Saturday and made good money. He could use your help after school if you are interested. Jack adds, "Yeah I seen him with a good-sized snow blower last year."

And he runs a snowplow and cleans walkways in the winter. He could use your skills to help maintain his equipment, Jack. You guys interested? I could put in a good word for you.

After school I found Mr. McGraw, and I introduced him to Steve and Jack.

At the C. Connection I start stocking shelves. Dan is doing inventory with Mr. Mustafa.

Bernie and Rabbi Hyman come into the shop and Rabbi says to me Staying out of trouble Mr. Faraday? I reply If I can help it. The Rabbi says this is wonderful Mustafa an Arab and myself a Jew in a free country having the freedom to live life to the fullest and to be able to pursue ones dreams truly this is a wonderful country. I nod my head in agreement.

Burney says to me in Hebrew I just saw a shoplifter and he points the guy out to me. I relay the message in Arabic to Mustafa He then grabs the culprit and the pocketed merchandise, and He says in English If you had stolen this in my old country you would have your hands cut off! Dan, finish for me I have to call this kid's parents. I guess you could call that a snake in the Garden of Eden. Rabbi shakes his head saying Spare the rod and spoil the child.

After work I go home and gather my clothes and I am invited to stay with Paul I'll stay in his older sister's room who went off to college. Because Mrs. Horton is having family and friends over. I catch a few minutes of it as I was getting my things It is like they are all saying goodbye.

At The Cooper's house.

Son, you want to be a gym teacher when you graduate right? Yeah, maybe Dad. Part of being a good gym teacher or athletic coach is keeping your players on the field. Next year you are going to be a freshman. If you practice some more, you could have a great arm for football, I will give you that, but the team is well mediocre. Well dad, next year we will have Paul hopefully. Hopefully soon? If Paul can't keep up his grades, he won't even be a bench warmer. Dad, that's not fair we are going to get creamed if we don't have Paul.

You might want to talk with your friends about tutoring Paul now. Ah dad why do you care?

I like Paul in a few ways, he reminds me of me. I got a scholarship to go to college.

If Paul wants to get an education after school he might try football. Paul is just 16 now He is going to have a college age body in high school. But all his size won't matter if you can't help him keep his grades up.

# CHAPTER SIX
### "Home Sweet Home"

August 1st Thursday 2002 I wake up and I have had the best sleep I have had since I have come home excluding the coma at the hospital. I have picked out where I am going to have my bedroom and I have a rough idea where I want to put my sports memorabilia.

My Ralph Shurlow's Mr. Nobody's T-Shirts man I have a lot of them.
Christ taking apart anger Through Prayer and Counting Tornadoes At A Trailer Park
Sometimes you have to laugh to keep from crying.
"Get comfortable in the boots you are in.
You may be in them a while."
"The world you leave behind is
the world you may be coming back to."
Rednecks driving around in circles at a Hundred and Fifty miles per hour
Not impressive.
 Rednecks at a Hundred and Fifty miles per hour going in specific direction.
Now That IS AWSOME!
"It is amazing
what you can get away with
when you pay the electric bill".
"Canada and Michigan are North Texas

New York is East Texas
California is West Texas
And Texas is Texas
The Whole World is Texas"
"Who needs coffee
 when you have a cold toilet seat."
"Self pity won't buy you a can of pop.
Get prayer and agreement
You might own the company. "
"The situation you are in
can either be your prison
Or your prayer closet.
Your choice."
"If you want to volunteer for thinning the world of stupid people.
Go ahead. YOU FIRST!
Don't take any innocent bystanders on your way out."
"Goofy will keep you going.
When other people are on
Happy pills."
"Long hours.
No Showers."
"We are Sometimes The only Bible people will ever read.
We are Sometimes The only Jesus Christ people will ever see."
"You can have all the head knowledge in the universe.
If you don't know the love of a good woman.
What the Hell do you got?
Lonely. Mr. Smart man."
"Why go through Spiritual Warfare
If you don't have too?"
"I ask the right dumb questions
That make smart people think."
"Garth Brooks has Friends In Low Places.
I have friends that can take care of a dead body."
"I am not being a Jackass
I am just being me
In my Natural Environment."
"Hopes and Dreams I have.

Life Experience
Not so much."
"Love this Michigan weather
If you don't like the weather
just wait Fifteen minutes and it will change."
"Who needs drugs?
When you are on
Imagination."
"The only way to have world Peace is
until Jesus comes back
The United States and it's Allies have the ability to kick it's enemies ASS.
Not just kick their enemies Ass
Kick their ASS for distance.
That our enemies have the full knowledge that we can kick their Ass.
Not "necessarily" know how we can kick their Ass."
"We are called Fly Over Country
Because we want
ASS Holes to fly over!"
"It is hard to get people to invest in the stock market
when they are too busy buying canned goods
shot gun shells running around screaming
It is all over we haven't got a prayer!"
"I don't blame you for everything.
What I blame you for I am very specific."
"If White People don't learn to talk with an accent.
The only thing we will be known for is
White Bread Mayonnaise and the Funky Chicken."
"Just because you can glow in the dark does not necessarily mean you should."
The letters on that one glow in the dark.
"There are some things they really did not teach me in Sunday School."
"Better ask The Good Lord to help me make it up as I go along."
"Lets take a five minute break and see if
Willie Nelson and Farm Aid will come save our ass.
Ho hum He Ain't coming.
I guess we are going to have to do it ourselves."
"I get paid by the hour
When I get home I need a warm shower

My little girl thinks I'm a safe strong tower
The kids want to play I have say I have no power
I get paid by the hour."
"Everyone looks shorter when standing next to
Achilles and Ajax.
Just remember who built The Wooden Horse."
"I am not defined by what people think I can do.
I am defined by what people don't know what I am capable of."
"Do The Eagle Song!"
"You can enjoy the view but you better treat her like your sister."
On Front. And on Back
"I kicked a many bad man's teeth out and I had to put them back in."
"Jesus was not apologizing for The Flood of Noah
when he was talking about putting a millstone around someone's neck
casting them into the ocean."
"You are not going to Hell if you say poo.
If you think you are going to Hell for saying poo.
You are not going to Hell.
You are already there."
"I know
I may be a little slow
But I know
When she is throwing me against the wall
And having her way with me
She is happy with me."
"Sometimes the best way to keep the peace
Is to remind your enemies
that they are a little lower on the food chain."

After I make our breakfast I can let Max out and she can run all the way to Paul's if she wants to and that is the first place she goes.

After Morning patrol Lunch break.

We sit at the Ice Cream and Fried food stand across from Howard's new and used and Garage sales. John Henry loves his fried chicken with BBQ. I am happy with a burger and fries. We are sitting behind the stand enjoying a picnic table with an umbrella.

Jack comes around the corner with his lunch and I say Hi Jack, how you doing?

He looks like he has seen a ghost. I ask, "Are you all right?" Max, can I talk to you in privet? I get out of my seat and I take him to the farthest picnic table near the trees.

Max, I have known for a little while now that Howard's Garage has been in the drug smuggling. Can you prove anything?

After a few minutes I ask Jack can I bring John Henry in and he nods yes. Jack comes forward to show how the drug dealers smugglers stay one step ahead of the Cavanaugh P.D. Jack shakes a bit when he tells us The Howard's Garage connection is. I don't know where it is, I think they have another garage outside of town and that is where they do repairs on drug traffickers' vehicles when they hit deer on the highway. Toney has a big mouth And I have heard him talk about a smashed-up car he towed. But they never deliver here and Toney rolls back the mileage on the tow truck. John adds Howard's Garage Repairs Cavanaugh & Carter City's and the county's police cruisers. Jack adds and installs tracking devices in them. I add My guess The money they make on the side is paying for the Remodeling and expanding show room and collision repair bays.

Why did it take so long for you to come forward? Jack admits After I lost my license for the accident and DUI, I lost my kids and everything. The Howards have helped me get a house within walking distance of the garage and I have been trying to get my life back together. I am not proud it took so long, but if you will help me. I don't know if there is something going on. Ok Jack, We will let you in, but for right now the less you know about what is going on the better.

Before he leaves, he asks "You going to AA tonight?" Yeah. Can I get a ride?

After my patrol I go home to get a shower and get ready for Alcohol Anonymous.

I pick up Churchill and tell him about Jack coming forward. I asked him, "What do you think, should we let him in?" Churchill asks Why Do you think he was sent in by the so-called Mystery Man to figure out what we are doing?

I hate to tell Churchill. My gut says we should let him in Churchill, but my gut has been wrong before and you have been around him more than I have. What do you think?

Churchill answers He is genuine he has been on my case to quit drinking before you came home. The authorities are watching him so close he even sneezes the wrong way and he will never have his kids back again. That bad? Oh, the judge had no mercy on him when he had the accident with The DUI well there, he is waiting for us. When Jack gets in the car, we share with him the information. Jack asks, "What do you want me to do Max?" I ask Do you have any vacation time coming? Yeah. Take it, Cooper is going to need some help with the renovations on The McGraw Farm. Kinda like the old days.

AA. Churchill has a week of sobriety.

October 17th Tuesday 1978 Jason brings up Paul and Football up during lunch. Ok guys, if anybody has plans for high school football, I think we better think of a way to help Paul get his grades up. What do you mean Jack asks? In order to play he is going to need to get at least a C+ average. Steve adds Well Paul is ok when it comes Science and History but Math and English. Pete comments He listens good, on items we discuss in class he does pretty well. I add Yeah but the stuff he has to actually read and do research on well.

Jason says It gets lost in the mix. Ok guys, you have seen what we have to work with. We need Paul on the field. Is it mission impossible or what?

Oh, here comes Paul, let's save it for later.

After my school job at the C. Connection, I am about to call it a night when I see the ambulance drive by, and I get that sick feeling in my stomach. Dan, I think that the ambulance is going for Mrs. Horton's. Mr. Cottager says Max you want a ride to the hospital? No, I can run their thanks. I take off my nametag and I am off. Along the way it goes through me there was so much I could have said and there was. There are things I could have done and there always are. I could have looked up her tombstone if I really thought of it, but I didn't. The ambulance passes me, and I see my mom in the rear-view window.

I reached the hospital, and she is waiting for me. She holds me saying I think this is it.

In a moment like this you bring an elderly dying person to the hospital. She is ready to die. But it is not your call to just let it happen. So, you call the hospital, and they send an ambulance. The paramedics do what they can to save the life. For a moment they prolong life. Then the doctors come, and it is like we ask them to perform a miracle. We basically say We have done all we can do before we give her to God, give it your best shot.

Dr. Churchill Smith had the day off and he had been drinking.. He gets the call about Mrs. Horton, and he comes in. Enough breath mints and coffee and he is ready to go? A last-minute operation behind closed doors and? Mrs. Horton dies at the hands of Dr. Churchill Smith Sr. She was ready to go. But behind closed doors the doctor's talk. Dr. Churchill Smith comes out to tell us I am sorry there is little we could do. We have seen that face before When Marcus was drinking. My Mom says I am sure you did your best. We leave the hospital; she begins to make her phone calls. It is nice to be home in my own bed, yet I know there is something missing here on earth a Saint is where she belongs tonight.

# CHAPTER SEVEN

## "Treasure found in the Chicken coop."

August 2nd Friday 2002 After work I go to Paul's as I pull in the drive a semi pulls out with a load of chickens. I see Paul standing there and he smiles and says to me It's all yours. What? The chicken coop go and get your stuff out.

I get out of my car and look in the chicken coop and ask, "Can I borrow some boots?"

I think your high school stuff is over here and your Marine stuff is here. Excitedly I yell Marine stuff I gotta get my bike out! We begin getting the tarps off. There she is my bike I built from spare parts "Maximum." Oh, Paul, she is dusty, but she is in good shape. Tires still hold air let's get her over to the shop. Marcy looks at Paul and says You painted Maximum on the gas tank. Paul replies, "Hey if he is going to call it Maximum it might as well look good on the tank." As we pushed the bike to the shop Paul asked, "So why did you come over?" Hey Pete, tell your mom I am having dinner out here and we are going to get Maximum going tonight.

Paul's shop is filled with all kinds of tools, and it does not take long, and I give it a push of the starter button and it starts, and she roars to life. I gave

Paul a big hug. After she is all greased up and ready to go, I hop on her, and I am off. "Music Born to be wild."

When I come home Bridge is there to greet me. Having fun on your bike? I comment If I remember reading the comics you can in an instant be traveling through time and space. I guess riding a bike is pretty limited to you. Bridge responds Wild Tail taught me how to ride a Harley. When I come to earth, I like to ride it from time to time. When the universe gets to letting me down. I ask It has been a while since you have talked to me? Bridge reassures All things in their proper time.

I am whisked to the past again where I find Wild Tail, Blue Bomber & Black Phoenix taking on a Gang War in New York Wild Tail whispers to Black Phoenix That Doohickey on your head will switch you to your Black Phoenix personality. Blue Bomber adds What we are going to do is switch you back and forth until your Max Faraday side has control of your Black Phoenix powers and personality. He I mean me asks Is that possible?

BB answers Hope so. This gang and its network have been distributing drugs all along the east coast. We are going to shake things up a bit before the Feds step in. Black Phoenix asks How?

WT answers When you are in Black Phoenix mode you are in Kill Wild Tail Mode too. I'm going to be over there you should start shooting up the place to get to me. BP asks, "What about the people here?" He hands Black Phoenix their files and he scans them drug runners smalls arms dealers and S.O.B.'s and the like. Wild Tail asks again What about them? If you are worried about them you will be firing knock out bullets. They will be firing real live ammo. Happy now? BP asks If am on my last bullet as Black Phoenix I may use that bullet on myself thinking it is real? Or knowing the information I know now I may take one of their real guns and start shooting at you?

WT reassures him We will keep that from happening Max. Then he hands me the files on the gang. Besides selling drugs and arms they deal in explosives providing potential terrorists with one stop shopping. After looking at the files he says Let's do this thing.

WT adds When you have control, I'll loan you one of my spares WT Pistols. It can shoot an energy stunner to knock a guy out without killing them or switch it to high and you can punch a hole in a tank.

Blue Bomber has left us and has snuck through the building and made it to the distributing center. Quietly knocking out the guards with his staff. Kapow! Chinese and Middle Eastern Immigrants process the drugs BB comes in using his Gauntlet's translator Whispering Get out of here in their native languages. As they leave another guard comes in yelling Blue Bomber! BB throws his staff, and it strikes the guard's head bonk! The guard is out.

He then sniffs the air smelling Explosives it does not take long, and he finds the bombs main triggering mechanism. This might take some time.

Wild Tail switches his Black Phoenix persona on and he sees WT and starts shooting! Dodging the bullets WT runs into the gang's direction! They open fire on them both as the bullets fly past them it is like a crazy dance. The rapid gun fire going off would distract anyone else, BB it makes his senses accelerate. He rips wires apart like petals on a daisy. His radar and x-ray vision shows him where all the bombs are, and he disconnects them. With the energy all stored up in his bio system he comes in through the noise & confusion and he just begins to move faster than I thought humanly possible. His staff ricochets the bullets causing them to strike back. WT's whip grabs them by the legs and he pulls them tripping them to the ground and yells Stay down if you want to live! I see Black Phoenix with reckless abandon mixing it up with the gang as he is trying to get a clean shot at WT!

It begins to happen he pauses for a second and then he gets control back and then pauses. A gang member is about to take a pot shot at him and BB knocks him upside the head! Blue Bomber yells Leave my little brother alone!

I see The Black Phoenix All of a sudden it hits him. I know who I am I am Max Faraday! He runs takes to the air and jumps over them discarding his pistols to stand by WT and grabs one of his spares. Causing them to fall to the ground. Stunned of course.

Black Phoenix says I hate to say it Wild Tail but part of me wishes this was not a stun gun, that it was for real.

WT says No you don't. There are several gangs represented here Max. None of the stun weapons we use today will be picked up by the Feds. They will most likely tell the Feds Wild Tail and The Blue Bomber came in here with this crazy man in black and shot up the place. The only injured or dead people were hit by friendly fire. It even looks like a gang war here, doesn't it? Perplexed BP exclaims You act like you have done this before? WT smiles replying All the time kid. BB comments Come here you gotta see this He opens doors and I see the biggest drug bust I have ever seen or heard about. How did they get this into the country? WT comments I don't think we will see this on the nightly news. BB adds "This is too big to put on the 11'o'clock news." And then he shows us the explosives. If the Feds had come in guns blazing, first my guess they would have blown the place up.

I am then back home at 11:00 p.m. and I go to bed because I am spent.

# CHAPTER EIGHT
## "Doctor Churchill has a car accident"

October 18th, 1978, Wednesday Dr. Churchill Smith Sr. has a car accident. It happened after midnight. Officers McGraw and Tom find the body. Oh God is that Dr. Smith's car? They get out and find the body dead. Drunk driving, how do we report this?

When I got to school, I get we are so sorry for you. Mrs. Horton will be missed. Churchill has been quiet all morning, his mother had visitors at 5 o'clock this morning.

I hate his father for not doing the right thing and staying out of the operation room. I could have said something to him, but I didn't. The report will say nothing about drinking and driving, he just had an accident. Maybe that is good, maybe that is bad I don't know.

I just know what I know.

After school job at the C. Connection. Mr. C. says You didn't have to come in Max. I respond with Yeah; I do Mr. C. Mom has been on the phone Mrs. Horton made her in charge of her Will and she has been making phone calls all day. I would just be in the way.

A pat on the back from Mr. C. saying Ok if that is the way you feel.

When I got home my mom asked, "How was your day?" I say Ok, I guess. I don't know how to feel about Dr. Smith and all, I guess. Mom responds He was drunk Max if he had any love for her, he would have asked another doctor to do the operation, if it would have helped any. The other doctors should have known he was in no condition to be there. I add everyone who knows is going to remain silent. That would be my guess Mrs. I ponder Horton is in a better place. The fact Dr. Smith died at his own hands there really isn't anything anyone can say to change the situation. For the living people will remain silent.

Mom asks, "Well what else happened today?" Jason is trying to figure out how to help Paul get his grades up so he can play football next year. Mom asks Is his father still planning on kicking him out when he turns eighteen. Yep. Mom shakes her head and smiles. I remember when I substituted for your teacher in the 5th grade Paul was a good listener. Yeah, I hear that a lot. What he isn't a good student when it comes to studying on his own. If it isn't something he is interested in the daydreams. Mom agrees Yeah that is Math and English. Paul's mother has been a good friend to us. I'll call her and maybe if I tutored him, we could find something that could help Paul get his grades up.

I Wake up in August Saturday 3, 2002 12:22 a.m. and then I go back to sleep.

October 19th, 1978, Thursday After school Piano class.

My Mom asked me if I could play at the Funeral, can you help me pick out a song?

Mrs. Horton's Showing the McGraws show up as a family and Mr. & Mrs. And their son Officer Indigo McGraw comes and sits by me. Their son Indigo whispers to me Thank you for helping out my dad. I felt a little guilty for becoming a cop, but I could not see myself as a farmer. I whisper back Hey you gotta do what you gotta do. I received the offer to join the Force in the Big City I am going to take it. Hey, that is great. I know we haven't known each other that long, off and on, but to tell you the truth I always wanted a little brother.

I Wake up August Saturday 3, 2002 2:45 a.m. and then I go back to sleep.

October 20th, 1978, Friday Mrs. Horton Funeral I get up get dressed the suit I am wearing is one that Mrs. Horton picked out for me, she picked the music she picked the meal that we are going to eat today she has the scripture that she would like to have read. The tombstone she shares with her husband has her the date of her birth and the date of her death and she added "to be continued." The church is packed, and I sit down to the piano playing When the Role is called up yonder, I'll be there.

I hear the Pastor say to the congregation "Happy is the Pastor that sends a Saint home."

I ponder Wouldn't he like to know she had a preview. I hear stories of happy students and college grants given lives changed and are still being changed. Someone asks out loud Who do I talk to about giving to The Mrs. Horton's Fund? I say Talk to my mom she is standing over there. I go home that night secure in what I believe is true. There is a God who has prepared a way for salvation. And he wants his children to choose him.

I Wake up August Saturday 3, 2002 4:12 a.m. and go back to sleep.

October 21st 1978 Saturday I get up and go work for Mr. McGraw's Lawn Care Perfection on Saturdays I go out to get the lawn mower started. And I look to the street, and I see cars from out of State License plates. Some with Military or Navy plates.

I kind of remember this time period from my past. I was recuperating from my beating. Uncle Sherman went to the funeral while he was watching me. As I finish my lawn and about to work on another one. Uncle Sherman pulls in the drive. I shut off the mower Come here Max! He gives me a hug. Boy you have grown. What are you doing here? I am here for The Churchill Smith Funeral. My countenances changes and I say I have to get to work. I would like to stay and talk with him, The Churchill Smith funeral is not a place I want to be.

Dr. Churchill Smith Showing

I mow a home near the Funeral home and I watch as cars are parked up and down the blocks. Service uniforms of Navy and Marines and a few Air Force and a couple Army.

I can tell by the way they walk a few of them have false legs and several are in wheelchairs. They are all saying He saved my life; I may lose my leg or arm but I came home.

Dr. Sam greets them with tears wearing his Navy uniform, and some give him a salute and others just keep their comments to themselves.

Big Paul drives in and drops his Dad Paul Chapel Sr. off and Comes in Air Force uniform and all. He shaved his beard off. As long as I have known him, he has always worn his beard. I am still stunned and Dale Chapel walks by and says to me He looks good in uniform doesn't he. I shut off the mower and get off and stand and Salute Yes Sir. He does. You don't look too shabby yourself. He smiles at me at ease Marine I wonder if your Uncle Sherman is up? Just pulled in this morning How come The Air Force and Marines are coming to see a Navy Doctor?

Dale says Because of a term you may learn of Some day if you are lucky that is Classified.

I smile back. Maybe I'll look it up when I get clearance when I grow up.

Father Michaels walks by and says Hi Dale sad that we are meeting like this today.

Dale says Yeah Father seems like yesterday we were just all talking about what the hell are we doing over here in Vietnam some Spook is going to get us all killed. By The grace of God go I, somehow some of us made it back. The good Father adds, and many didn't. Many that lived left much of ourselves behind. Dale nods his head and walks to the Funeral home.

Father Michaels says I hope you will come to the service tomorrow Max it will be held at The High school. I reply I don't know if I should go the way I feel. And that is? Angry, he had alcohol in his breath when he operated on Mrs. Horton. Father Michaels shakes his head saying That makes sense the police are very respectful of the family. No one wants to disrespect the memory. I ask, "What about Mrs. Horton's Memory?" The good Father says "How about we concern ourselves with the living. Churchill needs a friend." You're right. Don't say anything unless you know the Lord wants you to speak it. Then I guess I'll be really quiet.

And they keep coming.

Wake up August Saturday 3, 2002 5:36 a.m. and I go back to sleep. October 22nd, 1978, Sunday Dr. Churchill Smith's Funeral I get up and go to church with the Pearsons Mr. Pearson is dressed in his Army Core of Engineers uniform. He asks me Are you going to the Funeral after church? Yeah, for Churchill's sake I'll go. As we leave Church there is a procession of cars headed to Cavanaugh City. They can't all be going to the funeral. They are the parking lot is full and it looks like still more coming so ushers in military uniforms usher us in.

Under normal circumstances Mr. Pearson would see if he could park closer. Artificial leg and all. Today there are veterans with no legs being pushed in wheelchairs and he is thankful for the one good leg he has. The last time I saw this place this full was when they used the high school for the conference final playoffs. I see Churchill off in the distance crying he is not holding feelings in bottled up.

The Funeral eulogy Dr. Sam begins.

I came to the United States from Vietnam in Forty-Seven to go to college and Study Medicine at The University of Michigan. I met someone there that would change my life.

Churchill welcomed me and treated me like a friend. He was from the small town of Cavanaugh City. I was from a small village I think few of you could pronounce its name. He worked part time on a tractor to help pay for college. I worked part time behind a water buffalo and my father was a chief and elder who had a good rice crop that year and looked into sending me to the States to become a doctor. You don't know how blessed you are in America. No let me change that statement We don't know how blessed we are in America. I am an American. While in the States Churchill Smith Helped me get my citizenship confirmed. I may talk funny at times, but you can't send me back. Laughter.

I became a doctor and the rumbles of thunder of the Civil War in Vietnam could be heard in my letters from home. I told him I had to go home to Vietnam. Churchill pleaded with me to stay.

So, I returned to my village, and it was burned to the ground because we were of the South Vietnam and The Vietcong of The North did not take kindly to sympathizers.

My Heaven on Earth I call Vietnam turned into Hell. Churchill joined the Navy Medical Core and shocked me because he hated war. But he loved life even more and as crazy as war is sometimes you have to fight for life. So many faces here and skins fighting the evil of Communism. So that others who you never met before might live in freedom. What greater love hath man than to be willing to give their own life. I tried to do what I could for my people. I was captured by The Vietcong and about to be killed for aiding my own people. When they found out I had medical skills I was forced to be Their doctor. Thank God the Marines came and blew up the place I sang God Bless America! I was not a Christian at the time. I sang God Bless America as best I could. And one of them came and picked me out. I told them I was an American Citizen I lost my papers along the way.

You know they tell you to memorize your Social Security number, but does anybody memorize their number? Well, I did after that I tell you.

I started naming off names of people I knew in The States that might verify my story.

When I said Churchill Smith, the guy who was questioning me his ear's perked up.

The Marines and The Navy kept me as a guest, but no one knew if I was telling the truth.

I thought to myself If they could not find anyone, they might treat me like a spy. And I was scared because they could kill a spy! I had missionaries try to tell me about God and Jesus I didn't see the use. I didn't know who or which god to pray to. So, I just prayed To who it may concern. He came in and I saw my good friend Churchill. I was half starved and he still recognized me. I went back to the States and healed up and joined The Navy. The Stories I could tell, but in Sixty-nine we had enough our tour was through. My home, my family my village was gone what could I do I wondered. The war had changed Churchill as it changed us all. He said he had this nice little town that could use a couple doctors.

Over the years I have learned Churchill was a friend and a brother to me and an instrument of Jesus Christ. Churchill grew up with pain towards God because he lost his mother at an early age. I believe that put up walls for him. But he was always searching for the truth.

He hated hypocrisy with passion. How can You say we are for life when we take life so easily? How can you say "Thou shalt not kill and then kill?" How can you call yourself a Christian and then live like The Devil? I am alive today because Churchill came to my cell and recognized me. In life we are all in a cell called life and I would like to think when my time here is ended Jesus Christ my friend and Savior will come to my cell and recognize me. Will Jesus come to your cell and recognize you?

A Navy Chaplin comes to the stage and embraces Dr. Sam then pats him on the back.

He walks to the podium and asks Will Jesus to recognize you? I look over to Churchill and I just see him sob he and his mother have no joy in this day. No peace. Ashes to ashes dust to dust.

I get my time alone with Churchill. How are you doing? "Man, that is a dumb question?"

Churchill says Max you are a Christian right? Yeah, last time I checked. Churchill continues My Dad never talked about the Navy or Vietnam. I just knew he was gone. You see all those people out there today my dad touched their lives. I heard it. He kept me alive he didn't give up hope, he kept me alive till help came. I agree Yeah, he did a lot of Churchill your Dad was a hero. Churchill tearfully continues I never heard him say he believed in Jesus Max. All the good he did searching for truth along the way. If he did not accept Christ as his personal Savior and he died does that mean he is going to Hell? Max is that what Christianity means? I whisper Churchill I am not the judge God is. Churchill with tears cries If I can't see my father in Heaven. Then I don't want to go. Churchill walks away.

# CHAPTER NINE
## "I just had the longest night."

I Wake up 6:30 August Saturday 3, 2002 and ponder the days that have gone on for me through the night. Mrs. Horton & Dr. Churchill Sr. Repeated history as it happened in my first time around. A lot to comprehend over coffee and cream. It is my and John Henry's weekend but that will happen tonight. I would go back to bed to rest up but after last night I think I will have another cup of coffee with extra sugar and a little less cream. I get up and get dressed and I go to the Floral shop and buy three arrangements of flowers. I then drive to the cemetery and lay them at their graves. Sorry mom, it has been a while since I visited you, seems like yesterday you were telling me to get up and go to school. God this is weird. I then go to Mrs. Horton's grave. I really have nothing to say. And finally, Wendy's. You shouldn't be here girl.

God, you will help me so she won't end up here.

Night Patrol. Me and John Henry stake out the highway that the drug traffickers use. It is not Wednesday or Friday, but our witnesses said sometimes they travel on Saturdays. That is when me and Reed got his pickup shot up. Listening to the radio we hear an old Counting Tornadoes song.

"I wish I wasn't drunk when you sang your song"
On Sunday I go to church.

Answers in The Bible I search.
When I leave The pastor shakes my hand.
Saying Thank you and please come back.
My nightly activities Mama ain't giving me no slack.
I am the Baby Bouncer at the local bar.
It is a different world I tell myself.
The Boss says Here you are.
At the Karaoke machine they like to hear me sing.
For a moment on the stage you can be a king.
I fancy myself a writer every now and again one of my songs I fling.
An old guy comes up it is time to call it a night.
You did pretty good up there son you did alright.
I wish I wasn't drunk when you sang your song.
I wish I knew the words and I could sing along.
The doctors say I won't be around long.
I have been on the Twelve step program and quit at eleven.
Only by the grace of God will you see me in Heaven.
I wish I wasn't drunk when you sang your song.

Going home I get the cold shoulder.
Mom don't like the idea of me Bouncing at a bar.
Her gripes are getting are getting colder.
Dad says Son your mom doesn't like what you are doing.
I have to live with her and you have her brewing.
Her church lady friends are stewing.
As long as you don't take up the vice.
You will get no complaint from me.
That is my advice.
At night I learn to bend an arm to make a bad guy go.
Someone shouts I wanna hear you sing!
Start with something nice and slow.
I do my best to sound like Merle.
Singing through my nose to do Willie Nelson.
I throw one of my own in and I am done.
Boss man says one of these days.
We are going to Nashville and have some fun.
An old guy comes up it is time to call it a night.

You did pretty good up there son you did alright.
I wish I wasn't drunk when you sang your song.
I wish I knew the words and I could sing along.
The doctors say I won't be around long.
I have been on the Twelve step program and quit at eleven.
Only by the grace of God will you see me in Heaven.
I wish I wasn't drunk when you sang your song.

I call it a night and head for home.
I get up in the morning not feeling the need to roam.
I came home with a full tip jar.
Thinking you don't know how lucky you are.
Mom gets the call and says You have been requested to sing at a funeral.
The old guy died in his sleep.
They went to wake him up not a peep.
It is an honor to receive the request.
I shed a few tears I'll do my best
After I finish Amazing Grace.
His daughter comes to see me with tears on her face.
He wasn't drunk when you sang your song.
I am sure He is in Heaven and was singing along.
The doctors were right he wouldn't be around long.
He has been on the Twelve step program to Heaven..
Since mom died he has been stuck at eleven.
Now He is singing with mama and the angels and I know.
He wasn't drunk when you sang your song.

John asks How much coffee are you going to drink tonight man? I reply as much as it takes to keep me awake. John shakes his head saying That is why you should've taken a nap. I smirk Say that after you have had the dreams I have had. We hear the sound of a speeding car. Get ready! It speeds right by us! John floors it and the siren goes off and we bolt on the highway!

Jack was right, there were three patrol cars staked out on the highway before us and he chose to put on the Nitro right in front of us. John yells, "Our cruiser never made it to Howard's Garage! I am amazed We are keeping up with them matching them speed for speed! Then it happens 'Drug trafficker hit a herd of deer doing 90 to 100 plus!"

We just about skid out of control as we put on the brakes! The drug trafficker's car is totaled stuck upside down. Deer parts all over the place. The driver had on his seatbelt it did its job. He is hanging upside down. John asks, "What are we going to do?" I call Dusty on my cell phone and tell him to bring a tow truck. Then Paul the driver is a big guy he is alive but still loopy now. "I'll be there as fast as I can." I then called Pete, remembering the fact that the drug runners had devices for tracking police cars they might have tracers on their own vehicles. Churchill and Dan. The driver is banged up by the herd of deer he hit.

Me and John Henry gave him First Aid, he will live.

As I look around the car on my own John gets a crowbar. I yell Wait! Let me see if the car is booby trapped! John pauses then mumbles, "The other cars were not?" I advise Nobody knew about the other cars either, if they killed their own before who is to say they won't kill again or leave something behind to kill us. Oh, shit John, Thank Jesus I took the time to check the car is wired with C4. The Car, can you disarm it? This one sure, but there might be a backup somewhere? John wonders aloud A backup Booby? I cut the wire and say I must be losing my touch.

Pete is the first to arrive. He gets out of the car with handheld devices and goes over the wreck and says I can't triangle the home base, but the car has a tracking device. I added I found a bomb. Pete looks at it and asks aloud Where in the heck would some drug runners get this set up? I was wondering the same thing. John asks, "What is it?" The bomb and tasks device has CIA practically written on it. John asks, "And you know this how? Pete smiles "If we give our competition a headache all we can say is "Ice Works". We make a better bomb. This is old Tech, but it is still U.S. government issue.

Dan and Churchill arrive. Churchill yells You should have called 911 this man needs medical attention! Dan adds, "Well they did a good job on his bandages and first aid."

Churchill murmurs Shut up Dan! John gets his Grrrs in at them and smacks the crowbar in the palm of his hand then opens the trunk! Drugs just pour out. Churchill is silent Oh this bastard will live I guess whose car is he riding in? Paul arrives and says Ah throw him in the back of my truck I can wash out the blood when I get home. Paul just shakes his head Man that bastard killed a lot of deer. Churchill says Works for me. Injured deer lay on the highway so I get out a knife. The ones that can't get up well, I don't need to paint a picture. Reed arrives and Yells That is the Son of a bitch was the one who shot up my truck! Churchill smiles saying Oh That is showing a good Christian witness.

Reed yells back Thou shalt not shoot another man's pickup truck!

The driver survives and he and the car are taken to the safe house and put in the barn.

When I finally get home in my house Bridge is here and I am taken back in time again. Wild Tail & Black Phoenix confronts Bent and Graves. He asks WT I have all the memories of Black Phoenix now, right? Wild Tail replies You tell me you are him now? The doctor at Genetics Unlimited Labs says you should be able to control your BP powers on your own. He relaxes and the white extra layer of skin peels off on its own. The questioner comes in saying We think we found Agent Bent. I am going to bed and I am exhausted.

# CHAPTER TEN
## "Summer Vacation Seventy-Nine"

Iwoke up and it is Summer Vacation Seventy-nine It was just October Seventy-eight?

I look at my calendar and my best guess is it is Monday June 18th, 1979. I can guess this much because I cross off the days on my calendar as I wake up. Now I have to ask myself, "What the heck am I supposed to do today?" Ah Mom this may sound like a dumb question, but what am I supposed to do today? She yells back Max you are working for Mr. McGraw. You help manage his Mr. Smith's Lawn Care Perfection. Are you sick?

I found my paperwork and saw the homes and yards I have to do today. Steve and Jack work for me. On my list of things to do Mr. McGraw wants to talk to me? That makes both of us? What about my job at the C. Connection? As I get breakfast, I look out the window and see a scooter on the front lawn. Mom says, "Still looking at that bike." You wanted to buy contact lenses so you could throw your glasses away. You don't need girls Max you need to get an education.

"I murmur Mom."

I got my list, and I started mowing grass. I like working for Mr. McGraw and all but what happened to The C. Connection? I saw Wendy and I shut off the mower and said Hi!

She comes over with a worried look on her face. I ask how are you doing?

Wendy says My "Father "Frank Pearson" and Mother "Martha Pearson" are having trouble with their marriage, and their foster care children. I am sorry. Can I help?

Wendy says You could tell Steve he does not need to look for an apartment and live on his own.

Steve gets his own apartment? He is only Fifteen. Yes, but with all the hours he is putting in he is looking for an apartment. He is not thinking of quitting school, is he? Oh no if he is not working, he is studying he says he wants to be a Police Criminal Psychologist. So that sounds pretty good, what is wrong with that? I'll miss him Max, he is my Big Brother.

Well, he is probably tired of not having his own space and he wants to be on his own for a bit.

Yeah, Dad is tired too with his new responsibilities at the factory he travels so much now I don't get to see him hardly anymore.

I am just silent I don't know what to say because I have seen how this played out in the first time around and it wasn't pretty. I'll pray for you Wendy.

You will Max, thanks that means a lot coming from you.

I get on my new scooter, and I find Mr. McGraw at his Farm. Houses are being built all around his place. I saw Mrs. McGraw and I said to her Ah Mr. McGraw asked to see me?

He is expecting you Max, he is in the barn. Hello Mr. McGraw, are you in here? Here I am Max. Oh sir. You are in the dark. Really, I can't tell anymore. I fumbled for the light switch and turned it on. He does not even flinch with the light coming on.

Mr. McGraw says You have been a God send Max you really have. I thought I would have to sell my Mr. Smith's Lawn Care franchise and you helped me and my wife hold on. I know you wanted to keep working at the C. Connection, all I can say is thank you for working for me.

I ask, "Are you selling your franchise?" No, if we can keep good help like you, Steve and Jack, my wife will be able to keep going after I am gone. Gone? The doctors found cancer in my brain I wonder if you could tell the others. Tears start to flow I ask How long? Possibly a year or two, maybe less, I hope not.

You see these pictures have been in my family for generations. I look at them they are farm scenes. They show how things used to be done, how we harvested wheat and corn by hand and then the steam engine. My family owned so much land I was told they were going to call our town McGraw Ville. Instead, they called it Cavanaugh City, and nobody even knows why? Promise me you will look out for your history. Take care of it.

I love my boy, Max; I can't blame Indigo for wanting a different life. A police officer is one thing, but to be in the bomb squad? That is insane!

I ask, "So what are the pictures doing out here in the barn?" My Great Grand dad had this section burrowed out of the ground for a cool cellar. It has been used for Storage of odds and ends mostly. I am going to put the pictures in here like a time capsule and maybe someday someone will find them and enjoy them and say Look at that history maybe we should take care of our own history before it is forgotten. I love this barn. I hope whoever buys this place after us will take good care of it. I jokingly say Who knows maybe someone will want to live in it? We both had a good laugh.

I go to bed that night and wake up at 2:am August 4, 2002, Sunday and go back to sleep Nineteen Seventy-nine Freshman Year I ride to school, and it is a scooter but it beats walking and I see Kathy is out of her braces and looks like a Barbie doll. I take a double look to make sure it is her and it is wow. Hey, watch it! I swerve to miss someone and tap a fencepost and fall over scraping paint on my scooter. Kathy looks back and smiles "She can't help it Baby got her blue jeans on." The boys are crazy over her.

Steve is just the guy who can play Mr. Cool around her, and she likes it and lets him carry her books.

# CHAPTER ELEVEN
## "Mad dash and put on my Sunday best!"

August Sunday 4, 2002 I get up and make a mad dash for the shower I have to do a special at the Baptist Church! I gotta get there! I almost completely forgot all about it!

I am on the way and getting dressed and putting on my suit running out the door.

I yell Paul, "what are you doing at my house?!" Paul yells back Oh I organized Local Militia to protect the safe house. One of the militia yells out-"Well Somebody should do something, they leave dead deer all over on the highway." I yell back Yeah, I get that a lot! Paul continues Until I see dime one this is still my property. It hits me Wait a minute shouldn't you be at church?

Paul says, "Oh I went to morning prayer at Seven I get out a little after eight. Since I didn't have to pick up Marcy for church, I decided to come out here for a few then head back for second service. I replied, "Hey that is nice you go to early prayer." Paul shrugs his shoulders I kinda feel like just a warm body there, but they are so happy to see me come, it is hard for me to say no to them. Mostly I share prayer requests and say I have several unspoken prayer requests. Lord, do I have some unspoken requests. Anyway Dr. Dan is here too he says the Mad Max Bambi killer is drugged up pretty good. Oh, any chance you could get a tape of your special Marcy wants to hear you play. Sure.

I ponder to myself, "This is my life I just shake my head as I drive." At church they ask Connie, "are you sure he is coming?" If Max says he is going to do the Special with me he will do the special. The pastor says Well this is unprofessional I just hope his song will be complementary with my sermon. Connie says I am sure our song will be. "I Hope it will be." There is no time for butterflies in my stomach. Terrorist I can handle, room full of Baptists maybe another story. I have not played in front of an audience in a while. When she asked me to do a special this is all that popped in my head. The last time I played this, it was for my sister when she had a lumpectomy. And the announcer says and now for a special.

I begin to play and Connie begins to sing.
"There is more woman in you than anyone can take away."
 You are my sister and my friend come what may in families we have
learned to depend.
Dark clouds hung over us all remember This is just the beginning and not
the end.
Christ The Son broke through the clouds to bring a new day
There is more woman in you than anyone can take away
Your kindness, joy and peace as The Lord gives you the path He will not
lead you astray.
Together we have held each other when we pray.
Our Father is the same yesterday today and forever.
There is more woman in you than anyone can take away
 I can't say I know what you are going through, all I can do is ask God
to protect you repay you and defend.
Some of the dreams you had are gone this is true.
Dreams are dreams and the dreamer of the new dream is you.
There is more woman in you than anyone can take away
Your kindness, joy and peace as The Lord gives you the path He will not
lead you astray.
Together we have held each others when we pray.
Our Father is the same yesterday today and forever.
There is more woman in you than anyone can take away
I lift my eyes up as I play and I see women raise their hands. I see tears now

and I am thankful that I know this song by heart because I could not see the sheet music if I had it in front of me. Their applause fills the church and the pastor says Do another song.
 I play "I WILL SURVIVE!"
Holy Spirit Watch my Back
Father God lead and go before me
Jesus Christ lives within me and that is how I pray
Holy Spirit Watch my Back
Father God lead and go before me
Jesus Christ lives within me and that is how I pray.
 In the darkness of twilight the bravest of soldiers know fear and fright.
Even the mighty must pray for the light.
Weary and dead tired not knowing whether I have the strength to go on.
Friends have died or have given up yet I still struggle on.
Wondering will I survive?
 In mid dawn I have a glimpse of my enemy.
Great is his number before me!
My armor is polished and ready.
My sword and shield are at my side my motto is
'No guts no glory' at this point I know its do or die.
Great may be the obstacles before me!
Great may be the challenges too awesome to deny!
Greater is he that is within me.
And He is greater than all my enemies combined!
So no matter the outcome my spirit will survive!
Whether today I live or die.
I have planted my seeds of faith in fields of fertile soil.
On that foundation I shall receive and claim my harvest and victory!
No matter the outcome of the day 'I WILL SURVIVE!
At dawn's sunrise there are no options.
So I march forward with purpose, and I walk with a stride!
Not knowing the future Faced with a battle praying for strength, faith, and wisdom to survive!
When many have fallen around me, the enemy surrounds me.
Then I hear the trumpets of the Cavalry and the enemy sees this, then they run and hide!
Then the Captain takes one look at me.

Then he gives me a smile.
Offers me his hand
And says let's RIDE!
Great may be the obstacles before me!
Great may be the challenges too awesome to deny!
Greater is he that is within me.
And He is greater than all my enemies combined!
So no matter the outcome my spirit will survive!
Whether today I live or die.
I have planted my seeds of faith in fields of fertile soil.
On that foundation I shall receive and claim my harvest and victory!
No matter the outcome of the day 'I WILL SURVIVE!

I finish the song and I get up, wipe my eyes and leave to find Connie. She is teary eyed too in the nursery and she gives me a hug and says thank you. As I look around the nursery and the junior church, I see a little boy that reminds me of little Jimmy. I smile and say He kind of reminds me of Jimmy. Connie asks, "Who?" I repeat it without thinking Jimmy.

Max, don't you ever say his name to me ever again. Connie, he was once a little kid, we used to walk him to school. At some point you have to forgive him for what he did. Max, He grew up and next to you he killed my best friend. Connie, at some point you have to forgive. Max, have you forgiven your father for what he has done? "Truth, is she got me."

I say Sorry Connie. She quotes "Don't take the speck out of another's eye before you take the rod out of your own." I guess I have been trying to think of Jimmy as an innocent kid that he once was not the killer he became.

After service. I get the thank you so much you are a blessing. The pastor comes to me and says You blessed me and my wife with that song. When Counting Tornadoes came out, I didn't think they should be serving man singing at bars and God at churches at the same time. When Ralph wrote that song it blessed my wife when she had a lumpectomy.

Thank you, Max. Connie asks, "Where, are you going for lunch?" I am going to get some fast food and go check on an old friend. No, you are coming home with me. No, you are going home and enjoying your Sunday before your kids come back from summer camp. I'll be fine.

Nobody says little brother like my Big Brother Indigo McGraw. After the fast food I drive out into the country to Indigo McGraw's place. He went to the Big City and became a bomb specialist I know that but something else I just gotta check out. Indigo was forced to retire due to his eyesight. He had the same degenerative eyesight problem as his father had, genetic, I guess. The way He said little brother has just been playing over in my head I have to check it out. I go to the door and knock, he answers. Hello? Hi Indy, remember me? Indy says little brother. He hugs me and says I feel the sun is shining its warmth lets go outside and talk. I was really thrilled you bought My parents' old place. I tell him Yeah; they are going to turn it into a bed and breakfast. Who? The Coopers and Adam, Steve and me.

Well, it will be tasteful I guess. I ask How come you never bought it. Indy answers It was home growing up, I could not live with the feeling Dad wanted me to stay on the farm and I couldn't. When I retired from the Force Mom sold me her Mr. Smith Franchise and here I am. My wife drives me in and I repair the equipment and she does the books. A nice little life all and all.

I chuckled Blind Man's Bluff. And he Stops dead in his tracks. Nobody calls me little brother like my big brother Indy. He asks, "How much do you remember?"

It is not so much that I remember it is what I have been shown.

Shown? Bridge has taken me back in time and has shown me as Black Phoenix when he fought Wild Tail. Indy states He is trying to trigger your memory of Selah.

I ask what happened? Why don't I have memories of my past?

Indy answers Because you as Selah asked to have your memories of him erased.

Why? I have said too much Max.

I ask So you are the Blue Bomber how did it happen?

I told you my origin once, if Bridge is showing you the past chances are you will see it.

Then why the cold shoulder? You asked us to help you forget Max, or should I say "Selah" did.

You or he wanted a fresh start.

I leave Indy's and head for home and find Max the dog having fun with the local Militia.

Local Militia protect the safe house. I guess as long as they keep quiet it won't hurt having them around. I ask have you guys had anything to eat? No Sir. Don't call me Sir it is Max Ok. I pass one of them a couple of Grants and say Go and get some Pizza and some pops and thanks for staying watch. I go to the barn and Dan is still here. How is he? Dan says Out, the bleeding has stopped, and I put on a real cast instead of the splint on his leg. This guy has killed how many kids with his drugs? I don't know. Tom is doing a fingerprint search on him; he should know by tonight. When he wakes up what do you want us to do? Keep your face covered so he can't identify you and call me and John Henry.

Churchill comes in I hate to say it Max but, I would like to see this bastard die. Why is that Dr. Smith? Because of What drugs has done to my son and other parents' sons and daughters. I want him dead. I am the biggest hypocrite I tell my son he is killing himself with his drugs and I am killing myself with my own. I put my arm around him. You are not going through this alone. Let's get this guy and his friends off the streets.

Paul rides up on his four-wheeler and asks, "What's going on?" I say Just talking everything is cool I sent a couple guys for pizza they should be back soon. Paul says Wish everything was ok, Maria is headed to the hospital to deliver another baby. Churchill says I better head to the hospital she had a hard labor last time.

I ask Why so worried Paul? I am going to be shorthanded tomorrow. The Mexicans will make it a holiday. Probably won't see them till Tuesday. I comfort Paul by saying, "Well I have Monday off I could come in and help." Can you be there around five? Well, I'll need a refresher course. Pete Jr. can walk you through it. Sure, I guess I can be there. Oh, that takes a load off my back thanks. Paul sticks around and talks with the guys and when the pizza is gone so is he.

When I come to Bridge is there and I am sent back in time again. Blue Bomber comes by and asks How are you doing little brother? Black Phoenix says Indigo? The name startles him, and he takes off his mask showing he was right in his observation. He asks? How? He says Nobody says little brother like my big brother Indigo. I have been thinking of it when you said I was from your hometown. So how did you come to be a Wild Tail Champion?

Blue Bomber tells his origin It started when I began losing my eyesight. The doctors said I had the same degenerative disease as my dad. Funny thing it came and went when I was around loud noises. The noise of the Big city or an explosion of disposing a bomb and I could see just fine in fact I went back and had my eyes checked again and the doctor said I was cured? I came home to visit mom and the quiet of the country and within days I was almost blind. I had friendly connections with Wild Tail, and I was able to get a message to him. I let his doctors put me under the bright lights and microscope. When we figured out the sound connection. They did a genetic search and found that I was what they call the Great One. It basically means I was born with superhuman powers. Usually, they show up at puberty mine shown up at about age 35 in1987. I didn't like the idea of having powers. I figured I could keep my eyesight by keeping as much noise in my life as possible. When I drive by myself to the Precinct, I would turn up the volume on my radio. For a time, it worked.

My team was called to disarm a bomb and it was like one I had never seen before. The more I examined it the more I had a sixth sense about it. My X-ray vision came into practice that day and it freaked me out a bit. I shared the experience with WT he suggested I learn more about my gifts and what all I could do with them. I began with my hand-to-hand fighting skills and found if I concentrated on my radar instead of my eyes, I could block anything with ease. I became so used to the radar I had to concentrate just to see with my normal eyes. The radar is good, but I can't read a road sign or a sheet of paper, it is just blank to me. Wild Tail suggested I take on the name Blue Bomber. The same name was used by a hero of the Gathering of the Guardians back in the twenties and thirties. I guess WT thought I could be part of a Legacy. I went out with him to see how it felt.

I did and I loved it. There is freedom that comes with the mask. During the day I was Indigo McGraw police officer on the Bomb Squad, off duty I was The Blue Bomber.

I had to get another physical and it came to my eyes getting checked again. I had to wait in an office, and it was quiet by the time I went in the doctor said I had the degenerative disease again.

You see my body can use sound to I guess heal me from a wound or even my eyesight.

But there was not enough sound to maintain my eyes, so the disease showed up.

I was given an early retirement option from the force. My mom wanted to sell her Mr. Smith franchise and I came back home. I repair the lawn equipment and my wife does the books. I learned how to read Brail and I found the more I allowed myself to actually be "blind" I could store my bio energies like a battery. Does she know? Yeah, she is my anchor when things get me down. During the day I am the blind handyman at night I fight crime in the Big City. It works out pretty good actually. WT comes in Yelling We found Bent let's go! WT sees that BB shown me his face and says I thought I told you not to show him your face. BB replies He is my little brother he already figured it out WT.

We are transported to a harbor seaport dock. Where we huddle behind large crates.

The Questioner whispers We have been following agent Graves and he led us here.

I just received word from one of my people Bent or one of his aliases has been spotted and we narrowed down the area and we are chasing the complex. WT adds Graves is the last on the list of agents that know you are Black Phoenix. I say I guess we are going to save Grave's ass.

Wild Tail suggests It would be nice to capture Bent alive too. WT Pushes a button on his Gauntlet and I ask what are you doing? Keeping a promise, I told Titus that if we found Graves and Bent to let him know. He should be on a fast helicopter here by now. My guess, a call to the local police has also been put out to secure the harbor. They ain't going far we are just here to keep them from killing each other. Waiting and watching the story play out is driving me nuts. With my enhanced Black Phoenix hearing I listen in to the conversation.

Bent finally says Hello Graves. Graves says This is a strange place to meet.

Can't be helped something happened to Black Phoenix best I can figure he was taken in by Wild Tail. That could mean a lot of explaining for you. If WT gets a hold of Max, you could be in a world of hurt. How do you figure Graves? Wild Tail has friends in high places CIA and The Agency. You had better surrender now. Oh, I don't think so because I still have a few more hiding places only thing is I have a few loose ends to deal with. I had Black Phoenix take care of the ones who created him and the nuisance Wild Tail, but the one who sent Him out on his missions. I have to take care of him personally.

Black Phoenix jumps into the air and instantly changes to his white skin! Bent in shock says Black Phoenix How? My name is Max, and he belts him across the face!

So Wild Tail was able to figure your Black Phoenix persona out. I came prepared for this!

Bent put a device in his face and pushes a button and blaring sound comes out and he says you will kill Agent Graves for me! He turns towards Graves and the absolute fear on Grave's face is priceless. Then he turns around and gives Bent a flying kick! Knocking the device out of his hands! Yelling You son of a bitch! What did you have me do by your hands? Bent pleads What I did, I did because it had to be done! Look at what you have accomplished Max, it had to be done! He slaps him across the face and yells, "You stole my life!"

Bent can see the writing on the wall now. The sound of Titus and other agents coming off in the distance. Max, you were the best mistake that I ever made. Shut up! Sacrifices had to be made. Not another word! Remember what I taught you about saving the last bullet.

Before he can get ahold of Bent's gun, he shoots himself in the head. Bent commits suicide instead of surrendering to The CIA or The Agency. Graves is tackled by Titus and the other CIA agents before he can get away. Black Phoenix walks away from them.

Titus asks, "Where are you going?" Black Phoenix replies I have to figure some things out before I am any good to anyone Titus. He leaves with Wild Tail and the others.

# CHAPTER TWELVE
## "I wake up another time jump?"

Nineteen Seventy-nine I wake up and it is another jump. I look at my calendar and look at my schedule and see after school we are going to tackle K. Ray C. As I get up and get dressed the time jump gives me little headaches. I am not going to be in order one day after another in a row. I have to rely on my calendar and my crossed-out days to get a balance of where I am at. I vaguely remember what happened yesterday, but I am jumping around?

It is like a countdown, I guess. I am not reliving every single day, maybe just the important days? By the way who is deciding what days are important?

After School we find K. Ray C. walking home. Here we are jumping out of Paul's Pickup!

We pile on him! K. yells nice touch Paul, I see you got the muffler fixed! Duct tape is stretched by Pete and K. asks Can I keep my eyebrows this time? Paul yells out, "Did you use the bathroom this time?" K. yells back Yes it was delightful I didn't get a Swirly or anything. Paul laughs and says If those Seniors are giving you a hard time you just let me know I beat them up in Kindergarten I can beat them up now. We tied him up and I yelled Ok guys let's put him in the back One two three. Reed says Hey I think you are putting on weight K. K. comments I have been taking my pills hopefully my body will keep fighting the cancer and I will have a good immune system. Churchill adds That is the plan we'll keep you healthy so you can be the life of the party. K. Asks Can we drive by the park There are some Sophomore girls I want to whistle at. Anything you want. As we drive by the park "Whistle" Hey baby hey baby I love you! And we brought him in the hospital. OK Dock take good care of him.

August Monday 5, 2002 I wake up about 2 a.m. and go back to sleep. Nineteen Seventy-nine Another jump in time. I know that the K Ray C Test results are negative. Pete is not in any of our classes today. He is being tested. I know he is smart, but his father has been looking for a privet school to send him to for years. And today is the day they are going to find out. K. asks Why so glum chums? Paul says I am going to miss the little guy when he is gone. K adds Oh come on-. Paul counters with He is so smart his dad is going to send the kid away to an Ivy League Privet school. I add He speaks Spanish English German French Latin, and he is tutoring Seniors on the side. And he is only ten.

K. comments Well hey you will have me to pal around with, you can call me "Sickly the Cancer Survivor." Paul says Ah it won't be the same and besides every time you open your mouth, I think you are killing brain cells. It might be funny man, but you are killing brain cells.

K. replies Gee Only a friend can be that brutal and honest.

After school we will see Pete. Hey buddy, how are you? Pete looks at his shoes and says Scared. Paul rubs his shoulder saying Ah little buddy don't be you are going to a great place where people respect intelligence does not fear it because it makes them look stupid and ignorant. Really? Yeah, like in history where they used to burn you at the steak or excommunicate from the church for saying the earth goes around the sun.

Or saying the earth is round when they say it is flat. I may not know who all those people are, but you do, and it will take you far, far away. We may never see each other again, but we can say it has been fun. Pete just grabs ahold of Paul crying I don't want to go! K. murmurs Run free little freak of nature run free. Everyone knocks him on the back of the head. Hey, don't hit Sickly The Cancer Survivor. Sickly The Cancer Survivor bruises easily.

# CHAPTER THIRTEEN
## "Cow Poo is a natural skin moisturizer."

August Monday 5, 2002 I take the day off and work on Paul's farm and I get up after four a.m. I find my "Let's take a five-minute break and see if Willie Nelson and Farm Aid will come save our ass. Ho hum He Ain't coming. I guess we are going to have to do it ourselves." T-Shirt. Old clothes that I can get dirty and not get too concerned about and jog out to the farm, I see a car with a busted headlight weaving from side to side "El Koo ca rotcha" is being sung by the driver and the passenger's crash! They take out my mailbox and keep on going! Max the dog barks at the same time as I am cursing a blue streak!

When I got to the farm Pete 2.0 age fifteen was there and says Hi Max, Dad said you were coming. Pete there are some drunk Mexicans driving up and down the road and they just took out my mailbox! Pete says Yeah well what can you do about it, Maria had twin boys and they are celebrating hopefully they won't kill anybody. Well, I can go and arrest them.

Pete says Ah follow me you and me we gotta talk as we walk back to the calf barn.

Don't go and arrest them, they will ship them back to Mexico. Well, are they illegal? Most likely they say they are from Texas or California but who knows? Well then, I think they should be sent back to Mexico. Ah Max, are you going to come tomorrow? No, I have to work I am a police officer. Well hopefully they will lay off the Tequila and sober up by tomorrow or tonight and be back to work.

What about my mailbox?

Tell Dad maybe he can get one of them to fix it they are pretty good at fixing stuff.

They get enough practice around here. That is not the point.

Max last year Hector and Orlando got in trouble when they pick pocketed or shop lifted an item at the Corner Store. They got so excited about what they stole they got into their getaway car and instead of putting the car in reverse they put the car in drive and nearly took out the front of the store. I have to laugh. Pete 2.0 says That is not funny because Immigration came and picked up Hector and sent him back to Mexico. The only reason they did not get Orlando was because Dad told him to go hide in the Corn field. Hector was in lock up in Detroit for a month and then sent back to Mexico. I rightly state, "Well he probably deserved to go." Pete 2.0 gives a reality check He was back here working on the farm in six weeks. He hitches hiked back here from Mexico. Oh shit? Do we really need to send Hector back to Mexico? As Dad would say it "If he wants to see his family so bad, he can buy his own damn ticket." If Immigration can't keep Hector in Mexico, How can they keep the Arab terrorist out? I think they have enough problems as it is, they don't need to try to send Hector back just to have him show up here in a few weeks again. Besides he gets all his mail here and the video conferences with his wife and kids in Mexico.

We walked back to the calf barn and the baby calves woke up crying we want food water and milk as we enter. Ok Max it is pretty self-explanatory empty the orange pales that have water in them. Give the calves sweet feed in the other pail if they need it. Do you remember how to bed up the calves' hutches? I think so. Good I'll go see if there are any new calves and if there are I'll bring them back here and check on you.

I started doing the chores Pete gave me and for the most part they are coming back to me.

The only difference is when I was a kid there were ten calves and now there are almost a hundred or more. Pete brings a baby calf back with the calf cart and says I have two more where this one came from and another one that might be having twins. Hey, how are you doing back here? Nice bedding up Max. Ah thanks. Tell me who am I replacing for the day? Orlando is the proud poppa. Right. Hey, do you know how to run a skid steer? It has been years, but I think I remember. Well, if you don't think you will destroy the farm, I'll let you drive, you can watch me clean one alley and then I'll let you try it. Do you let Orlando drive a skid steer? Not anymore then he has too. You have seen how he drives; it is not that much better when he is sober.

A bit later Pete comes back with twelve five-gallon pales of milk on a pushcart and shows me how to feed the calves. Little by little it comes back to me. Stick your finger in the calf's mouth and let it suck. Come on baby, suck that nipple. That's it you are a natural.

Hey Pete, how come there is no high school kids besides you working here? Pete says Danny Cooper helps out but that is because he is trying to get in good graces with Dad and see Maggie Max. Ah young love.

Yeah, but he won't show up till after eight and mom will have him working in the garden.

He is the exception, mostly they are too lazy to work much around here, I guess. If they can get a job at McDonalds or Wal-Mart or The C Connection, they will go there before they would work here.

I add I worked here when I was a kid? Then you are special Max. I guess if you are not born to work hard you have no get up and go to do it.

That is why Dad hired the Mexicans. It is hard to get anyone who is dependable. I worked the whole time Hector was gone, didn't miss a day. We had a White Trash guy work for us. Wouldn't come to work on time. Tell us he was going to take a week off, which ended up being two weeks. That was when Paul 2.0 was a senior. You couldn't leave your lunch in the cooler because the guy would steal it. Dad finally told the guy to go. "Ain't going to miss you when you are gone." One guy when Troy asked him to do something told me and Troy, I am nobody's slave. I said to him get off my farm and Troy backed me up and told the guy Get out of here you are fired!

I ponder things have changed saying You have some interesting workers. Pete replies, "That is an understatement." I don't know how Dad and Troy are going to do it if I go to college. It ticks him off how the government tries to regulate things. So, mom keeps him in the dark most of the time. Keeping Dad busy in the shed painting and doing comics. Also, Dad needs to watch his blood pressure. Paul has a bad heart. No, as far as I know mom is a bit paranoid, I think. Never met my grandparents on her side of the family. "Heart Attacks and they smoked."

Yeah, I wish my mom would quit smoking earlier too.

So, the Mexicans have worked out for you? Some have worked out. Some will work no problem then they get their paycheck, and they don't come back. Dad got a house for the family that worked for us. They Stole paper towels instead of buying their own toilet paper and plugged up the septic system. Big ass mess! Stole my lunch out of the cooler too. Come to work drunk. Get another member of their family to work here he learns how to milk cows. He then goes to another farm and finds one that pays a few cents more. They leave without even a notice.

Oh and just say Border Patrol and Immigration and they run.. All in all, right now we have a pretty good crew. Fun thing is I can speak Spanish and Peppy told me to my face in English that he couldn't clean calf hatches tomorrow because he had to take his wife Maria to the doctor. I overheard him talk on the phone in Spanish to a friend.

I have this white lazy farmer I can do whatever I want, we are going to party tonight.

You got the Tequila? What did you do? I cleaned all the calf hutches while he was gone. That was a whole day's work and several hours he could have stretched it out milking the clock. He was pissed when he came back. He was nervous, he needed that time on the clock for payday. He was crying. I have a wife and kid! I told him in Spanish "You should have thought of that instead of Tequila." The look on his face was priceless. Don't call me a white fat lazy farmer. I am Mr. Chapel to you.

He was telling the truth about the wife though. Maria helped out in the calf barn too at the time. And she laughed at her husband because she treated me with respect. I hated taking the money away from them by doing the work myself. After that when there were calf hutches to do, he did them right that day and did not say I'll do them tomorrow. Uncle Pete has helped a couple work towards their green card and citizenship. You call him Uncle Pete? Well, I am named after him. He might be of Mexican decent, but he is American as anybody. I am not prejudiced against anybody. I just don't like people who will not work. Why should I or anybody else work 365 days a year just so someone else can sit on their butt and get a welfare check?

By nine thirty /ten the calves calm down as they get fed and are almost happy and content now. We finish up by cleaning up the barn and watering the calves. Maggie Max Paul's oldest daughter brings little Benjamin in a red wagon and her younger brothers and sisters. She says Ben wanted to see the calves. I look at this precious life and I thank God he is alive. Here he is with a cast on his leg. Happy he just wants to play with his calves. Pete sheds a tear for his little brother and says Come on Max lets go up and clean pales and bottles. I keep it to myself under my breath, I say I promise I am going to get the ones who did this to you. As we walked up, I asked, "When is breakfast? Pete's answer is, "What is breakfast? How about a coffee break?" Pete says I guess Dad has coffee in the office, but I don't drink it. Coffee tastes to me like the water that Jon Valdez soaks his feet in after a hard day picking coffee beans. Pete takes me into the parlor, and we clean bottles and pails. The family is pitching in and helping everyone catch up with their chores.

Hey Paul, your Mexicans took out my mailbox. Paul looks at me with shock. Oh, I am sorry I am a bit busy taking applications for replacement workers. I have fifty of them waiting outside the door and I have to interview them. I miss your sarcasm where can I get some coffee? Marcy makes a fresh pot, by the way you missed breakfast where you were? I look at Pete and he says Dad's sarcasm gotta love it. No breakfast, right? Yeah, but I hear mom makes pretty good coffee, but I don't drink it because-. I ran to the house, and I get a cup of coffee and buttered breakfast rolls.

On the way back I take a look at the workshop and a couple of Paul's relatives are fabricating The Trebuchet. Whoa you guys weren't kidding when you said you wanted to build it. Troy says, "We are going to be able to fling a cow with this." The kids are blowing up old tractor tires and tying them together making an inner tube cage?

What the heck is that for? Troy explains Oh what we are going to do is strap a couple people in here and launch them with the Trebuchet and they will land safely in the water.

We have a couple mannequins and dead waits to test the contraption. When we feel it is safe you want to be the first volunteer?

By the time I get back to the parlor Pete is already gone. I find him moving cattle outside so he can clean barns. If you want Max, I'll bring the tractor around and you can load shit into the spreader while I get straw and bed the barns up. I am so excited to drive the skid steer that I rev it up and run into a pile of wet stuff and it splatters back at me big time! Oh SHIT! I shake my hands and shut off the machine. Take it is easy Max you'll get a handle on the controls just relax. I'll go get you a wash rag and some water and you can clean yourself and the skid steer off.

I could leave here, and it is tempting Pete is being kind to me a city slicker. But I offered to help, and I clean myself off and I go back to work and I do take it easy and when I am done it is a pretty good job if I do say so myself. Besides I am having too much fun.

After the barns are cleaned, He shows me how to flush barns and occasionally I get a wet sloppy cow's tail in my face. It is a lot cleaner than a Perp who got off on a technicality and curses in my face, a lot cleaner.

Lunch time comes Marcy, and the kids are in the garden harvest and canning season is in full swing. Marcy has Maggie Max's boyfriend Daniel Cooper in the kitchen running the pressure cooker. Hey Danny, how you doing? Sweating but the Chapel's all organic garden is worth it. Marcy comes by and gives him a thankful kiss. What would I do without you? Danny asks Max try my BBQ sauce. I try a taste This is good, but it is still a good second to Sodom and Gomorrah. Yeah, they are the best I just can't get the seasoning just right. I admit, You have a good start. I walk away and I look back and see Danny and Maggie making goo-goo eyes at each other. I nudge Paul and say They make a cute couple.. Paul adds He figures out the secret to Better than sex BBQ and I'll give him my daughter's hand in marriage.

I find Pete drawing at a desk looking over his shoulder I ask Who is this guy? Oh, I am just playing with a costume design for a new Wild Tail Champion character out of San Francisco. His name is "Copycat" He is a Martial arts expert and a beat cop with a Great One Power that enables him to make multiple copies of himself. I am impressed by Cool. In theory he could have a copy of himself as a cop, another who is our hero Copycat and another who is learning more Martial Arts and hand to hand combat and another doing something else who knows. Sounds great. Yeah, if I give my dad a decent copy maybe if he likes it I'll be able to help him draw the series. You want to be an artist like your dad? Paul 2.0 When he is not studying and doing stuff for The Air Force. He is great at computer graphics and stuff like that, and editing and nobody is as fast and as good as Dad. I just want to find my place in where I fit in, I guess. I like the farm and all, but I would like to see if there is something more out there.

How old are you? Fifteen. That is a lot of dreams to hope for at Fifteen. Troy Comes in and asks Max any chance you could help Maggie milk right now? How long? From now till five. When do you people take a coffee break? Pete chuckles and says, "Go on I'll feed the calves tonight." I add and check up on me, so I don't mix the cows up.

I start milking cows at around noon and Paul's daughter Maggie "Fourteen" gets things started. Ok Max let's get this party started! She begins milking by putting her Garth Brooks CD in the player and turning up the music and then pushes the button that starts the milkers. Cows are loaded and she watches over my shoulder as I put on the milkers, and I take a look at her, and she flops that milker on a cow so quick I know I am going slow. She looks at me and says Oh you will pick up the pace Max. You just need practice.

On the last group I start dragging my butt and Pete comes in and helps us catch up.

After five P.M. We get done milking and Maggie almost carries me up to the house. I am beat and tired. Marcy feeds me well and I am part of the family again and it feels good.

After supper a Chapel cousin says Hey let's go take a swim at the pond. They load up pop and snacks on the wagon and Paul drives the tractor, take a leisurely hayride to the camp site and they pile out and jump into the pond. I wish I had shorts on I would take a swim, so I roll up my pant legs and get my feet wet and enjoy the company. Sun sets and I walk home and Hector, Orlando and the other Mexicans drive by and Maria is driving and I watch as she drops them off at the Parlor and they stagger in to Milk. Troy has learned how to speak Spanish and has some words for them. I have to smile when he talks to them about a certain mailbox. And the owner of that mailbox is a Carter County Cop.

"Oh Shit!"

I am tired when I enter my house Bridge takes me back in time again. Black Phoenix asks Wild Tail Where is this place? Wild Tail answers I can't tell you until you are a full member. But I can give you a tour. Over here this is our Hospital if a Wild Tail Champion or an ally or any paying clients is injured or wounded he or she can be automatically transported to the Emergency Room. We may be able to do a lot of stuff, but we are still human. Transported? You can transport matter by energy? We transported you.. Actually, it is not energy or matter we use earth's magnetic field to transport. We don't use it on a regular basis, it costs a lot of money to operate, and we don't want to take the chance of being traced. The FBI CIA KGB NSA ISA MI6 Israel's Masada SECRET SERVICE S.I.G.H.T. And the whole alphabet soup agencies might not have a transporter, but it doesn't hurt to be careful.

WT looks both ways to see who is watching and smiles and snickers Ok just between you and me. It does not cost a thing for us to use. We just put a price tag on it so our clients will purchase our vehicles, and gadgets. As for being traced oh that is a laugh.

This is our Wholesale Warehouse we have just about anything a Wild Tail hero could want or need. The way I see it why should James Bond have all the good toys? Here is one of our designers. They will create a uniform that will fit you to a T. Max replies I already have a designer, if He will take me that is. WT asks by the way what are you going to call yourself? He rolls up his sleeve to Show the Tattoo SELAH. That is a good name, but there is already a comic book by that name. Max replies He named it after me, Paul Chapel is one of my best friends.

Wait a minute, I can't do this, I have a job. I work for The CIA and the N.Y.P.D!

WT says This can be a career and an adventure! Wearing funny long underwear?

WT snaps Flex Cloth Max. Flex Cloth. All right Flex Cloth but that's not a real life. Wild Tail says Like what you have been living is a real-life sleeper agent for the CIA. Ok I have to pay my bills. Can you write? NO. Paul and Marcy have been writing and drawing a pretty good comic, all you have to do is tell them your adventures and they can do the rest. After you beat the crap out of the bad guys, they can write the story for you. Of course, we change the names and faces because they deserve a fair trial. We make a comic book out of your adventure. Sell the comic book after the bills are paid you get to keep what is left over. Left over? Well, that's after medical taxes an insurance uniforms lawyer if you ever get caught and other niceties. If you are really popular we make T-shirts toys baseball cards and lunch pails you name it we sell it. Sell it? What happened to protect and serve?

Protect and serve yes, but I have houses planes and cars to pay for. And some of the other Wild Tail Champions have family and kids to send to college, ex-wives and alimony to pay. Besides I give to worthy charades. They ask for money, and this is my way of earning it. Did I mention the retirement fund?

Have you ever had to kill anyone? WT pauses then answers In order to protect the innocent. It's not an act anyone wants to do. It is THEE last option. We do everything we can to avoid that and when it happens everyone, even your friends, watch you. They are making sure you don't or didn't go over the edge. When someone has gone over the edge, we take care of our own.

He puts a smile on his face saying I want you to meet the crew some of them should be in the Training Center. Is that really? Yep that's Exclamation!. There is Cockroach He is only visiting the Training Center He likes to keep in shape and test himself against the Training droids. His Cockroach's armor enables him to grip most surfaces, jump great distances and rip through almost anything.

Wild Tail pushes an intercom button. If you destroy those Training Droids you are buying them! Cockroach answers back That is what repair crews are for! Yeah well, they have a union now, and I will hear about it!

Max asks, "Is that The Void?" Yeah, with his computer linked to his brain he is an expert in just about anything and everything. He has that cape that is just about like having a warehouse on your back. He can store limitless stuff in the thing. Tanks, motorcycles, helicopters, jets, boats, cars you name it, and he can teleport too! His army buddy created the cape and jury-rigged the brain computer. Now they basically live inside the cape. That's one way to get an apartment in New York City.

I just watch him as he watches the other WILD TAILS for a while, and he knows he is hooked. WELCOME TO THE WILD TAIL CHAMPIONS FAMILY.

But what do you do? "We keep the world from blowing up on a daily basis." Yeah right. How? We watch, we keep an eye on things. Like what? Let's put it this way Max there is a lot of people in this world who don't like us. Meaning The U.S.A. / and The Western world and culture in general. And they want us dead. Plain and simple. And the way the world keeps going is there are a lot of things the world does not know about.

You must really think you are so superior. And above all. WT asks Tell me Max does the world need to know about The CIA trying to create you as secret weapon?

No, I guess not. Then don't give me psychology, or moral lessons on feeling of being Superior. I say my prayers and ask God for wisdom and strength and a little help every now and again. If you really do become a Wild Tail Champion, I suggest you do the same. Sorry I. You're young Max, you will learn if you live long enough.

WT hands Max a little black box. What is it? We call it "Gravitational Communication."

What? Do you have Cable TV? No. Well, you do now. Actually, it is a lot better than cable. This is the basic unit you connect it to your TV or VCR, and it will give you a clear as Digital Satellite picture and sound. How? Let me show you. They both get into an elevator and they go down. This is the bottom of The Bottom of the basement.

What is a Satellite dish doing in The Basement? And turned upside down and facing down? We found multiple uses of earth's Gravitational field. The Transporter you know.

But we can also send TV Radio cell phone and just about all the Wild Tail communications go through the " Gravitational Communication ". You have to have pretty high WTC clearance just to know the details about it, and how it all works. But let's just say I am halfway around the earth I can have a conversation on a G.C. Cell phone with someone else. At another point. And there is no satellite and no loss in signal strength. Cell Phone, TV, Radio, and wireless Internet. Max asks how come you don't market this technology as a way of communicating instead of using a Satellite?

WT answers Well for many reasons. One, My Boss does not care too much about The F.C.C. I ask Who is your boss? Two, My boss "William Wildtale" owns a Satellite Company that makes Satellites for communications. Three, It is secure and sound technology and nobody knows that it exists. "WOW." Oh, you think this is wow. Stick with me kid and we will go places.

They get back on the elevator and head back up. And he asks, "So what now?" WT comments You have control of Black Phoenix now. But I have a life as a Police Detective, and I don't want to give that life up. WT responds Everyone here has a secret life.

I hate what Bent did, but I did have a life. Is there a way I could have you separate my personalities. You want to be a sleeper agent again? I want to keep my life. There are some things I would like to forget. Selah can carry the burden of it all. WT adds A Max Faraday personality to live your so-called normal life. Can it be done? Yeah, from what we have learned, yeah it can be done. But at some time Max, your personalities will merge. I have seen it before you might as well be one mind from the start. Alright let's see if we could split your personalities who would have control over them? Max answers "You could give me a call like Graves or Bent did." It could be done, But Max? When you have control of your powers it heals your internal organs. He says, "it is either this or you erase Black Phoenix from my memory." WT shakes his head in the end Ok this is it. So have you spoken it, so shall it be done.

They get out of the elevator.

Take this Selah comic to the tailors down the hall and they will make a uniform for you. While you are waiting Call your friend Paul Chapel you have a lot of explaining to do.

He might as well know the truth. Set up a meeting tonight if possible. He suggests How about The back room at The Sodom and Gomorra Saloon Bar and Grill ok for you? WT agrees Sure they have the best ribs. But I won't be going. My boss "William Wildtale" will be making the introduction. Indigo overhears the conversation and asks Mind if I tag along? He says Sure more the merrier.

Later that night I see them, and they are all in casual dress. Paul and Marcy have just arrived. I watch as he leads them to the back room. Paul recognizes Indigo as a good friend, but the other guy? Paul shakes his head, Marcy we are leaving. Marcy asks Paul, "what is it?" I don't know why he is here, but I ain't staying in the same room with him. That is William Wildtale. He comes to Paul's side Paul you are my guest please. Ok for you Max, just for you. The doors are closed behind them as a buffet is placed before them. Silent prayers go out and they talk amongst themselves.

Paul asks him, "What is going on I like a free meal and all, but what is going on?" Max says Paul I have something to say. And he tells our story to Paul. Stunned amazement Paul says No shit. Indigo is on the other side of the room, and I can imagine with his sensitive ears he probably heard the whole thing. He just can't keep from smiling. Paul looks over to him and tosses a dinner roll in his direction? Indy catches it? So, let me get this straight you are not just Indigo McGraw you are The Blue Bomber? Indy nods his head. Max here wants to be The Real Selah. What does that make you William Wildtale The WILD TAIL? Mr. Wildtale gets up and says Now wait a minute and Paul Cold Cocks him and he is on the floor.

Indy gets up and says You just Decked the Wild Tail. Paul says I have nothing against The Wild Tail, but William Wildtale had that coming! WT wakes up and asks, "What hit me?" I did how do you like that! Indy asks, "What is wrong with you Paul?" Paul yells When I first submitted my artwork to Wildtale Comics I got back a damn nasty letter! His name was at the bottom of the letter. And it, it hurt! I was tempted to sell my Wildtale comics and give up my art! You ticked me off! Indy heard I submitted to you and got back a bad letter and he said he had a friend who wrote for the Blue Bomber. He gave me a script and said If you draw it, I'll pass it on to my friend. And I did. I have been drawing Blue Bomber ever since under a pen name.

WT rubs his jaw When did you send and get the letter? Paul, we get hundreds of letters every day from people submitting artwork. I don't get to see hardly any of them because I am too busy. It had your name on it. Well, that editor has been fired and I am sorry that was very unprofessional. Well, I am sorry, but it hurt. Well, you have done well for yourself. Now you want to have my Selah? Max stands up and says Paul, "I thought it was ours?" Well, If I work for Wildtale who has creative control?

Will Wildtale says Everything will go through our editors. Working for Blue Bomber you have had to do editing? Paul smiles I work with a blind guy I pretty much have creative control of the story. Well now you will have another set of eyes looking over your shoulder.

When do I get a story? Max is going to wake up in the hospital tonight. Seems he has been sick in bed and has not been to the police station in a few days. That should be a good cover for his absence. After a few days I'll call him up and activate Selah.

We should have a mission by then. You sure you can handle His story "The Real Selah" and Blue Bomber? Paul snickers I should, I have been doing Twilight on and off for over a year. Bridge brings me back. I am so tired I can't get mad at Paul for not telling me he knew who I was all the time, so I go fast asleep.

# CHAPTER FOURTEEN
## "UFO Aliens are here, they ain't going anywhere. Get used to it."

Nineteen Eighty Max and Jackson Reed witness a UFO sighting!

At lunch Reed asks Hey it is Thursday anybody want to watch the UFOs with me?

Jason murmurs Ah man not the UFO thing again. Paul adds Hey I have seen something, but I don't know if it was a UFO or a weather balloon or what? Reed pounds the table See there I told you there is something.

Steve states Yeah something, the idea that there is life on other planets? K. Ray C asks Hey Why not? Adam remarks, "Well he has you there why couldn't there be life on other planets?" Churchill comments Because if there were life would the only ones to see them are people like Red Neck Reed and not people like me. Reed smacks his fist on the table, Hey I said I saw something I am not certain is was anything. To say the only ones who see UFOs are Red Necks is a racist statement. K. Ray C says You were just waiting to use that word in a sentence weren't you. Just because I am a Red Neck "Sickly The Cancer Survivor" does not make it true that we are the only ones. It just is the case.

Dan says Hey wouldn't it be neat if there was life on other planets? I mean we could learn from them and maybe it would put an end to all our wars on earth. Churchill adds, "What if they are having a war out there and we get caught in the middle?" Paul wonders aloud Hey that would be neat just like in the comics and the TV show The BRAVE UNIVERSE! I add Just because you have all the technology in the universe does not mean there is peace in the universe.

 K. says Maybe they could cure all our ills? Steve comments Maybe we could cure our own ills if we weren't trying to blow each other up? Reed mutters Well I don't know about illnesses I just want to know if anybody wants to watch and see if they will do a fly over tonight? I say sure what time do they fly over? "8:30 - 9:00." Jason asks, "Isn't that a bit predictable?" Reed replies I don't know but they do great fireworks show, man they can move.

So, after I work at my after-school job I go home and have some dinner and get on my scooter and drive out to Reed's. Hey you came cool! It is 8:30 on the dot and nothing.

Reed offers me a pop and a candy bar. Nine forty-five I am about to leave. Thanks Reed but I think I better get home. Oh, come on Max Stay. Then I look up to the East and there they are dancing in the night sky! Doing maneuvers like nothing I had seen before? I have seen a lot in my day. Up and down loop tee loops and barrel rolls? I shutter at the thought How can they do that? Then they are gone just as rapidly as they came. Wow. What do you think Max? How come nobody has seen that and talked about it? Reed says something profound for him at least Maybe they think people will think they are goofy or a Red Neck or something if they talk about it? Maybe they know better and know there are some things you should be quiet about. You think? Hey, you gotta do what you gotta do Reed. What people think about you is one thing. What you know about yourself is another. I ride my scooter home and enjoy the springtime air. When I got home my mom asked, "Did you see anything?" Yeah, we saw something but I don't know what?

# CHAPTER FIFTEEN
## "The Gospel according to Paul"

August Tuesday 6th 2002 I wake up get a shower I should have had one last night my sheets smell. Get dressed grab my breakfast muffin "Thanks Marcy". I meet two Mexicans at my driveway who are putting a new post and are pounding the dents out of my mailbox. Hola caballeros. Orlando dice por favor que somos tan arrepentidos que queremos hacerlo derecho con usted. ¿Yo los entrego un "Alcoholicos Anónimos" tarjeta está allí en una base regular? Ah Señor. Trabajamos tercer cambio y yo no pienso que podemos obtener el tiempo de también. Yo'discurso de ll al señor Paul usted obtendrá el tiempo lejos.

"English Translation." Hello gentlemen. Orlando says Please we are so sorry we want to make it right with you. I hand them an "Alcoholics Anonymous" card be there on a regular basis? Oh Sir. We work third shift and I do not think we can get the time off too. I'll talk to mister Paul you will get the time off. But We speak very little English.

Do you understand deportation and I show them my badge. I am not in the mood. Don't mess with me today!

I did my duty, nothing new happened and when the day is done, I head to Paul's.

I see Paul working alone in his office at the drawing table. I look at him straight in the eyes and ask Paul Why didn't you tell me I am Selah? He looks down at his drawing and says "Because you asked me to help you forget." I ask, "Why did I do that?" I pounded the table yelling Paul answer me! He barks back I won't answer your question, because you asked me to help you forget! I turned away from him in my rage That is not an answer Paul! Well Man that is the road you chose not me!

I pause and take a deep breath, breathe in, breathe out. So, I went against your wishes? Paul, I have always respected you and your opinion. He adds Yeah right. What did I do that would make me want to erase Selah? Paul let it slip out It wasn't Selah that did it, it was Black Phoenix. Black Phoenix? But I am a Black Phoenix? Hey, I already said too much. Please Paul. No, you said you wanted a fresh start, well that is what I intend to give you. But Paul, I am remembering please give me more to go on. Paul replies Max if you don't have it. All the knowledge skills and powers, you are going to get yourself in deep shit! I know you; you will go off halfcocked and get yourself killed. I plead Who else knows I am Selah? Paul responds Oh man that is a loaded question.

Ralph knows, doesn't he! Paul chuckles Max what doesn't Ralph know. Marcy knows you tell her everything. Yep, but don't go trying to get anything out of her, she didn't like your choice any more than I did. Indigo McGraw the Blue Bomber knows, and he won't tell me either. Yeah, he is pretty tight lipped too. Pete knows because of Ice Works. Yeah, he and Jason built and ran the computer network for us. Oh shit, that one slipped.

I realize That is right he has his video game system with Wildtale Corp. Jason knows!

Then I look on the wall and there are comic book characters called "The Bull's Eye Duo" Bull's Eye Red" with a sniper's rifle. Steve was a sniper during the attack on the safe house? Steve is Bull's Eye Red! I look at another Character on the wall with a Bow and Arrow called Bull's Eye Green? Adam is Bull's Eye Green! Damn it Who else knows?

Well Reed does. How? He is probably one of the best fire fighter / Arson investigators in the State if not the country! He has a nose for fire and smoke, you know that.

They call him all the time for opinions on stuff. It hits me, I was doing an investigation as Selah, I needed a second opinion, and I didn't trust my Gauntlet's scanners, so I brought Reed in.

Jamie and Ellen don't know who I am right? Paul laughs Little pacifist Baptist boy! Shoot, he is the reason we can't tell anybody what is really going on in the world. If he owned a gun he would be out buying shot gun shells and canned goods and screaming It is all over we haven't got a prayer. He doesn't even like the idea that I am drawing comics for Wildtale Comics. Too violent.

It hits me I did a mission for The Special Intelligence in Israel as Selah. I met Abba Rabbi Hyman there. He had an intelligence contact being held captive by the Palestinians that I rescued. Paul adds, "Yeah, he has been managing your Selah account for years. You haven't even tapped your hidden cash yet."

 I was Black Phoenix, Israel made arrangements with Bent in the old days. . I did Wet Works for Israel? Paul admits, "Yeah, I read your Black Phoenix files that The Questioner saved. You worked for just about everyone at one time or another."

John Henry and Connie? They don't know anything. Graves! He knows I am Selah! Paul chuckles Ah no he doesn't, we erased his mind about your whole Black Phoenix history. The same way you erased me?

Link did it with a little bit more English and elbow grease in the erase part put into the mix.

Titus knows who I am too. Paul adds Yeah but, Bent did such a good job of cleaning up The Black Phoenix files before he shot himself. Only Titus and only a few people at The Agency like Gather know who you are. I wonder And Titus was for my erase of Selah?

Paul comments Max at some point you have to make your own decisions and that was your choice. Max you can't ask me any more questions Ok.

Fine, I guess I'll just have to remember on my own. By the way Paul remember when we were kids Freshmen in high school and one night Reed and I saw lights in the sky?

Paul sits back in his chair and ponders Let's see that was way back in 1980, You were most likely seeing a dog fight between The Brave and The TRI. I ask, "But The Brave takes place two hundred years in the future?" Paul responds No they just say that to keep most people from snooping around because it really takes place in the here and now. I give a stunned look Every Thursday night? Not really once they were identified and caught in earth's atmosphere The TRI were relocated via The Magnetic Transporter. The WTC have the ability to hold matter in a "N Space stasis." They could capture them on Monday and let them go on Thursday. I read the reports that when they attacked on Thursday they were relocated to Michigan.

Any other day they were moved to different locations. Why Michigan on Thursday?

The dog fights were kinda like a Brave Space Air Forces commercial. Those who knew what was going on in The Air Force would pass the info to young pilots. "You see what is going on up there. You could be doing that."

You see The Tri cannot trace Magnetic Transporter actually nobody really can because the energy field exists in normal space actually it is called N space. For a time, the BRAVE and The Wild Tails couldn't track the new TRI's cloaked star ship. But when they would launch a TRI star fighter attack. That is a little attack plane. The WTC would capture the TRI star fighters, hold them in stasis then release them. The Brave would launch an earth based BRAVE squadron counter strike attack. All the destroyed fighters debris would be caught before it might hit the ground. Or in the confusion the surviving TRI fighters would "bee line" it for space.

High above the Skies in Michigan? Oh, that was just on Thursdays. Hey sometimes the whole dog fight was moved to Japan, China, Area 51, and Russia. The Wild Tail and BRAVE Tech boys moved them around till they figured out their TRI stealth / cloak Technology. For the most part The lights in the sky are earth's own so called secret planes now.

What about The Roswell crash? Oh that was some aliens out in a student driver flying saucer. If you translated the marking on the side of the ship that is basically what they say.

"Caution student driver." I shake my head saying- Paul I came home thinking there was nothing I could share about my life. I mean The CIA and my Black Ops. You know everything about that stuff don't you? Paul bluntly says it Hey when you find out there really is a group of so-called Comic Book Heroes out there. That they are keeping the world from blowing up on a daily basis. And there is life on other planets and every day there is a war going on in the stars between the BRAVE and the TRI. And the unknowns of the universe. Your old CIA file of secrets is kinda a drop in the bucket. Good reading, but still a drop in the bucket.

I wake up and it is still Nineteen Eighty? When I meet everyone at school Wendy looks concerned. What is the problem? She explains My Dad says He enjoys his job on the West Coast. He wants us to move out of there. Me, mom and Steve but mom won't go.

"This makes me remember this time in my history." Wendy's Father & Mother get separated, and The Mother keeps going with the Foster Care. Or in better terms she practically kills herself trying to keep the foster home going.

Over lunch Pete says I have been invited to go to a special school for the gifted. K. says Like the X-Men? Paul taps him on the back of the head. Hey, bud it will really be great for you where is it? Pennsylvania. Oh nothing in Michigan? Yeah, but my dad says he wants the best for me, and it is kind of hard to say no to him. I mean the life he lived in Mexico. He is sending for Grandma to come live with them as soon as I leave for school. Jason sympathizes I know how you feel as soon as I turn eighteen, I am out the door. Churchill says It is not the same thing. Jason continues I know I am just saying I know how he feels all my good stuff is in my room. And since my Grandpa moved his glass blowing to our warehouse I think my dad is planning on giving him my room when I am gone. I ask How is it going with your grandpa? Great I was working on the side with my dad after school and when I am not working with him, he is having me learn the glass blowing trade. The things he can make. Bowls goblets vases he helped me make glass figurines. Dad even has a guy making neon signs.

Dan adds We are going to have a new neon C Connection sign. Pete adds, "Wish I could be here to see it, but my dad wants me gone to Pennsylvania as soon as possible." Paul asks, "When are you going?" I start packing as soon as I get home from school. Pete just opens his arms and holds on to Paul and does not let go. Hey little guy, don't cry someday when you become rich and famous you can buy that old farm house down the road and live next to me. Pete dries his tears and says Really!

# CHAPTER SIXTEEN
## "I am a Mystery wrapped in an Enigma.
## Something a conundrum?"

August Wednesday 7, 2002 I wake up with the knowledge that my once secret life that I thought was so secret. Is common knowledge to my friends but is an enigma to me.

I do my duty with John Henry and on lunch break I check my messages and I find I got a call from the bank that Marcus used to work at. They left a number and I dial it. Ah Hi this is Max Faraday you left a message? Oh hi Mr. Faraday this is The Cavanaugh City Bank, as far as we can find you are Marcus Faraday's closest relative? "Yeah, that would be my guess?" Well, we are tearing down the old bank and we found a deposit box with Marcus's name on it. We would like to give the item's ownership to someone. Any chance you could come pick them up? I get off duty after six, will you still be open today? I can wait for you. Ok, after duty I'll be there.

Max saying "That was strange Marcus leaving something in the bank?" John H. wonders Maybe it could be Stocks or Bonds or something? I replied, "I won't hold my breath." John asks, "You have some bad feelings about your father?" To put it lightly yeah, just ask Connie I don't care to go down memory lane when Marcus is involved. Hey it's on our way let's get the box now and get it over with.

When I get to the Lucrative Opportunities Key Investments "L.O.K.I." Bank they are in the middle of moving and tearing it down. A bank manager says Oh you must be Max.

May I see some ID just to make this official. I gave him my driver's license and a couple other ID's. Ok here is the box thank you for your time.

I open it, in it are baby teeth of my brothers and sisters all except for me? This is another slap in the face. I do my best not to make a scene and head to the car. John can see my tears. You want to talk about it? He didn't even include me in as one of his children? What? He saved their baby teeth and their first hair clippings, there is nothing for me? John tries by saying Maybe he was tired of doing that kind of stuff. I am the youngest in my family and there are a whole bunch of pictures of my older brothers and sisters but there are hardly any of me? I thought I was adopted because there were no pictures of me. Kinda silly when I think of it. John Henry looks at me with a dumb looking smile, he takes one look at me turns his head straight forward and does not say another word. "If looks could kill."

After duty I go to Father Michaels and ask What should I do? He advises Well with your connections you could have this looked into to compare DNA. Testing the waters, I ask My connections meaning CIA or Wild Tail Champions? He replies Both are very good, but The WTC would get the information in hours not days. So you know too. Max, I know a lot of things and I ask God to help me deal with these things one thing at a time. And I suggest you do the same. You knew I used to be Selah.

Max the idea is you confess to me, I don't confess to you. I am about to burst and point my finger! Now before you have to say a bunch of Hail Marys just calm down.

Just think of the opportunities you have been given.

I explain Reed Jackson invited me to his church as a kid and I felt the Holy Spirit led me to go in the pastor's office and I found porno there.

The Father says I remember the commotion back in seventy-eight that was your doing?

We made K. Ray C. go to the hospital by hog tying him and making him go the to check up.

We all prayed for a miracle Max, it was the Lord's will. He is still dead. It was God's will Max you have to let go and let God be God. I see my mom when I go back in time and Wendy and Jimmy, and it rips me up inside. Maybe it should Max. Why?

Because God has given you a great gift and responsibility cling to him and be sensitive to him, he knows you can do this because he can see too the end of the story before he even began the story. Your life is a living Gospel and how you live your life will affect countless others.

Yeah, I have heard this story before. Well, you may hear it again.

I came home and I am tired.

Churchill is checking up on the "hostage in the barn". I ask, "How is he?" He is eating now, but he won't talk. The militia put a bracelet with a twenty-foot chain around his leg.

He can stagger to the makeshift bathroom.

 I am too tired to interrogate him. Tomorrow will come soon enough. I stare at the prisoner You are going nowhere.

Nineteen Eighty The State officer comes by, warns Wendy's Mother that her husband should be their when she is not at the home. "They do not know?"

Frank Pearson needs his freedom "burnout" his Boss's company wants him to move to another state, he wants his wife and daughter Wendy and Steve to leave. "Fresh start" The Foster Care home, they both don't want to go, and he leaves without them.

August Thursday 8, 2002 I get up early and head in town and find The Mr. Smith's Rent All is open so I pull in the parking lot and go in. Indigo is working on lawn equipment, and I say Hi. Hey little brother, how you doing?

I respond Your radar sense is like a lie detector so if I told you I was doing great you would know. He chuckles My Radar sense is not a Lie detector, you must be thinking of Dare Devil a common misconception, it happens. So, what is going on? I have baby teeth and hair of my brothers and sisters saved by Marcus. I want to compare DNA with my own and see if Marcus is my biological father or not. Can you send it to Genetics Unlimited for me? Sure, I guess I can do that. Why not Paul, he is at the very least a Trouble Shooter? I would be tempted to ask questions that he does not want to answer.

And do you feel I might answer your questions? I have not asked any questions; I am just asking you to send something to GU.

Indigo asks, "Any chance you could mow for me Saturday?" I have a worker who can't show up due to the fact he and his wife and kids are in witness protection. I ask Jamie works for you? Indy responds He is raising two kids on a teacher's salary, during the summer he mows lawn for me. I ask Indigo By the way Who mows your lawn? Actually, I mow it myself at night. For a blind man I love to have a manicured lawn. I live out in the country with a long driveway from the road. What can I say I like my privacy. Yeah, I have Saturday off, I should be able to work for you.

Elsewhere Drug runners find out who Max Faraday is and begin to get scared!

The Mystery Man has made his contact. Ok Badger I have been hit on all sides I need information on Max Faraday now. Badger yells You think I am here just to give you information you son of a bitch! Get out now while you still can! What? Max Faraday is the Terminator. If he finds out who has been making his friends live a living Hell he will hunt you down. I don't know how he did it, he is out of The CIA and if you have not noticed he has your Mafia friends looking for you. Get out now.

The Mystery Man yells I can't shut everything down now, I have too much at stake here to pull out!. I lost a load last Saturday and a driver. You lost a driver, damn what does the driver know? I have never spoken my name to any of them, nobody knows who I am relax. Then the Mystery Man pauses saying Only Toney knows who you are. Yeah, and he knows about you too. Should I have him taken care of? No, not yet, have him snoop around Max for now. He is good, he got rid of the body and the car for you. Why kill a good man when you are not done using him.

After I finish my shift, I come home and Max the dog is the only one here.

I ask my guest How are you doing tonight? He smirks saying Good you have fed me pretty good actually. Well, we would not want you to starve on us. You mind telling me a little about yourself? Hey, I was just out of prison and a guy I have never seen before offered me cash for moving his merchandise. He offered me some drugs that I can use for myself, or I could sell on the side. The deal was Ok for me. Who were you working for? I don't know who I just know the job, he provides the car and I drive. Can I have a smoke I am dying for a smoke.

I look him in the eyes and say You don't get the picture, if you don't start providing me with some names it won't be lung cancer that will kill you it will be me. He yells Fuck you. I know my rights you can't hold me-. WAM! Punch to the face and he is out! I know my rights? He has a prison record. Whoever this Mystery Man is, he just waits outside the prison doors for his drivers to get out and put them to work. He comes to and says Son of a bitch what happened? You said some nasty swear words I had to remind you watch your mouth when talking to me. Fuck you! WAM! Punch to the face and he is out!

Ok I am not a gentleman; I really don't like to hear Fuck you in any tone of voice.

I throw water on his face, and he comes to. Watch your mouth or I am going to start kicking where you feel it and your daddy will feel it and his daddy will feel it.

A scared "Shit" comes out and he starts blabbing I don't know any names. I get half my cash when I show up and the rest when I deliver. I am given a map and location to memorize, and I deliver. Sometimes I am given a passenger to ride shotgun, sometimes I ride alone.

I reply, "Sometimes you are the shooter also. You shot at my friends fire truck."

Hey, I lost my car thanks to those damn deer! Your friend's truck what does it have in it Nitro?

I replied, "You don't ask questions here, I ask the questions. Where are the drugs stored?"

I don't know I pick up the car at different locations. I have never seen a warehouse.

Do you know what happened to the other driver? The one that hit a deer on the highway and totaled his car on Friday July 12, 2002? He thinks about it answering No I was never told what happened to "Bob Black?" "That's our dead guy." Get some rest I'll be asking more questions tomorrow.

I got in my car and drove to Paul's, I find him in his office. I say to him our guest is talking.

Paul looks up and asks What has he said? Not much, I punched him out a couple times, that felt good. Maybe I should bring Indigo in and he can play good cop I am already the bad cop.

Paul smiles asking, "You want to scare the shit out of him?" With what Paul?

Paul smiles stating I got a dead guy in the freezer we can show him.

I state Hey that is evidence not a scare tactic besides we didn't shoot him.

Paul asks, "Does he know that?" I smile and say, "Tomorrow night good for you?"

Sure, I can bury him in my compost pile he will never know the difference.

"Nineteen Eighty" Final warning from the STATE.

I come home from Basketball practice with Steve and Adam, and I see the police officer and Mrs. Pearson and Wendy crying. Steve runs to them in their time of need.

# CHAPTER SEVENTEEN

## "Confessions at The Compost Pile"

August Friday 9, 2002

Me and John Henry passed The Howard's Car sales and Garage. Toney is working in the shop. John murmurs I'll never have my car taken there as long as Jack is not working at the garage.

I ask Bad service? No service is more like. You think after going to prison for heisting cars he would at least learn how to fix a car? Toney had some prison time? That is where our dead guy Bob Black and our guest both went to prison. May be that is where our Mystery Man went to prison too? That is our connection.

John reminds Ah Max That is where Jack was sent too. For his DUI and car accident.

It is dark and we bring our guest out to the compost pile. John Henry is handcuffed to him; he isn't going anywhere. We take the blinder off, and he says "So you have a lot of shit so what? I take a shovel and uncover the face of "Bob Black." Our guest freaks out when he sees the face! Oh my God! You killed him didn't you! I smile. He just continues to freak out. I heard about your country people "shit" but I never!

I ask Where is the drugs coming from? He yells, "I don't know! Who is paying you to deliver the drugs?" I don't know! John H. asks How about Toney Howard what do you know about him?

He is a middleman for the Boss or the Mystery Man as you call him. If a car needs work, he gets it fixed. He is my contact. Yeah, I can tell you a few things about him, we went to prison together.

"Nineteen Eighty" It is a summer Saturday I call Mrs. McGraw and tell her I need the day off. My mom asks Max why haven't you left for your job? I told Mom I think you and me have to talk. About what Max? Martha is about to lose her house it could easily be condemned if the State agency really looked at it. Mom, we have this whole big house, and it is just sitting empty. Please mom we have to help them.

Mom wipes her eyes saying Max I have been praying for something like this. If the Devil can't get you to do something bad, he will terrorize and overwork you to do something good and get no peace from it. Her husband has done all he could, he needed a break from everything and so does Martha. I ask You don't blame him for leaving? Max, you don't know everything. He came to me for advice, and I agreed if he felt the need to move, he is the father and the bread winner of the family Martha had better realize this and make arrangements. You know the story. She chose to stay. He sends home twice as much money home, but she hasn't had time to call or make repairs. I guess you see the big picture more than I have. Mom says Maybe I should see if I can take a more active role. I'll call Martha and see if we can set up a meeting.

# CHAPTER EIGHTEEN
## "Personal Revelations"

August Saturday 10, 2002

For old times sake I am working for Mr. Smith's Lawn care perfection. It is early in the morning the sun is coming up and Indigo and his wife are there to greet me. Hey you are the first one here. That is good because I am giving you the big lawns to do today. His wife hands me the list. The Home Hearth complex and The McGraw farm. I slap my head Oh I forgot all about the McGraw farm! Well, The Coopers haven't, they are doing measurements of the place and said it needed to be mowed.

Mrs. McGraw informs You are all loaded up and ready to go. I start at Home Hearth, and I just can't get over the place where the back yard has a stream and a waterfall and little ducks in the pond. And over there is a wishing well. How cute. Parents and children are coming out to play on the jungle gym and swing sets. A little boy is bald, my guess he has cancer. This place is beautiful in more ways than one. Steve comes out as I am finishing up and hands me bottled water. I am thirsty and say Thank you and drink it down. Adam comes out and says I have fresh buttery rolls want one. I have not had breakfast and again I say Thank you. After I have finished my water and rolls Steve says Maybe after you are done looking for the so-called Mystery Man you could come back and work for Mr. Smith's Lawn Care Perfection again.

I ask, "So how long have you been two been Bull's Eye Red and Green?" Steve nervously spits out his water and Adam almost chokes on a roll. Steve pats him on the back and he relaxes. Steve then whispers in the house now. I follow them in and down the basement we go past a secret door that opens with a touch and closes behind us. I ask, "Is this The Bull's Eye Cave?" Steve explains This is a sealed environment no listening devices can get in or out except WT communications. So, do you remember?

Little here and there, I guess. How long have you been Bull's Eye Red and Green?

Adam answers with It all began in Ninety-four when I was being black mailed for a crime when I was on the "Seattle Washington" police force. I was a pretty good detective and some bad cops tried to make me look dirty, I guess they chose to blame the new guy.

I was suspended from the force, and I called Steve up and asked for some help.

Steve continues I was at The FBI academy teaching Psychology and marksmanship.

I couldn't be out in the FBI field, but I was good enough to teach recruits. We did our own investigation and brought the bad cops to justice. Adam adds I got my badge back, but I was given the cold shoulder for bringing down the bad cops.

Adam continues I was blackmailed again and this time I was asked to be the fall guy. I wonder aloud Asked by who? Gather of The Agency and reluctantly Wild Tail also. I went to prison and the bad cops got caught while I was there. In order to get the ringleader, I was told I had to go to prison. In the end The Agency says We are sorry we can't clear your name and so sorry for prison shit happens. Steve adds "On the side I was setting up Home Hearth with Kathy and we bought this place, and I invited Adam to come home and look at it." Adam commits This place needed a makeover and an exorcist really quick if you know what I mean.

Steve adds Before Adam would commit to working at Home Hearth, he wanted to bring down the bad cops that The Agency did not get. So again, we went undercover, and we almost got nailed if Wild Tail didn't save our hide. He said I like what you two are doing, but you need the right equipment. Wild Tail set us up with costumes and everything. Paul designed them, I think they are great. You don't remember?

Max admits It is kinda fuzzy, yeah bits and pieces. Wild Tail told me that it would be for the best that I have one mind not two separate personalities. He said that the two minds would most likely become one. I made the choice that I wanted two personalities Selah and Max Faraday. I guess he was right the personalities are merging. Steve comforts me with If it happens it happens, we'll deal with it like we always deal with it as it comes.

"It makes me wonder what was so bad that I did not want to remember?"

Thanks guys I don't know how I would be able to deal with this without you.

Adam hugs me and says Hey you saved our butts a few times it is nice we can return the favor.

The Old McGraw Farm I unload the lawn mower and start going at it man this place is big. As I begin, I see Jack pop the hood and tinkers around with the pickup. This lawn is big and thick as it is I go over it twice in order to make it look just right we are called Mr. Smith's Lawn care perfection not lawn care half ass. As I finish up, I go into the barn and find the Coopers. Jason is setting up a device that looks like a mini tank. Mr. Cooper is at the computer saying I hope this contraption is worth it. Dad, I will get an exact measurement of this area and we will be able to feed the information into the computer and compare it to the blueprints you drew up. Hey Max, put on the protective glasses the laser could blind you if you don't. Ok Dad, turn it on!

The device starts shooting lasers everywhere and moves inch by inch. Slowly the information is showing up on the monitors. All I can do is say wow. Mr. Cooper says, "Oh you think this is wow look what we are going to do to the place." The blueprints show up and the finished product or the hoped for result is put before me. Steve is investing a good chunk into this project. He thinks he might even turn this place into a conference center or a TV studio and compete with Oprah and Dr. Phil.

I am impressed adding Maybe I will have to do some jobs on the side like I used to do. Then again Paul says I have my secret stash from Selah to play with. They stand there quiet in wonder. Mr. Cooper asks, "You are starting to remember?" I replied, "Bits and pieces." And like Paul Steve Adam and Indigo you are probably not going to give me any details of my past right? Jason admits A part of me wanted you never to remember Selah.

Maybe you shouldn't even try Max, you deserve a break. You helped to save the world enough times already.

I reply, Maybe Jason, but there are forces involved trying to help me remember and maybe I should.

Mr. Cooper says Let me guess Bridge, right? Yeah? Oh, like he has to get involved.

I don't know if it is his will that I remember or is it God's will that I remember, and he is just helping me along in the transition. Jason adds Well with Bridge you never know sometimes. He might be almost all powerful, in the end he is still human at the core.

Mr. Cooper quotes If you don't learn from the past, you may be destined to repeat it.

I look to the corner of the barn and say, "What does that look like to you?" Jason says A wall.

I say to them, "You know what it looks like to me?" "Hidden treasure"

I go for the tool shed of the barn and come back with a big heavy crowbar. I start pounding at the wall! Mr. Cooper and Jason begin shutting down the machine and yell calling out Max what are you doing!? I strike a hole in the wall! Mr. Cooper utters, "Hey there is something in there!" I keep pounding as they clear the plaster and rubble. Then I stopped and we get a look inside. Mr. Cooper states These are McGraw's old paintings. I see them before when I was invited over for dinner once. I smile and say, "Don't forget your past. Wow dad these are great!"

Mr. Cooper ponders aloud It has been staring us in the face and we just have not seen it.

What Mr. Cooper? Max, we have been neglectful of where we have come from our history our family heritage. We forget where we come from. This barn has a heritage too.

I remember barn dances and good times told of by the old folks. I guess I will be one of them sooner or later. This is our heritage staring back at us. Maybe we can get some antique equipment and park it outside and do demonstrations. Jason adds Anything to keep Home Hearth's guests away from Paul and the Amish. I chuckled and said Yeah.

As I leave the Coopers Jack is doing repair work on Mr. Cooper's old pickup truck. Jack says Hey you haven't lost your touch. Thanks. Ah Max I am getting my kids for this afternoon I wonder if it would be too much to ask if you might, I don't know take us out to dinner I'll buy of course. Hopefully you will say yes. When I asked to see my kids, I put you down as my co adult. A little shocked by this They really have you on a short leash when it comes to your kids.

Jack admits, "Hey I have a criminal record in their eyes. I have to play the system and jump through the hoops to get my kids back. Reed helped me get going. Man, he is a God send Max. I didn't have any close relatives and he and his wife took my kids in. Until the State took them away from him and put them in a foster home.

They said because he was a fire fighter, he could not be a Foster Parent for them till I got my life together. They are in a good home, but it is not my home.

I tell him Hey someday Jack someday. What time? About five Ok for you? I have a couple more jobs, if it was six that would be better? Sure, here is the address we will be waiting for you. As I leave The McGraw farm, I call Indigo. So, any more jobs?

His wife answers. Howard's Garage called and they want somebody to do mowing.

I should be done in time, I guess. Jack asked if I could take him and his kids out for dinner. They are watching him pretty close these days? Indigo replies they sure are. Hopefully someday he will get his kids back. I'll check in later.

Howard's Garage I unload the mower and get to work I don't want to be here any longer than I have to be. It is like checking out enemy territory. Nobody offers me a friendly water, I am not surprised. Toney stares at me through the glass of the show room and I try to act like I don't care or don't notice.

It is like "I am going to get you look" or "What do you have to hide" followed by "What do you have on me that I don't know about?" I trim the hedges and do the bushes.

I loaded up and I am gone. It is a hot day, but it felt cold like a tombstone at a cemetery at Howard's Garage.

The Smith Mansion Churchill has kept up the family estate. Ever since I started mowing lawns in the back of my head, I always thought there was something wrong if you couldn't or wouldn't mow your own lawn. But I'll take your money and I expect a good tip because I do good work. Because it is called Mr. Smith's Lawn Care Perfection not Mr. Smith's half ass. Maybe it is because I knew that Churchill never had to mow, and I was jealous. No there is just something wrong if you couldn't or wouldn't mow your own lawn. He comes out and offers Lemon aid. Ah thank you Churchill and I drink it down.

He says Paul says You scared the shit out of our guest the other night. I drink my lemonade saying Yeah, he gave us everything, but who his boss is. I doubt if any of his men know who he is either.

A true Mystery Man. All of them went to the same prison. Churchill adds Yeah, the same as Jack from what Paul told me. You two talk a lot don't you? Churchill looks around and says, "Well I am your doctor." You were my doctor when I was Selah. And he nods.

I can hardly grasp what you did for me. Churchill lowers his head and puts his hands in his pockets and whispers I failed you when you needed me most Max. You were there when it mattered I, It is coming back to me. What is it?

I get off the lawn mower and get in the shadow of a tree. And curl up like a ball. What is it Max? I am remembering when I was Black Phoenix and Graves sent me on a mission to South America Brazil. I was sent there to take out the leader of a Cocaine manufacturing Cartel. It was supposed to be a quick assignation. It turned into a blood bath, and I was caught by a drug cartel in the jungle. They shot me up and left me dead. Oh my God. I did die. Black Phoenix is not just a name, it is who I am! The moment the body can't repair the damage done it begins recreating a new "me" The white extra layer of skin that covers me foams up and becoming a cocoon. Then a Black exoskeleton creature comes forth ripping through!. Oh God I remember!

Churchill holds me and asks Do you want to go into the house? I shake my head. It is like being in two people at once I am dying and I am being born? I am dead and I am alive. The jungle is pitch black, but I can see thanks to my enhanced eyes. I hunt animals eating them raw because I am so hungry. A primal force controls me a will not my own. When I am satisfied, I again survey the drug Cartel's compound. A guard is patrolling the compound, and I eliminated him and took his food and clothing and supplies. I am on the hunt. The guards see something, and I charge at them! They shoot at me, and it does not even daze me! My body armor is my own, I can take hits and my body bleeds white blood then covers the cracks or holes created by gun fire or grenades! Nothing can stop me. What am I? I bring the fight to them one at a time and in the end, I take out their leader.

The beast in me is satisfied and it takes to the river and swims like a fish and breathes air in the water because of its gills. Piranha attacks and it just grabs them and crushes them till it gets annoyed and comes to the surface.

Back on land it stretches out its hands and fingers grow then it sprouts leathery wings like a bat and takes to the air. When all is finished, I shed the exoskeleton, and I am healed?

Black Phoenix's mission was preprogrammed. I came to a village I steal some clothes and find a phone. I then called Graves on the phone, and he sent a black helicopter to pick me up. What am I?

As Selah I got into a fight. And I lost an arm, and I could feel the process about to start all over again. I am transported to Paul's safe house where he draws my story. I used to know where it was. Churchill adds Paul called me and I left the hospital, and I came to you. I didn't want to go through that again. I said Churchill you have to keep me alive!

Churchill tells his part of the story I bandaged you the best I could. Paul was able to transport blood in and somehow, we were able to reverse the process.

I remember My arm grew back in days. I went out and finished what I started. You kept me alive.

Wait a minute. If I am a new creation every time my body dies, then how come I still have my tattoo. Not that I am complaining. And my old burn from my arm when I was a kid?

Churchill answers I wondered that too, your body has made skin pigment that resembles your tattoo. My guess your Max Faraday side of you does not know that you are supposed to be healed. So, it reverted back to the way it was not the completely so called healed Black Phoenix or Selah. Mind over body? Something like that, I guess. You know Max if you were severely injured it would stay with you. And your body would mend it the best it could. When you changed to Selah it would repair the damage and you would do your mission and when you were done it would change you back to the way you were.

I ponder Churchill has given me more information and comfort than even Paul. I compose myself he helps me up and I give Churchill a pat on the back. Thanks Man.

I drive out to Pete's he is last on my list. He is rebuilding an old farmhouse a half mile from Paul's farm. I unload my mower and I can see this place will take a while.

Satellite dishes and antennas are going to be obstacles challenges at best. I get started and when I get about half done Pete comes out to check on my work. Pete shakes his head So that is where I threw out that Apple Computer. Hey Max, how are you doing?

I am going to ask you to do something. What Max? I need you to bug and tap Jack's phones. Why? Because after I get done here, I am going to be taking Jack and his kids out to dinner and when I get a moment alone, I am going to share information with him.

If he is part of the gang, he may call our Mystery Man after I tell him what we know.

Pete nods his head saying Yeah, I can do that, but Max he shared with you information.

I remind Pete Most of it we already knew, and he might have been just feeling us out to see what we know. Pete defends Jack with but if he is caught up with the drug smugglers, he can kiss his kid's goodbye. They might have such a hold on him he might have no control.

And if they have the Cavanaugh Cops who knows who else they control. I mean they watch him so close as it is. Who knows if The Protective Services could be in it too? Do what you have to do Max. I'll set up the trace on his home phone.

I hate doing it and add You better add his cell phone too, here is the number.

Pete asks Ah Max if he is on it what are you going to do?

I start the mower and finish the job and head for Mr. Smith's Lawn care Perfection.

Indigo greets me. Well I can take it you did a good job nobody called and complained.

I ask Indigo, "Any chance you could do a favor for me tonight?"

"What?"

Watch Jack for me after I take him and his kids out for dinner, I am going to share with him some information. I need you to watch him in case he leaves his house and uses another phone instead of his home phone or cell. You think he might be in on it? I reply Even Jesus had his Judas. Indigo agrees I usually do a patrol around town before I hit The Big City. I'll stay in town a little bit longer. I ask Don't you ever sleep?

Indigo chuckles Let's just say I get around and I have been around some explosions recently and stored up some extra bio energy that I have not spent it out yet. I can tell that Jack gave your pickup truck a tune up from a mile away and there are some houses in this town that need some more insulation. I am about to go into information overload.

Oh, by the way I had your G.U. results you wanted sent to your house.

I walk away from him and I silently whisper thank you. And he says Your welcome.

I start up the Trans Am and it backfires, and I cringe, and I head for home I need to take a shower. Feeling kinda dirty thinking my old friend could be a Judas is a filth I can't wash off very easily. I have been fooled by Judas and his friends too many times. How does it go Fool me once shame on you. Fool me twice shame on me. Fool me three times? I think I'll bring Max the dog, the kids will have fun with her in the park.

As I drive to the address that Jack gave me, I can't help but think there has to be a better way then treating foster kids like cattle and when they turn eighteen let them out in society. The Pearson's Foster home did their best through the trials and stress, but everyone has a breaking point. I have seen the successes like Steve the failures like little Jimmy. Jimmy is dead and Steve runs around in funny long underwear and shoots bad guys. Oh, sure he solves mysteries like he used to play poker, but he still runs around in funny long underwear and shoots bad guys. Me I used to, but for the life of me I can't remember all of it. And I am starting to wonder if I should.

Jack is at the curb; he waves to me, and I park the car and he takes me to meet his kids. The Foster Parent looks like a prison warden to me. Jack makes the introductions Max these are my kids Bobby and Sarah and Busy Bee. I wave my hand and say Hi. Max The Dog barks and the kids say with glee Oh you have a dog! The kids pile up in the car, and we get out of there and I ask is there a curfew because she looks like a warden to me?

Jack asks, "So where do we want to go?" I yell with glee Sodom and Gomorrah I am so hungry for BBQ! Jack looks at me like I am the bad guy A recovering alcoholic does not need to go there look. The kids yell out wow yeah lets go there! I can't take it back now. I sheepishly say I think we can get takeout and bring it back to the park. Max the dog barks in agreement.

Jack begins talking with his kids and from here on I listen in but don't say much.

At S&G we pull in the drive and see the parking lot is full. Jack says Maybe we should go to What's its name? They are too full. "He is really scared to go to a place serving alcohol."

I let it be known Ah I have some pull with Sam, I'll get us some food to go. I'll park in the back where you and the kids can play with Max.

The place is going ballistic, and I mean that in a good way. "A little less talk and lot more action by Toby Keith" is playing I see Sam at the Bar and I yell out I need some BBQ to go! Sam Yells back Get your butt over here boy! He comes from behind the bar and gives me a bear hug. Ah Max, it is good to see you! I hate to say it, I am in a bit of a rush. I have Jack Hammer and his kids out in the car, and I need some BBQ. Can you help?

Hey that is wonderful. Charley, I need a BBQ party mix to go! Now what are you going to do to get The Counting Tornadoes back together? What?

Back at the car Busy Bee asks to go to the bathroom Daddy I need to go. Jack Logically asks Why didn't you go before we left? The child answers I didn't know I had to go then, I have to go now? Jack looks around for a tree. Dad, it is number two. Bobby Sarah stays here in the car I'll take Busy Bee in.

I see them walk in and Jack says Busy Bee needs to use the bathroom. Sam points the way It is down the hall in the back where it always is. As they head in that direction Sam explains. I refused to sell him a drink and he wanted to get plastered. And he went to another bar, and they let him drive away damn it. Max, I hope you can help him out, he really needs a friend.

They enter the bathroom, and a drunk is puking hung over one of the toilets. Oh God I will never do this again if you "spew"! Busy Bee asks Daddy were you ever like that?

And Jack gets down on one knee and says Yes son and with The Lord's help I won't be that way again.

Sam continues Them boys need to get back on the road. Oh, sure there are the two 2.0's but they need to be one band again. Ralph is writing his Ice Soldiers novels and doing God only knows. Damn Republicans won't leave him alone. Reed he may be a big-time fireman, but he needs to take time off and tour. That wife of his has him wound up too tight!

I reply What am I supposed to do Sam? Sam yells Get The band back together!

Jack and Busy Bee head back to the car Busy Bee with his fingers pinching his nose. Sam hands me two big bags of stuff and I say Oh boy what is that going to cost me? Sam says Nothing, your money is no good here you just get them boys on the road touring again. Have a good time with the kids. See yah Sam.

That woman that I just can't remember her name is Oh it is Missy. She is talking with Jack. Jack looks really happy around her and I think it is mutual. As I get to the car their eyes bug out when they see the bags Wow how did you get all that stuff? I told them I was head of security for Counting Tornadoes Sam thinks I can get the band back together. Can you?

Jack asks, "Is there a way we could give her a ride back to town?" I remind him it's a Trans Am not a minivan Jack, if she can sit on your lap sure, I guess. She does they make a cute couple. On the way back to the park I tell old stories of Counting Tornadoes on the road. Man, I miss those guys. The kids think I am so cool. Busy Bee kinda stares and smiles at Jack's lady friend? He is cute, he just keeps smiling at her. He blurts out, "Are you going to be our new mommy?" Everything goes silent. Jack doesn't know what to say and neither does she? They both blurt out No we are just friends. Breathing a sigh of relief.

Picnic at the Park I love BBQ! At the park the kids have a ball with Max. I guess she missed being around kids not being at Paul's so much. Jack's lady friend gives him a kiss and walks away. He enjoys the moment then looks at his watch and says Hey we better get going.

I thought you were kidding. The kids have a Curfew? As we take the kids home Thanks Max, they all say Thank you we had a great time. A Cavanaugh City police car turns his lights on and pulls me over.

I ask, "What is the problem officer?" The officer says You have a broken taillight. As I hand him my wallet and other information, I look in my rear view mirror and I see Blue Bomber reach in the patrol car and turn the video camera on. I say I can't believe I am being pulled over for a broken taillight? Mind if I get out and take a look? I open the door and say, "There is nothing wrong with my taillight?" The officer murmurs I would be careful of the people you associate with Mr. Faraday. I stand my ground saying I will associate with whoever I wish to officer, it is none of your business.

He kicks in the taillight smash! I state Oh you are a bright boy doing that with the video camera on and all. He looks back to the car seeing the red light on the camera and says Oh shit. I add If I wish to see the video and if it is erased, I would be very careful of the people you associate with. The officer yells "Just get out of here because you only get one warning!"

I drop the kids off and Jack goes in to explain why he was late. Jack comes back to the car and says Thanks for the evening; I can walk home from here. I say Get in we have to talk. I tell Jack all I know to bring him up to date. Jack says I didn't know. Max the dog cuddles up to Jack as though she can trust him. Jack explains When I was in prison someone, I never saw his face, came to me and offered me a job. I told him to go to Hell. He said he would make my life a living Hell once I got out. I didn't think what this guy could do? When I got out everything went up in smoke, my kids my life everything, I couldn't get a break for nothing. I thought it was just my record, but my parole officer said he compared my case to others, and it was like I was being unfairly treated. How far does this thing go Max? I don't know?

I wonder if Jack is in fear for his kids' lives, I can see it in his eyes and asks me Could I stay with you till this is all over? I drop Jack off at his place and he goes in to grab clothes and a sleeping bag and stuff. When we come back to my place Jack goes out to the barn to talk to "the guest." Out of the silence Blue Bomer says I think we can trust Jack. As I go into the house, I find the test results and Marcus Faraday is my father. I don't know either to cry or laugh so I get to my cell phone dialing Reed to talk. He answered Hello? Hi, it's me, Max Reed, I really need someone to talk to. What is it? I just received the information about Marcus that he is my Dad and I just went out with Jack and I was all prepared to think he was in on the drug smuggling and all and he is not. Reed reassures Ah Jack well the Lord is doing a work in his life Max. And if anyone can bring them bastards to justice hey bud it is you. I hear an Et hem in the background from Reed's wife Deborah. Reed says I said bastards and I meant Bastards.

Reed continues Yeah after he got out of prison, I helped him go to his first AA meeting.

I wish we could have kept the kids a bit longer than we did. We pick them up to go to church on the bus. The one thing that has not changed is Jack can fix just about anything.

I have shared it all with Ralph, he and I have written a song about it all.

I say Funny you should mention it I took the kids to S&G's. Stunned Reed murmurs You did what? I was having BBQ withdrawals. Do you have any left the woman won't let me go there anymore. Yeah, I have a bunch of leftovers. In the background I hear I won't let you do what? Eat BBQ you put me on a diet. Deb declares I did no such thing!

Well then, "I'll be over to Max's then and have some leftovers."

Less than ten minutes Reed is over here going through my leftovers. That is pretty good timing for a fireman. With tears of joy Oh I miss S&G! I hand him a napkin and he take it and says Thank you. You know Sam wants you and Ralph to get back and tour with the band. Reed? Yeah, I would like that too, but I have more responsibilities now. I quote "I won't let you go where?" Reed smiles and winks Am I going bald because sometimes I feel henpecked.

To change the subject Reed picks up his guitar.
 "Jesus I don't know why you took my Mama"
Sometimes it is hard to remember mama.
She used to call me Busy Bee.
She got cancer when I was three.
I wanted to go to the hospital but they would not let me see.
Mama went to you in Heaven.
Daddy was left with brother and sister and me.
 The State came and took us away from Daddy
I was scared and sad as I could be.

Daddy said You have to be brave Mama is looking down from Heaven my little Busy Bee.
Jesus I don't know why you took my Mama.
Daddy comes to the Foster home and says he is so proud of me.
Brother and sister say he lost his job and got lost in the bottle.
And he could not take care of me.
Jesus I miss my Mama and I know she is in Heaven.
Please send Daddy a new Mama and maybe she can teach Daddy how to pray again.
Jesus I miss my Mama and I know she is in Heaven.
Please send Daddy a new Mama and maybe she can teach Daddy how to pray again.

"The father's voice" Jesus I don't know why you took Busy Bee's Mama
Sometimes it is hard to remember my Ruth Leanne. She used to believe in me.
She got cancer and I got down on my knees.
I wanted you to heal her but the anger I had towards you would not let me see.
Ruth Leanne went to you in Heaven.
I was left with Bobby and Sarah and Busy Bee.
The State came and took the kids away from me. I was scared and sad as I could be.
I told them You have to be brave Mama is looking down from Heaven my little Bobby Sarah, and Busy Bee.
Jesus I don't know why you took Busy Bee's Mama.
I come to the Foster home and say I am so proud of them.
I lost my job and got lost in the bottle.
And I could not take care of them.
Jesus I miss my Ruth Leanne and I know she is in Heaven.
Please teach me how to pray again.
Jesus I miss my Ruth Leanne and I know she is in Heaven.
Please teach me how to pray again.

I just shed a few tears and said, "You have to get back out on the road."

# CHAPTER NINETEEN
## "One Big Dysfunctional Family"

Nineteen Eighty Monday after school" My mom is on a board that manages Mrs. Horton's Endowment Fund Program. It has been set up to send people to college and donated to worthy causes. Father Michaels, Marcus, and my mom Maxine Faraday and Rabbi Hyman and a few others are on the board. Marcus says Ok we shall begin the meeting with Maxine Faradays suggestion.

Mom gets up starting. It has come to my attention That the Pearson Foster home is in need of expanding. I believe that they provide a needed service to our community. As the pictures show, their current home is in need of repairs. Marcus asks if I thought they had work done on their house not too long ago? Mom replies They did, and I believe Martha has been taken advantage of. Mom submits the paper receipts. Marcus passes the receipts to Rabbi Hyman. And says the house is in bad shape what is it you intend to do the children can't stay where they are for very long.

Mom answers, "That is why I intend to move them to my house while the Pearson's house is repaired properly this time." Marcus is stunned. So is everyone in the room.

Steve looks at me and I can only wonder what he is thinking If Max's Mother decides to turn her home into a new Foster Care Home.

"Max & Wendy & I will under the same roof cool"

Marcus asks, "Will this be a permanent arrangement?" Mom says It may be, what is it to you? Marcus bewildered at it all I think it is a wonderful offer what else do you wish? Mom says I wish that the ministers of the area would not just marry people, but that they would follow up and direct the couples in the way they should go. Just about all the children in the home are from this area and only two of them are from single parents. Martha and her husband have been at this alone with little help from the community. I think it is time we changed that. The board begins its recommendation.

Rabbi Hyman submits names of people who can look into the poor work on the Pearson's house. He always has names. Cheers fill the room for my mom and as we get up to go.

Marcus comes by me. Hi Max I have been watching your progress in school. Honor Roll and Basketball I used to be pretty good when I was young myself.

I mumble Yeah well that is nice, but you never played ball with me so how would I know? He wipes tears from his eyes I know Max, I would like to try to make up a few things if I could. I have changed. I smiled, whispering I found your money you left in the lawn mower.

Marcus' eyes bug out. Really, I almost forgot about it. "I am sure you did."

I say Mr. Grant is managing it for me. Marcus replies He is a good man I hope he is investing it well. I add Yeah can't go wrong with stocks like Apple Computers, Microsoft IBM.

Picked them all just as they were starting up too. "I had a little help, but Marcus doesn't need to know that." Marcus says Well I am happy for you Max maybe a little good from me rubbed off on you. I grit my teeth murmuring You rubbed me the wrong way Marcus that is all that you ever rubbed off on me. And I walked out.

Wendy is excited Yelling We are going to be one big family!

# Chapter Twenty

## "Who is your Daddy?"

August Sunday 11, 2002 I get a call early in the morning from an officer called in sick, and I am lowest on the totem pole. I pick up the cruiser at the station and I am on patrol. The countryside is quite peaceful too. Reed's church bus is doing seventy-five, so I follow him, and he slows down to fifty-five. A kid asks Hey Mr. Jackson we are going to be late for church. Reed looks in his rear-view mirror and sees me winking and waving at him. I follow him all the way to town. Reed says Officer Max must have had to work this morning. Must be thinking if he can't have any fun neither can we.

As I drive down Main Street some Cavanaugh City things have changed. My old house is still there, and I see Reed waving at me from the church bus as he picks up Jack's kids. I almost swerved and hit an oncoming car. Howard's Garage moved to another location. I then turn around and drive to the cemetery and I see the flowers that I put on her grave. Wendy is still dead.

As I leave the cemetery, I see Reed's church bus and Martha Pearson is at a window seat.

She still runs the Foster Care Home. The bus stops at the light and a black car with dark tinted windows comes along the side. Reed opens the door and calls out Hey you want to drag?!

An obscene gesture is given, and Reed revs the church bus engine. Then they rev their engine. The light goes from red to green and they haul asphalt! I see all this and hit the siren and I am in hot pursuit! That bus hauls I should know I helped build it. Now going faster than the speed limit is a no, no but in this case, I think God will let it slide. I know I will. The black car pulls over and Reed is gone. I start by running the plate and registration through the computer and things don't match up. The car of its description has been at several gas station robberies, but the license does not match up. I call it in, and I get out.

I don't hear it over the radio, I do hear it in my spirit "Use caution."

I see a gun and I pull mine and Yell Get your hands up now! Keep them where I can see them! I recognize them from wanted posters they are wanted for murder. They get out. I yell get your hands on the vehicle and spread them! Now! I read the Rights to them as I get the cuffs on one the other moves to strike me. Wam! If you cannot afford an attorney, one will be provided-. I then heard a banging from the trunk I get the keys from the guy still out on the ground. "It is easier to handcuff them that way." So, I roll him over and find the keys in his pocket.

Reed and the bus are coming back. I open the trunk and a teenage girl is tied up inside.

I get her out and untie her and Reed comes to a stop to check out what is going on?

She stands there stunned and happy to be alive. Repeating Thanking God Jesus and me for rescuing her Then All She can do is stare at the long and lime green bus and read in BIG letters is John three sixteen. For God so loved the world, that he gave his only begotten Son, that whosoever believeth in him should not perish, but have everlasting life.

She remembers the verse from her childhood.

Written on the sides are other sage inspired messages. "I hope you know Jesus" She cries because it has been a long time. "Do you know where you are going when you die?"

For all intensity and purposes, she should be or could be dead. In tears she gets on the bus.

I need her for asking questions so I ask Reed can you get her name and what happened for me and I'll let you go.

Reed smiles saying I think we have a testimony and burns rubber leaving the scene.

I on the other hand can't chase after him because I am keeping the guy on the ground from crawling away.

I come back with breakfast, and I find Jack spending Sunday with "the guest". He says to me Having him tied up like this helps him detoxify from his drugs. I have been telling him he better talk.

Max goes to bed and Jack gets a call on his cell phone. We know you are talking to Max Faraday. Who is this? You know who this is. Accidents can happen if you talk. You can't be there to protect your kids. Jack grits his teeth saying If You lay a hand. How about Missy Chambers who is going to take care of her kids if something happened to her? Who is this?! The phone goes silent.

# CHAPTER TWENTY-ONE
## "Family Drama"

Nineteen Eighty I wake up sharing a room with Steve and it is like one big happy family.

One dysfunctional family with baggage to spare. We are there for each other and that is what counts. Martha and my mom are downstairs making breakfast for us all and I come down and set the table. Wendy is helping the younger kids get dressed for school.

It is a nice day, so I decided to walk.

There is little Jimmy he is in the 2nd grade now and Wendy still shares her lunch with him for his breakfast a good number of us do. He gets lunch at school now and sometimes his parents feed him at night. His father had a job as a janitor till they caught him stealing from the store. My guess they were just waiting for an excuse. His mother will sometimes get out of the house and do errands for people within walking distance; she has no real motive to do anything. Little Jimmy has found friends in the wrong crowd too.

At lunch time K Ray C. says The Test results are still negative. Churchill says Hey you went and had a checkup. We all say That is great. K. Ray C. explains Well I can't have you guys tying me up all my life as short as it may be.

I say Don't talk like that you may live to be a hundred. K. Ray C. says, and your life expectancy is seventy-two and then I'll be all alone.

Reed taps him on the back of the head. Ouch.

August Monday 12, 2002
Reed's wife receives a call and when her husband comes home, she tells Reed I have a thirteen-year-old son that I have not told you about. She sits him down and tells her story.

Afterward Reed goes to his personal computer and puts his feelings down. I turn on my computer and check my e-mails. `The Counting Tornadoes still talk to each other for support and for old times' sake. They consider me as one of the groups and I am so blessed because of this. They send each other songs amongst the group. As I look through my files Reed sent me something and I click on it.

"She was born in the Bible belt"
He was the guy she loved in High school.
Listening to him saying he would love her forever she played the fool.
He was the summer lifeguard at the pool in his sunglasses he looked cool.
He said if he wore a condom it wouldn't feel right so they did it one night.
And it didn't take long and her clothes began to get tight.
She packed her things in a couple bags and she was gone.
She had to get out of there leaving this town has been coming for far too long.
She bought a ticket on a bus and said I gotta get out of here.
My Daddy wants to whip me my Mamma wants me to abort.
Dear Lord help me with the fear.
As she passed the county sign she began to tear.
When the bus went as far as it would go on her dime
She saw a help wanted sign.
She found a job at a Saloon bar and grill cleaning off the grease and the grime.
Her new boss treated her good.
Helped her out like a father should.
When regulars asked about the new girl this is what he would say.
She was born in the Bible belt.
Her father took it off his hip.
With liquor on his lip he used it occasionally.

Her mother said how could you?
You know what you are going to have to do.
Abortion was not the solution and she cursed at her mother for the notion.
She was done crying tears that could fill an ocean.
She was in the family way and was asked to go to church one day.
She had hit rock bottom and needed to pray.
Redeemed by the blood of The Lamb and was cleansed by the healing stream.
The child was born and was given in open adoption.
She knew in her heart this was the Lord's option.
She was lead by a teacher and went to seminary and became a preacher.
Counting Tornadoes at a Trailer Park came to town and they liked to rock it.
Christ Taking a part Anger through Prayer came to her church and she was
perplexed because they had the Spirit.
She asked How can you serve both God and man?
And the leader of the band said If you are half The Prophet you think you are,
you can go right to God to get your answer.
The Lead Singer of the band thought the preacher was cute.
He had some questions about God that his friends couldn't answer.
So he asked her on a date and he began to romance her.
They were married not too far down the road.
Together they learned how to carry the heavy load.
She got a call one night the parents of her baby boy born
died in a car accident their car was torn.
There was a history she held back from her husband.
And she sat him down and told her best friend.
She was born in the Bible belt.
Her father took it off his hip.
With liquor on his lip he used it occasionally.
Her mother said how could you?
You know what you are going to have to do.
Abortion was not the solution.
She cursed at her mother for the notion.
She was done crying tears that could fill an ocean.
She was born in the Bible belt.
Her father took it off his hip.
With liquor on his lip he used it occasionally.
"Oh Reed."

Nineteen Eighty At school I see a new or old face. Ruth Leanne moves to Cavanaugh City and when Jack sees her, he is girl crazy over her. Do you tell someone that you know how many years you may have together? Or do you just let it play out. Another thing I wonder is one of these days I am going to wake up and it may be the day Marcus gets shot by the bank robbers. Do I just let that happen or do I act? The bank in question is in Carter City. I could ride my bike there if I had to but.

After school I go to see a friend, Father Michaels. I told him I found out I am Marcus' son. He asks, "Have you told anyone?" Not here in the past, in the future I have shared it with a few people. So why are you here? In the past or what? In the confessional. The Father asks again, "Why are you here?"

I respond I know that Marcus will be shot and killed, and I don't know if I wish to save his life or not. Can't you tell anyone? I have told you; would you believe me? No, if I have not seen events, you have described pass as I have. So, what am I supposed to do?

The Father says If you get me blueprints or draw a lay out of the bank and remember as many details of the crime as you can. I may be able to help you plan a rescue in order to save Marcus' life.

Later that night I sit out on my porch and look to the star filled sky. I decide to go for a walk. Bridge walks by. He says You have some thoughts you wanted to talk about.

I replied, "You a telepath on top of the nosiest being in the universe?" He chuckles Ah yes and no, but when you ask questions even in prayer don't be shocked if someone can help give you some answers. I whisper, "Why do people have to die?" Bridge says Let's take a walk.

I sarcastically say Gee you can go back and forth in time you like riding Harleys and you like taking walks. It is a wonder why you are single. Bridge chuckles and ponders aloud I always wonder Why do mortals always dwell on death, they only live for a short time. Why not dwell on life? I answer Because death is always out there, and it can be an enemy to the living. Then again thanks to Black Phoenix and Selah I may be an immortal only God knows, I guess. What is so good about being immortal when the ones you love die? You have had that happen to you a lot over the years?

Bridge put his hand on my shoulder saying, I would be callous if I said get used to it.

Do you… Are you used to it? Bridge answers When David Roth "The Infinity" died you know what they said to him in Heaven? What? Take a good look around you won't be staying long.

Maybe someday I'll go a little deeper. You ask because people around you here in your past are alive and when you wake up in the present some of them are dead. I state I am planning on saving someone's life and there are others I can't save. Isn't there?

Bridge explains Well in the flesh people die for many reasons. Their environment. Age A hundred and twenty seems so short. I say, "Try seventy-two I think is the average."

Bridge says Oh that is even shorter. You are born, you live, you die. Choice, you choose to do something harmful to your body. Smoking, tap dancing in a minefield. Running in a black jogging suit at night along a highway at night. Don't get mad at God, he gave you free will to make choices. Ask for wisdom to make the right ones. He loves to talk, and he is waiting for so many to ask and listen.

I state Mom and her smoking. Being at the wrong place at the right time. That is Marcus. Not caring if you live or die. That was K. Ray C.

Bridge says Then help give him something to live for. Jack he wanted to die with his wife gone Max. Having his kids taken away woke him up. I say He was prepared to die without her? Despair can move people in damaging directions.

Bridge continues Flesh dies the spirit and soul live forever. Sometimes Max people die because others need a sign. A sign? Able died so that others would wake up and know there is evil in this world wake up! Do you think Able wanted to be a sign, Max? No.

Then let God be God and you be you and know He is in control.

I admit If I had my choice K. Ray C. would live and Marcus would be the one who is dying. Bridge somberly states That is why it is God's choice and not your choice Max.

I then tell him Then Let him save Marcus. Bridge lowers his head saying He also allows us to do his will. Remember Max the Lord's will be done.

And I am again alone.

# CHAPTER TWENTY-TWO
## "Even Heroes get sick"

August Tuesday 13, 2002 I Wake up sick, so I call in and tell them I need a sick day. Tom says You sound pretty bad Max. Better take it easy. I ask Is there any chance you could get me any and all information on The Bank robbery that killed Marcus Faraday. Tom asks, "Why do you want to see that, they caught the robber?" Please, I just want to see it, if you can that would be great. Tom says That stuff is pre computer, they may have it at the library at least the Carter City newspaper any way.

I get up and Jack says, "You don't look so good?" I feel even worse, I think I hope it is a 24-hour Flu. Ah Max there are no leftovers? I'll get some supplies, did you get anything out of our guest? Jack says He is a user that is all he is, but he is going to talk to save his ass.

You sound like a cop. Jack replies No, a concerned father I don't want that guy on the streets. It was bad enough being in prison with him. I pat Jack on the shoulder and say I'll see if we can get him out of our hair. I have a guy in the FBI, an agent I can call. First I have to go to the Bathroom before I go anywhere.

As I make it to the Trans Am I stagger all the way. I am sick. I hope I don't have to go again soon.

I make it to the Carter City Library, and I ask the librarian, "Where is your bathroom?"

After I take care of business, I then head to the newspaper files I'll remember all I can and take notes drawing diagrams and stick figures. I am hoping with my photographic memory I'll be able to take this all back with me whenever I can get some sleep. It might be soon I can hardly hold my eyes open.

I then go to the bank it is being torn down. I walk in looking at the structure mapping it out in my mind how the robbers entered and exited. A well-placed sniper could take them out just by looking through the front window. Markus was shot in the back near the vault? And they entered the bank in the back.

A demolition worker asks Ah may I help you? I am here just looking. And you are? Max Faraday Carter County Police. I am off duty. "Cough" I just thought I would take another look at the bank before you tear it down. Oh, that is right you are Marcus Faraday's kid. Something like that. Is there any way I could walk through the bank? I kinda would like to picture how the robbery & murder happened. Oh, you mean when he got killed right, Kinda local history. I guess they are just about to set up the explosions for tomorrow. I know if Marcus was alive, he would never allow this place to be demolished. Well, he is not here, we have to get rid of the old and make way for the new. Some call it progress.

I take a walk from beginning to end and between dizzy spells I can see how it all happened.

I then go to my car to rest a bit.

I woke up at Nineteen Eighty the day after the State came and got Jimmy.

Jimmy Thomson is put in the Foster Care program. There is not enough room in Martha's and Maxine's foster care, so Jimmy goes to another Foster Care home. "A bad one"

Mom, we have to get Jimmy out of there. Max we are full, I'll let it be known to them that we are interested in taking on Jimmy, who knows with the State system.

After school I go to Father Michaels and show him the details. He says, "You had a good teacher in your Ops training you covered all the bases." I say I can get past security before the robbery before it takes place. I could set off the alarm as they were coming in, but they would get away. So, what do you wish to do? They have murder in their criminal records. I say take them out and be done with the lot of them. That so. If I set the alarm off and they get away I may save Marcus's life, but I am responsible for any crimes they commit. The Father asks, "You are at peace with this?" I say The Commandment is Thou shalt not murder, not thou shalt not kill.

The Father states You are planning to kill these men?

I reply No, I can't do it alone. I could at one time; I am going to need some help. As far as I am concerned, they already killed Marcus once. If I can risk my life for millions of people in Chicago over a small nuclear bomb. I can at least try and save the bastard that gave me life.

The Father shakes his head pleading Max you must forgive. Father I am going to risk my life to save his…. I forgave Marcus a long time ago. It does not mean I have to jump into his lap and send him Christmas cards and call him daddy. The road to Marcus' redemption starts One step at a time. Maybe he will get a chance to take that step I don't know. The Father says I pray that Marcus has been on that road and will continue on that road The Lord willing. I could be there early in the morning I have my long-range rifle ready to go. There will be here in the entry keeping people on the floor. I add at some point killing the guard, who went for his gun. The Father shakes his head. Yes, he is one of my flocks. The one that will try to kill Marcus will be all yours. I nod, "let's do it."

We will pray for this, and we will go over these plans till we have this down like clockwork. We have been given the time let's use it.

"Time" I say, ever since I have sent back in time, I have been forced with the question would I save Marcus if I ever get the chance? I open my arms and he open his and the good Father says I can only imagine the pain Marcus put you through. You must forgive Max for it is right. And Jesus would not have it any other way.

I go to bed and wake up August Tuesday 13, 2002 back in my car. One of the workers at the bank asks Sir. You don't look so good? Sir? Am I that old looking to this kid or just sick? I start the car and head for the grocery store. Pick up a few things in the pharmacy dept. I got home and Jack has been doing repairs on my house. Jack shows his concern in his voice Ah Max you should have stayed in bed. I had to go to the store, and he helped me in the house. Jack do not argue I'll make some dinner you just rest up and I'll call you when it is done. "I think I'll keep him." Can you bring me some water I have to take some pills.

I called FBI agent Andrews he answered and said Hello? Hi, this is Max Faraday. Oh Mr. Faraday, what seems to be the problem? I wonder if you could come by for a visit. When and where? I am living in the safe house now and I have some evidence I wish to give you? What kind of evidence? Oh, the kind I find lying out on the highway? Of course, you can't share with the local law enforcement? Certain law perhaps. Listen I am not feeling the best, can you show up tonight or what? Sure, you are always good for a laugh.

I took the pills, and I am out again.

"Nineteen Eighty" Martha's Husband Frank comes back. His Company has made him manager for the Cavanaugh City plant. August Tuesday 13, 2002 dinner is ready I eat it and then Jack helps me back into bed.

"Nineteen Eighty" Jimmy is moved to Martha's Foster Care Home. One of the kids that lived with us has gone to live with his grandparents. The opening space is soon filled. When I get home from work. Jimmy! We celebrate like it is a birthday party and it is his birthday. Jimmy is a happy kid. He goes to bed about eight and wakes up about nine thirty. Steve is there for him. Hey buddy its Ok you can cry if you want too. I'll take care of it. Here are some fresh sheets and blankets. There isn't that better. As Steve walks by our room, I ask whispering What happened? He smiles Jimmy wet the bed.

August Tuesday 13, 2002 Jack wakes me up. My so-called FBI friend shows up. Max, you don't look so good. Ok Max what do you have to show me? I take him to the barn where the guest is? Oh, shit Max you got this guy tied up! I add Bandaged he has been fed and watered and we set up a bathroom for him too. The guest is quiet and turns over in his bed.

The FBI recognizes him. This guy is a drug runner who has dropped off our radar. I take the tarp off the car and open the trunk. Showing the drugs. Max, I don't know what to do with you? I show him This is the signal device that tells the drug smugglers where the police are. And you know how? Jack, you can come here. Jack says I know I have a history how about you help me clean it up. Jack explains the devices.

FBI guy says You coming forth like this. That will go towards cleaning up your record. I don't like the way you went about this Max. I respond, "You left me no choice." Andrews admits I was wrong I won't argue that now, but you are doing good here. Nobody knows who this Mystery Man is, you have the best lead on him. Are you still thinking the FBI could be in on the Drug smuggling?

I showed him the bomb I took off the car. The agent says I am not familiar with it.

I say I am It has CIA written all over it. The FBI agent says shit.

Oh, by the way there is a dead body over in Paul Chapel's freezer. A dead body?!

Its blood matched the driver of the first car "Bob Black" that crashed on Deer Crossing Alley Valley Highway.

Where did you find the body? In a compost pile on a farm outside of town. The Agent shakes his head. I don't know whether to deputize you or what. I say Call Paul and tell him I'll send a refrigerator van to pick up the body. I'll take this guy with me. The agent puts his cuffs on him. Before he leaves, he says Max keeps me informed of any and all information. You have a friend at the Bureau.

After The FBI Agent moves out, I call Indigo / Blue Bomber. You still have a signal on our guest? Indy replies Yeah, he is taking him to the Michigan FBI offices as we speak.

I say Thanks for watching him for me. Hey, it is nice to see The FBI doing their job for a change. I'm going back to bed.

"Nineteen Eighty" Smokey Joe's Parents separate, and Joe becomes a ward of the state.

He comes to live with Max. August Tuesday 13, 2002 I wake up and see my clock. I felt a lot better and go back to bed.

"Nineteen Eighty" Mrs. Faraday and Smoking Joe both quit smoking at the same time..

Jimmy becomes Max's little brother.

# CHAPTER TWENTY-THREE
### "Then Came Suddenly"

August Wednesday 14, 2002

I get up early something has happened I just feel it in the air! I head straight to my old house! The first person I see is Jimmy! Hey Max, how are you doing! I gave my little brother a big hug! Jimmy works at The Foster care facility and Wendy is alive and well they are married, and she is still a counselor at the high school.

Well, it is about time you visited your mother! Mom is Seventy-six and alive! All this time since you have been out of your coma, and this is the first time you have visited! Mom! "Mom "Maxine" is alive and well helping out at the Foster Care Home." Oh honey, I am sorry really. It is my fault your sister had another baby and I had to go see my grandchild. Speaking of grandkids, when are you going to get married or adopt a couple? I am so happy my mom is alive I am not going to tell her to get a life.

I go to the high school and see the library. It now reads Karl Ray Chambers Memorial Library. Wendy comes by and says I miss him too. I give her a big hug and a kiss whispering, "There is so much we have to catch up on." Wait a minute if Joe is alive my Trans am? As I leave for the parking lot I look on the back where there used to be in memory of Smokey Joe I now have "Maximum II" I guess I can live with that.

John Henry is happy to see me. Well, you look like you got up on the right side of the bed this morning. I exclaim I feel pretty good actually. Now I brought Jack into our investigation Saturday night, and he felt fear for himself and his kids. Our guest is gone.

Jack can stay at my place tonight. Besides I need him to look at my car. That Toney really jacked it up.

"Nineteen Eighty" Monday summer vacation. 4 a.m. For the life of me I know I have prayed over and trained and planned for this day. I am out the door and ride my bike to the bank in Carter City. I have collected the tools necessary to break in the bank by crawling on my belly through the air vent. I am here, all I can do is wait. Marcus is here by 6:30 a.m. he begins doing paperwork. He then stops and folds his hands in silent prayer and tears fall down his face. Every now and again I hear a Dear God forgive me I am so sorry.

Marcus hears people coming in and he takes Kleenex and wipes his face and blows his nose. They start coming in about seven thirty / eight and the bank comes to life.

9 a.m., they come through the back door! This is a bank robbery get down I don't want to see any heroes! "You won't see any heroes because you will be dead."

I said get down!

The robber looks at Marcus yelling You come with me we are going to the vault!

He takes Marcus to the vault. I come out of the vent and silently follow. The other three remain and watch the hostages. From a building a significant distance away, The Father takes aim with a silenced sniper rifle. Aiming through the window he picks his targets. Whispering Father God "pep" The first robber goes down. The second and third robber wonder what happened to him?

The second looks at the window and sees a hole. The Father aims again through the hole and shoots the robber in the head by saying Jesus the Son Pep. The third does likewise and The Father does it again by shooting through the same hole. By finishing by saying Holy Spirit Pep. Thy will be done.

Markus is at the vault trying to get it open he is so concerned by this he does not hear my Pep! To the robber's head. Marcus turns around to see him dead on the ground?

I can't be sure, but he might've seen me leave I just have that feeling. I crawl out the way I came in and the Father drives by and picks me up and takes me to my bike. I Go home a different way then I came to town.

With the summer I am working at Mr. Smith's Lawn Care Perfection. I drive the lawnmower from my place to the Coopers. I began doing my job and about noon I got a visitor. Marcus gets in front of me and says, "Max I have to talk to you." I yell, "Can it wait?" He grabs the keys and turns off the mower. That was a no, no. Max I don't know how but I know you were there at the bank. I say Good for you. Max, I am sorry. I grabbed the keys from him, and I turn walking away and he grabbed my shoulder. "You don't do that to me." Max! I turned around and I let Marcus have it WAM! He is out cold on the ground.

I checked his pulse, and he is ok. Mr. Cooper came home for lunch he came out to see what was going on and says to me If he doesn't wake up in fifteen, I'll turn the sprinklers on and that will get him up. I go to my next job.

Fifteen minutes pass and Mr. Cooper turns on the sprinklers. Marcus awakens.

Mr. Cooper says Get off my lawn Markus or I'll call Pearson over to kick your ass again.

Marcus is soaked. Mr. Cooper says Now get. And he does not take any chances and gets in his car. If Marcus can't talk to Max Here, he decides to wait for him at home.

Maxine is there sitting and relaxing on the porch trying not to think of cigarettes.

Marcus still soaked, gets out of the car. She asks Markus, "Have you been drinking?" What happened to you?

Marcus says I saw Max mowing the lawn at Cooper's and I just wanted to talk to him.

Maxine says Maybe you should have made an appointment. I took the keys out of the lawn mower to get his attention. She smiles That did it. He got off the mower and took the keys from me He turned away from me and walked away. Maxine murmurs In other words he was turning the other cheek. I put my hand on his shoulder, and he nailed me and I was out until Cooper turned on the sprinklers!

Maxine states Max has some issues, Marcus. He is not the little boy you used as a punching bag when you were drunk or angry with the world. Marcus says I am sorry.

Maxine says Well maybe you should say that to Max yourself. I did and he knocked me out and-. Well try it again and maybe you will get in and I am sorry out before he knocks you on your butt.

Maxine you are really snappy! It comes from quitting smoking. Marcus, I have been helping out here and all I can say is you were a piece of work. I am sorry Maxine, I have changed. Apparently not soon enough Max can beat the crap out of you now.. Would you talk to him for me Maxine?

When I get home my mom says You and me, we have to talk Max! About what I innocently ask? Marcus came to me and we talked. I could not let him in the house because he was soaking wet. I add It took more than fifteen minutes for him to wake up then. Mom is smiling and then she remembers she is supposed to be mad at me.

She says That is not funny. He came by and said he wanted to talk to you. Tell him to make an appointment. "Marcus Faraday is saved from bank robbers and now I have to talk to him."

After dinner I find mom out on the porch sitting and relaxing still trying not to smoke.

I asked Mom was it hard raising me with people wondering if I was a bastard child or not?

Mom says Max, I never. Answer the question. With tears she says, "You are my son I love you I raised you the best I could baby."

I say That was not a yes or no but it will have to do. What do you mean it will have to do?

I state Think back nine months before I was born mom what were you doing? Max I? Marcus was doing it at the same time and who knows, you two could have been doing it together.

Mom ponders it aloud Max how could you think such a thing? I blame sex education that put the thought in there; I was hoping you had a fling with a traveling Marine, Semper Fi. But Jackass Marcus.

She says Max don't say such a thing he is your father! Oh…

I go to bed I had a long day.

Mrs. Faraday goes to her room and searches for her diary for the time in question. She read her own quote That Son of bitch is nowhere to be found and I am hiring a babysitter and going out and having some fun. "Well, I went out and had some fun." I went out and had some fun and I promise God I will never do that again. She gets in her car and drives to Marcus's, she knocks on the door, and he answers. What is it, Maxine? Look here in my Diary this is nine months before Max was born. He reads her own quote That Son of bitch is nowhere to be found and I am hiring a babysitter and going out and having some fun. Well, you went out and had some fun. I went out and had some fun and I promise God I will never do that again. You were out that night having fun too Marcus We were both drunk at the same time we could have you know, and Max came nine months later!

Marcus falls into his own chair whispering I am my own son of a bitch.

# CHAPTER TWENTY-FOUR

## "OK I know who my Daddy is now what?"

August Thursday 15, 2002 I wake up and I drive to work, and I see the bank. The same bank that was being torn down is getting remodeled with a name change "Faraday Savings and Loans." The first thing John Henry asks Why are you so quiet this morning? Oh, I am just thinking Marcus Faraday has his name on the Carter City bank. John says That is nothing Marcus Owns Most of Cavanaugh and Carter City.

Marcus wakes up in his house he is a seventy-eight-year-old man, and it has changed from what he remembers. His calendar says it is August Thursday 15, 2002? It was just Nineteen Eighty something yesterday. He gets out of bed and asks, "Who the hell are you?"

Your personal aid Sir. I have been working for you for years. "I think the old man has finally lost it." Marcus comes to think Max hit me on the head and I am having a nervous breakdown. The aid says I have your breakfast served. Marcus eats his breakfast and takes a bunch of pills then gets dressed and goes to the bank Faraday Savings and Loan? Finds his way to his office.

Marcus says to his employee Ah I need to be alone for a while. By the way is there any way you can contact Maxine and or Max Faraday? The mother or the son? The son. Ah by the way what is that over there? That sir. is a computer. You can access all the bank's records from here. Yeah I have seen a computer before I bought the first system for the bank. I just never saw one this small. Marcus begins accessing the computer. That will be all, just find Max Faraday for me.

In the middle of giving a driver's speeding ticket my cell rings. Hello? Marcus pleads Max I need to talk to you. I ask, "Who is this?" Marcus. "He is alive I thought he would be dead by now?" Max, can we talk tonight there are some things that have happened, and I need to talk to someone, and you are the only one who may understand what I am going through?

I ask Are You having a heart attack call nine one, one.

Please Max I went to bed at Nineteen Eighty and woke up in Two Thousand two! "Oh shit" I ask Where and when? My place tonight.

After work I go to Marcus' and he has aged but haven't we all. Marcus welcomes me Thank you Max. How did you know I was going to be robbed at the bank?

I reply, "You and your guard were going to be killed at the bank." How did you know? Because I lived a life without you in it. As far as I know you died the night you beat up me and mom for the last time. With tears he says I am so sorry Max. And you died at the bank in Nineteen Eighty. How did you?

I tell my story on Friday July 12, 2002, I had an accident that put me in a coma and when I went to sleep I woke up in Nineteen Seventy-eight. When I went to sleep in Nineteen Seventy-eight, I woke up in a coma back in Two Thousand two. Marcus comes to realize So you changed history? Something like that. It was tempting to let your part of history happen over again. I changed circumstances, I guess. I encouraged Dan Cottager to become a doctor and when I woke up in Two Thousand two, I was out of my coma.

Marcus asks, "So what have you been doing in Two Thousand two?" I am a Carter County police officer, and I am having an investigation on the side. What kind of investigation? Drug smuggling murder the usual. Really? I could do some investigating for you? See if they are moving money in my banks. Do you have Howards New and Used Cars account? I just glanced at them today as I was going over the books my body may be shot, my mind is still pretty good.

I think about the offer I have all my records at my place at The McGraw farm.

Marcus asks That reminds me Max how did you gather all that money over the years?

I worked in The CIA and I did Black Ops and collected hazard pay. Some security jobs, I also had some good investments.

Marcus realizes So that is how you made your money "Just as they were starting up." Then you also know that I have given a good portion of it away too. Yep, and I applaud you for it.

I bring Marcus to The McGraw Farm He says I can't get over how this town has changed!

What are you doing in the barn? Setting up a conference center TV Studio and a Bed and Breakfast. A what? Bed and what? It is a small business that people start up when their kids move away, or retired people want to remodel a home and rent out rooms for the night instead of going to a motel. And people make money doing this? There is too many people doing this if you ask certain people. And you are? Undecided when you get a chance look up Home Hearth on the Web you will be shocked. Web? Internet the telephone connected to the computer. Oh that is right you have to catch up. I lay the investigation in front of him and I go over it with him. Marcus says I am going to have to look into this tomorrow. You mind if I can get Pete to help you look at the bank's records. Pete you mean that Mexican kid? He grew up and Bill Gates asks him technical questions. After you mentioned Microsoft, I looked it up and invested in it.

"I hope I did not create a monster."

"Nineteen Eighty" Marcus wakes up looks at the calendar then goes for the mirror he is happy to be fifty-six. I am taking the day off, canceling appointments. I am mowing as usual, and Marcus finds me by driving all over town. I see him and I turn the mower off. I asked, "So what happened?"

Marcus answers I am back here in the present. Yeah for me it is the past. Max, I want to get another chance at being a father.

I am guarded My initial feeling is I want nothing to do with him. I say one step at a time Marcus. Lets talk after a bit at the Diner you can buy me dinner. Marcus agrees Ok that is fair mutual ground I can understand that. I finish work and clean up and I meet him at the diner. We get a booth way in the back and we sit down. We order our meals and I break the ice by asking So how have you been since?

Marcus shrugs saying Mr. Frank Pearson knocked me on my ass and cracked my skull.

To put it bluntly yeah.

Marcus continues I was laying on the hospital bed could have been dying for all I know, and feeling bad for myself. And a Black Pastor walked by and said--Lord I don't know why you want me to go in there that Son of a bitch deserves to go to Hell just get it over with and move on.

One more chance? Lord you are full of grace and Mercy this guy gets one more chance and then I am leaving. I ask, "What are you babbling about?" Son this is it nobody wants your sorry butt here on earth! You have a bad heart you smoke and drink and if you died right here, they would have a party for the funeral.

The Lord has sent me to your sorry circumstances and for the life of me I don't know why? Just die right now you would do the world of good and get it over with.

The reality of it all just then hit me, and I cried dear Lord forgive me!

The pastor cried Oh now you have done it you asked the Lord to forgive you. Lord you are going to have to give me strength, this baby is going to need a lot of cleaning up.

When I got out of the hospital your mom finalized the divorce and that part of my life was over. It was over a long time ago but your mother hanged on and I dragged her with me. Max can you forgive me? "I am silent." I went to the bank, they wanted to fire me but I had enough clout and rank I was back to work as soon as I was well enough.

I snicker Mom said you knew where all the dead bodies were. Yeah something like that too. I went to church they did some things different at that church that I never seen before. But they let me in and me and the Pastor became good friends. He didn't color coat things and he laid it out plain. Don't screw up this time. The Lord has grace and mercy but don't push it. And from then I have been doing my best with the Lord's help to stay on the straight and narrow.

# CHAPTER TWENTY-FIVE
## "The Voices in my head are getting louder"

August Friday 16, 2002 Pete goes to the bank with Marcus. Ok Mr. Faraday let me set up my scanner to see if there is anything we should look into. Marcus asks, "What are you looking for?" Pete responds, "Oh seeing if there are outside computers taking a look at things they are not supposed too." Within moments Pete whispers Ah this is interesting? I think it would be a good idea if I copied the files and your computer and worked on them elsewhere? Marcus asks why? Because you have some encryption and tripwire software that will send an e-mail to certain files and accounts on the net or web saying a tripwire has been set off and they will know we are on to them. I can copy the bank's computer files to my portable system, put it in my Glass Jar lab and take it apart. It will send out a signal but then I can trace it back to its source. Marcus asks This is bad? Pete replies Ah, if I went any farther my guess it would delete your entire computer network. Crashing the bank big time this is some techno terrorism here. Astonished Marcus asks You have seen this before? In a round about way I designed part of the program for The CIA. Before I was hired at Ralph Shurlow's Ice Works. This here is a 2.0 version with a few extras. It is good but I am designing a 10.5 version for The Agency. Ah you are not supposed to know that, try your best to not remember what I just said.

Later At Pete's Glass Jar Lab. Pete explains Ok it looks like Howards Garage are laundering money through the Bank. And So is another account? They are the ones who set up the encryption program. Where did it send the trace signal? I tracked it Ten places, most likely a few more. Definitely a CIA agent trying to earn some cash on side. When you think about it if you were looking for his money you would look for Swiss accounts or an off shore bank not Faraday Savings and Loans. I'll call up Max we better get the guys together and he should bring in his FBI friend.

Marcus looks up Home Hearth on the internet and makes an appointment to meet with Steve.

Pete has been gathering the digital evidence for us and has everything displayed on Power Point. Gathering the evidence The FBI included Marcus out of his good will caters the gathering. Paul adds At least someone else is bringing the food. Good eats Marcus.

Pete explains I did some looking into Toney's criminal record and found he had a cellmate in prison that has been erased from just about all records. My guess Toney's cellmate was The Mystery Man himself. It may take some time but whoever the Mystery Man used to erase him from the records was well? Lets put it this way makes my work interesting. Pete concludes by saying And that brings us up to speed.

Marcus asks Ok what am I supposed to do about them laundering money out of my bank?

The FBI agent says Nothing Mr. Faraday We want The Mystery Man and his little CIA friend too.. We all ask, "So what are we supposed to do?"

I say Let them come to us One of Cavanaugh's finest pulled me over Saturday night for a broken taillight. I got out of the car, and he broke it right in front of me. And the officer had his video camera on and didn't know it.

Jack adds I saw Toney's car drive by Sunday while you were gone Max. Steve adds So they are sending Toney out to scope out the territory. Paul adds He'll slip up and we will trap him.

The FBI agent agrees And when you do call me. We have some questions for Mr. Howard. The best thing we can do is let them think they have everything under control.

Jason speaks up Excuse me But I am a parent and a school teacher getting those drugs off the street is! The FBI barks Listen we have been searching for this guy and you are not going to screw it up for us! I am including you in this, but if you make this difficult!

John Henry gets in his face and says, "You will do what?" The FBI agent declares, "I will have your badge."

J.H. promises If you let them get away one more time you can have my badge because it won't mean a thing to me. Me and my friends will take care of this personally. You dig.

Later that night when I am all alone in my house Bridge shows up. He says it is time Max. I ask Time to what? Time to start from The Beginning. "Black Phoenix Origin" the year Nineteen Eighty-four. Bridge begins this history with me at The CIA Training grounds. I pass with flying colors. Bent comes up to me and asks Max remember your Eye operation we talked about? "Never let them put you under the knife and always leave one eye open when you sleep." Me and Bridge are in ghost forms again. I watch him I mean "me" go under anesthesia and I am out. Bridge what are they doing to me? Just watch my friend.

He is moved to another room where machines of almost alien Dark Age design appear to be everywhere. He is strapped down. The Russian doctor explains to Agent Bent. We cloned the perfect specimen from him. Bent adds The Genetics Unlimited program that The KGB stole will be the beginning step. The Doctor adds And The Russian Mind control will be the second Agent Bent. I recognize all the doctors and specialists here, Bent had me kill them as Black Phoenix just before I went after Wild Tail. Bridge can't you do anything? All you can do is stand there and watch?

I look at him and he tears up and is about to almost break down and cry. He watches because that is all he can do. There are times and that is all Bridge can do. Because there is a greater force in the universe that controls him. If tears come down from Bridge what must my Heavenly Father be doing? The Doctor says If you don't pull the trigger I will.

Bent declares Strap the child in.

The child is a cloned me, that is strapped to what looks like a magnifying glass that hangs over head of me lying on a table. The child cries I know he can't see me, but in this ghost form I try to consol him. A blinding light strikes the child, and it vanishes? The Doctor Yells it worked The child made the transfer into the genetics of Max Faraday! The doctors celebrate and Bent applauds clapping his hands.

I yell I am going to get you all! Maybe not today but some damn day your ass will be mine! The doctor nods her head, Bent removes his pistol and shoots him in the chest Bang! Silence, his heart stops beating, the room goes quiet. Then it begins beating again.

Wires are drilled into my head and the programming begins. The extra white skin peels off leaving him as normal looking as can be. Bent orders Move him back to his room and allow him to wake up. When he awakens to his amazement, he does not need glasses and thanks the Russian Doctor. Over and over for what she has done.

At night when he goes to sleep the process starts again. Bent shoots him, he again he dies wires are drilled into his brain. He is being programmed. Then training begins dodging bullets. When he is killed he dies and then again he comes back to life. During the day my CIA training begins and at night my Black Phoenix training continues. He may die at the hands of a gun or sword but By morning He wakes up not knowing what went on the night before. Then it starts happening He isn't dying he is fighting back, and he takes the skills he was trained and takes it to another level. Under his white extra skin layer. What scratches there are, heal on their own. Bent declares He is going to be perfect. During the day he will do reconnaissance as a CIA agent. At night we will give him a call and wherever he is he will come to us and take orders as Black Phoenix. The Russian murmurs A shame we were only able to make one.

The Technology to create this one cost Billions doctor. We were fortunate we were able to at least create only one. The other subjects did not survive the process in Russia did they. He alone is unique. I Almost think Providence had a hand in what we're doing.

The Russian doctor murmurs If he dies or is injured as Max Faraday, he will remain that way. A factor of mind over matter. Lord's will be done. The Russian turns away in disgust. You know I met The one known as Infinity AKA Forever Young in the Vietnam war. I saw him use his skills to help us track a V.C. general who was torturing downed pilots. He took a bullet right in front of me it was amazing. I offered him a full-time arrangement with The CIA. He passed. Turned me down. Black Phoenix won't do that, he is mine. This time Bent does not kill him. He wakes up unaware of what went on the night before.

Bridge brings me back. I whisper, "That is how it began? The rest you may remember."

I say The rest you may remember? Bridge reminds me In life you are given free will. Inside you may have the free will to remember and you may have the free will to forget.

I yell at him Free fucking damn will!? I, and then it hits me. Not all of Black Phoenix's recall programming were erased from me. The bridge then takes me back to that time and places it all happened. I received a call from a so-called wrong number and before I took the phone from my ear a sound went off and I received instructions. I watch him as he goes to a bus station where he opens a locker with a combination lock. Inside he finds files on certain Russian scientists who recently defected to the United States. Cash and unmarked weapons are provided. The CIA were not the only ones with a file on Black Phoenix the Russians had a few secrets of their own.

Bridge explains The Defectors from the KGB to the CIA came to the U.S. with plans and expertise to create a New Gravity Bomb. I ask What is a gravity bomb? When the CIA start missing their defectors by assignation. They begin to get worried. And when they get worried. They Call The WTC this time "**SCOTT STYLES** Wild Tail" shows up for the briefing on the go. Titus explains We can't find Max so you will have to do! WT replies Gee I am second banana around here? Titus answers No we just prefer working with "Selah."

He gives it to him straight We acquired some Russians not too long ago and placed them in witness protection. New names the works. WT says And they are ending up dead? Yes, but how did you know that? Because you called me. Right.

Titus lays the files down before WT These are the Defectors. WT comments The ones with red X's are dead I take it? You are correct WT? I need this displayed on a map. Titus waves some agents to do as WT requests. WT says Well whoever it is they are using a car for transportation. That is what we feel also. Whoever it is they don't take time to sleep. So, who or what does that eliminate? They have access to CIA clearance and knows about our defectors.

Or someone in The CIA who has clearance and letting our mystery person know where the targets are. Have you moved them? Agent Gaines says We were hoping you and your people could find this target and eliminate it. WT asks What did the defectors come to you with? Gaines murmurs You are not classified to know. WT answers Then I am leaving because I don't do the impossible without knowing why. Titus says Damn the classified level just tell him. Gaines explains They came to us with a Gravity Bomb. WT says The Russians? Don't we already have a gravity bomb. Gaines asks How do you know that? WT says You don't have the clearance. Titus smiles and hands Gaines a WTC comic book and says The WTC went to Russia to destroy a bioweapon.

The memory of that comes to me. The year is Nineteen Ninety-Two The place Top Secret Russia A multi basement floor Biological Warfare lab facility has made a successful experiment come to life. Success comes at a very high price. "Translated from Russian " Contain The area! It must not escape! On orders from the Doctors in charge causes the guards on the outside to take proper procedure and lock everyone inside.

Days later officials came to investigate. What do they find? They open the main gate's massive steel doors and enter in containment suits. This facility that was at one time crowded with staff is empty? Where did they go? The cement floor is cracked in places as if something hot was dragged along it? Where is everyone? Da? What were they working on here Gorky? That is Classified. I have clearance Level 8? This is Level 12 with my personal knowledge. Then why do you need me or my men? To carry the equipment General, You can't be a man of my level of Clearance to carry equipment.

Science Officer what have you gathered? The air is clean no biohazardous materials present? Good. Shall my men take off their gas masks? Neit ,better too play it safe?

Over the radio Sir. we found something in the lower levels! What? Can't describe it?

We will join you. Come General I have something to show you. In the lower level they find it? What is it? It has no classification yet. It is a new life form. But the treaties? Are how you say made to be broken. Besides the ones who are paying for our research never signed a treaty. The Arabs? Yes. But where are the scientists? Where do you think. All life must consume something General. The General's does all that he can to hold in his anger. Laughter comes out of the Secret Agent. Why so angry General? You should be happy! We will give this weapon to our enemies and they will use it and we will be there to pick up the pieces when their anger and hatred consumes them all we will be the Masters OF OUR DESTINY as we are meant to be! The General looks at the ground in shame, and says You are Mad. A youthful soldier takes off his helmet to breathe the air of success. NO PUT YOUR HELMET BACK ON! The warning, It was too late.

The life form comes to life again, and the creature attacks! It hungers!

It strikes out with a tongue like shape grabs hold, and sucks the soldier in as his companions try to grab hold of him or what is left of him! The Secret Agent makes himself one with the wall and does not move! Guns are fired, but nothing stops it!

One soldier runs and gets away and makes it to the Top Floor screaming Let me out!

Protocol for the situation is not kept and the doors are open!

Crisis Room Russia.

It is terrible. What happened? The creature was successfully reproduced and is free and it has made it to the surface. We have lost contact with the nearby city. What shall we do?

Call The Wild Tail Champions. What? They have abilities we do not, and it would be well to see how they deal with such an event. But they are Americans! And if they die here we can say they were working as covert agents for The CIA and they intended to cause millions of deaths of the Russian people and so on. If they manage to secure and destroy the creature good. If they die in the process good, one less headache I have to deal with.

Wild Tail Champions Headquarters New York. The Wild Tail yells out OK People we just got the call The Russians have asked us for help.

Skate yells, "Has Hell Frozen over?"

WT replies back Keep your comments to yourself SKATE! Rose adds He has a point WT.

WT takes the lead OK ROSE The point is this. Shit has hit the fan in Russia. BIG TIME. I am asking for volunteers for the mission.

Rip Tail agrees I am in. Always wanted to visit the USSR. Void adds Count me in.

Brute speaks in Russian. Skate shakes his head and asks, "What did you say?"

Selah has just arrived and just finished a mission and answers Skate's question. -To Mother Russia I go ,I am in Comrade.

Skate says Well if Brute and Selah are going Ditto for me.

Rose adds Well someone will have to make sure you don't make fun of the natives.

I guess I have to chaperone you boys for that matter. Thanks Rose. WT comments This is not a full group, it will do. Wally I am going to need you to get the Mobile Lab ready for air transport. Wally asks Hey Don't I get to volunteer too? WT yells back You can't volunteer you are my little brother, you are drafted. Let's go!

Rip Tail asks WT Why Air Transport we can Mag Transport to Russia? WT answers It gives the appearance that we need air transport wherever we go. In this business never show anyone friends or foe all your cards. We will Mag transport the Wild Wing to Russia's airspace and be escorted the rest of the way there. Fifteen minutes later.

WT & RT prepare for takeoff Wild Wing's engines are revving up. On my mark turn the throttle up all the way. In the cargo bay? Skate asks, "What are we doing?" Brute smiles We are conducting a science experiment. Say What? We are going to be Mag Transported over X thousand feet over the Coast of Russia. Thus, causing us to drop rapidly. What the?! A flash oh of light! SKATE Yells!!!!!!!!!! We are falling!

Brute calmly says Yes, as to be expected the force of gravity is. The Wild Wing begins to level out. Voids laughs You screamed like a girl. Et hem! Ah no offence Rose.

Skate's comeback is Hey I always yell on the good roller coaster rides.

WT's voice comes over the speakers Remember people " It is not the drop that kills you it is the sudden stop!"

Wally says over the intercom We have entered Russian Air Space!

Thanks Wally, for the newsflash. The monitors show the Russians a plane has just shown up on their radar.

Where did it come from?!` And it was not long and. We have company!

Selah comments Remember to smile and wave they are our friends, I think?

A Russian escort flies by. Bang Bang Bang! Wally asks aloud Somebody is knocking at the door? WT answers I think we should open the rear hanger door. Why? Because if we don't it would be rude. The door is opened and then closed. His name is BEAR Part Russian Soldier / KGB mostly machine Cyborg. Put the plane on auto pilot, we need to talk to our guest. Hello Bear. Ah again I see we are Comrades Wild Tail. Give me co-ordinates and give me details. Bear states I am accomplished pilot perhaps I should fly the plane.

WT asks Can you fly and talk at the same time? Yes of course, Comrade. Let's go up front.

As Bear takes the controls The Russian escort separate. We are alone now Bear.

Comrade, we are having hard times as you say. Some of our scientists have taken it on themselves to find work elsewhere.

Selah says Never let a Nuclear Scientist go hungry or they will nuke for food. Bear growls Quite Comrade Selah. Quite. Fortunately, this accident was not nuclear. It is Biological in nature. Void comments You mean a crime against Nature!

WT says Down Void pointing fingers right now won't help.

Thank you, Comrade. Gentlemen, I must warn you to brace yourself if what you will see is unsettling.

A massive sight, it is the size of the modern coliseum, and it is slowly moving. Selah and Rose both ask in awe What is it? WT whispers A Parasite that consumes all life leaving behind empty? Oh God. The buildings apparently untouched cleaned leaving no trace of human animal or insect. Only Plant life is left behind. Convenient Bear who are you / they working for? Who else Wild Tail Who else.

Wild Tail takes the lead Set us down, Bear and me will get a cell sample of the creature.

Rose Whispers WT that thing?! WT replies That is why I asked for volunteers. Me and Bear will get the cell sample you go to research facility.

Rip Tail comments, "But that thing could have left a part of itself behind?"

WT replies No when this creature was created before it never divided itself up into separate parts. Whenever it was separated or divided it would rejoin itself. That mass out there is all one giant life form. Bear is stunned by WT's knowledge. How do you know this?

WT answers I have Trouble Shooters in Russia they keep me informed. This Life form is highly Classified, it seems they didn't think you needed to know all the details.

Within minutes Bear and WT are in the air. Bare yells It is going in a straight line why? WT-using a jetpack shouts The closest distance between two objects is a straight line! Bear comments It knows where the nearest city is? That would be my guess. WT asks Shouldn't we warn the city Bear?

Neit we must try to contain or kill the creature before it reaches the city!

The creature was created in a remote area far from telephone or radio communications.

The cloud cover hinders satellite, they would only find the creature if they knew what to look for. Wild Tail states I see you are a gambler Bear. Let's see how its motion detectors are doing? See if it has a one-track mind or it if it is active? WT lowers a live lab rat by using a fishing pole and line. Just a few feet above the creature and it grabs hold of the rat!

Oh, it's active all right! Da!

So, Comrade, how do you say we approach the creature? WT states You have the best chance of getting a sample. Bear replies, "It can sense life I am more machine than flesh."

WT realizes I guess I'll be the bait you just have to make sure you get a piece of the creature in the glass and steel box when it reaches out for me.

You are a Cowboy WT!

Ready Bear! As WT adjusts his jetpack, he takes a dive with Bear right behind him.

Just then the creature lashes out and just before it can touch WT Bear slices a section off and the rest in secured in a glass and steel box! The creature comes to a stop! What is it doing? And then it continues. Wild Tail yells Come on we have to get back to base.

Rip Tail takes control. What are you soldiers doing? Selah translates for him. We are under orders to guard the base. Rip Tail is that you? Gorky? They both say What are you doing here? "Gorky is an old friend of Rip Tail." Your Bosses called The Wild Tail Champions and asked for help.

The Russian soldier Ah they want to cover up everything. Well, they called the experts. Any suggestions? RT says You have a whole lot of soldiers guarding a whole lot of nothing?

You better get them to drive cars up and down the street to make this place look alive.

Yes, you are right U.S. Satellites monitor this area. Good. Gorky then passes the suggestion and turns it into an order.

Rip Tail continues Gorky my people need to go inside now to get data and information.

Then you just came at the right time my friend. We were about to seal it up.

I'll give you thirty minutes. Two hours Gorky! We don't have two hours I give you one!

RT yells Brute Void Rose Selah get in there now we don't have a moment to lose!

Wally sets up the Mobile lab and says I'm going in to look around RT my staff can do most of the stuff. Wally goes in, and it is a good thing Wally is not afraid of the dark because it is pitch black. Where is the light switch? His Gauntlet answers All power has been shut off from the complex. Luckily all the doors are open, Wally commands G led me to the Master computers.

When they reach the Master computer G you are going to have to make this monster come alive. The G comments Monster is the word. Just below ground level.

Void Breaks out two high powered Laser Cutters and says OK People we have to make this quick! They put on mining clothing and equipment breathing apparatus and such.

Brute you cut west side going north And Selah you cut east going north.

Skate and Rose will follow stretching my cape and I'll stay here and anchor and finish the south. We will take this facility all at once. Selah asks What are they going to do if they come back here and find the facility gone? Brute answers This place does not even exist, and the bio weapon they created they signed treaties that they would not create such weapons. Void comments So you can't steal what does not exist.

Wild Tail and Bare return to the Base. Where is everyone? A WTC staff scientist comes out and explains They all went into the Complex do you have the sample? When Wally's G is done accessing the computer Wally gets back to the surface. What The? Where is the Damn Ground Floor?  The Ground Floor has been cut completely off leaving only The second to the ground floor and the entire basement below. A helicopter piloted by Selah comes by and Brute and Rose yell Come on get in! Wally asks What happened?

While you were in the Basement complex, we put The Underground complex in the Void.

Didn't you notice? Wally explains When I get doing my research, I wouldn't notice an earthquake!

They come out of Void's cape. Void says You know I used to arrest people for doing what we just did. I never thought that becoming a hero I would become a thief.

Brute adds Not just a thief, An extraordinary thief. Thanks Brute I feel lots better.

When they gather at The Mobile Lab WT asks Did you have any luck? Wally tries to hold it all in, I did get some information from the computers. Bear asks How? I was told all power was shut off?

Wild Tail says Forget that Bear let's see what they have. Wally exclaims, "Look at the cell structure amazing!" We have separated into groups we tried fire water cryogenic freezing it. Oh we can freeze it, once it thaws it is back to eating, or absorbing everything that moves. WT asks Gorky So how did you kill the original? Gorky answers It was starved to death and turned itself into a powder. WT adds That proved to be a good source of fertilizer. Bear does a double take How? WT comments We can't contain it? No. Can we? Wally is looking at his microscope and asks Rose would you hand me the Creature sample on your far left. Get Both hands don't drop it. She puts both hands on it and carries it over and Whoops! She trips on a cord! Did it break! Wally picks it up and says I think it's dead? What?! I detect no life signs, it is changing? Selah says Apparently it can't take the stress of a fall? Skate looks at WT commenting "It is not the fall that kills it is the sudden stop." WT just smiles as he offers his hand and he picks Rose up.

Gorky yells We tried Fire water Ice nuclear tests and she trips and falling down kills the creature! Are there any mountains? Not the way it is traveling. Wally suggests Perhaps the force of Gravity is just what we need. A Gravity Bomb? Wild Tail says A Gravity Bomb.

Bear questions and yells A Gravity Bomb! Bear declares Gorky Get us a Gravity Bomb.

Gorky asks WT How do you know we have a Gravity Bomb?!

Wild Tail yells Forget that I know, I know just do! Gorky yells If we used a Gravity Bomb it would create a crater and they would see it from space!

WT explains So we say the crater was a meteor and to the untrained eye it will be a meteor's crater. Gorky Barks back But to the Secret Intelligence of the world it will be A Gravity Bomb's crater! WT explains Not if you let the CNN and other news agencies turn it in to and document it as a Meteor that crashed. Gorky before WT can explain sees where He is going. Bear I need you to -.

Within the hour The Gravity Bomb Explodes In the explosion the creature instantly dies. Leaving a crater as was thought of in the theory. We called CNN as you suggested.

And on the 6 o'clock news people see A meteor has impacted in Russia.

It made the news as reporters and news media were welcomed to see the crater.

The Russian Government did interviews asking the world to join together to create agencies to watch the skies so that the people of the earth might have some future warning about asteroids and meteors. "Think about our children." Those who knew or could guess what really happened kept it to themselves. That was a Gravity bomb look at it! The Stock Market is up, consumer confidence is up, and the world did not blow up.

How did they do it? As the CNN cameras pan around, they watch as a soldier lights up his cigarette with a shiny blue lighter. Get a close up on the lighter. And the close-up shows the insignia for "What's it's Name ."A Wildtale retail store franchise.

WILD TAIL!

Gaines explains The Bioweapon was like a blob that consumed everything living in its path people you name it. So how did you kill it? The Russians used the gravity bomb because the bio weapon is unstable to sudden stops do to a fall. The Gravity Bomb caused The earth's gravity in that area to intensify. It looked like a crater so you had CNN come to Russia and say a meteor hit. Titus adds Perfect Cover If it didn't happen on CNN it didn't happen. Gaines says Well The Russians have been developing a new Gravity Bomb.

Wild Tail asks And our Defectors came to us with information. Software? Titus answers Human intelligence. And you wanted to keep the Russian scientists safe so the Powers that be could make a bigger, better Gravity Bomb. M.A.D. Mutual Assured Destruction.

WT yells You don't go around messing with earth's gravity BAD STUFF HAPPENS!

Gaines yells back If we don't stop this assassin from killing our defectors, we won't have a gravity bomb! WT leaves and Titus follows WT are you on the case or what?

WT discloses A gravity bomb was used about a half million years ago by a now extinct advanced culture. Debris from that planet are scattered across the universe. The CIA Agent realizes You are talking about Tales of The First Force. The Elders warned them not to mess with their planet's gravity then and I am warning you now. Don't mess with Mother Nature when she has PMS caused by Mutually Assured Destruction everyone dies. Gauntlet plot the next likely attack on the defector. Confirmed. When WT is away from the cameras at the CIA HQ he vanishes.

At The Safe House WT arrives. And waits for the assassin to show up. And he does?

Oh no Max. G contact GU I need a tranquilizer gun for Max it looks like he is Black Phoenix again. WT calls the CIA agents inside the Safe House. Gentlemen get the Defector out now while you still can! Who is this? Wild Tail! WT jumps into action and attacks Black Phoenix! He punches him but he simply knocks him out of the way!

The CIA agents opens fire on him, and he goes into action! Wild Tail yells Come on G get me that tranquilizer! G answers with The mixture in question is being processed as we speak.

An Agent gets the defector to a car and makes a run for it! The Agent yells get down!

As they Leave Black Phoenix pulls out a rifle and takes aim shooting the Defector through the rear window and then the driver! The tranquilizer appears and WT fires it and he goes down. The remaining CIA agents then begin firing into him out of sheer rage.

WT yells NO STOP! And jumps in front of him and takes a few hits himself!

G materializes them out of there and sends them both to the Emergency Medical Ward of The WTC.

WT wakes up hurting but alive. WT asks How is he? "Wally" William Wildtale's brother answers He died, but he resurrected himself before he could turn into the Black Phoenix creature, and we have him sedated in the med lab. The CIA have the remaining defectors.

Wild Tail asks Who did this to him? Wally answers Someone in the KGB. The mind control was Russian and Black Army remember. Wild Tail murmurs We told him we had everything under control how did this slip by Wally?

"SCOTT STYLES* WILD TAIL aka Rip Tail" we are only human. Ouch! You better lie down for a while you took a few bullets yourself. Max is not going anywhere.

Scott is both Rip Tail and Wild Tail in training. When William Wild Tail can't be The Wild Tail Scott is his replacement.

Later Paul comes to his bed side saying We are going to get them Max. Steve and Adam are there too. It is not your fault you had some Black Phoenix programming left in you.

Scott a.k.a. Wild Tail. And William Wildtale the original Wild Tail wheels himself down to his room. Stating Ok Max it is your call what are we going to do?

I hear him say it You have to erase Selah and Black Phoenix from my memory.

Indigo says Now hold on Max!

Or you kill me here right now as Max Faraday because if I die as Selah or Black Phoenix I will just come back!

Scott consents Make the call to The Genesis Agents if we are going to do this Link II is the only one who can do it right.

Paul pleads No Max you are better than this to give up!

I am Selah Paul I have to make this decision. Paul proclaims I don't have to be here when you make the worst mistake of your life! You have done better than this mistake can ever take away!

Then it is my mistake to make Paul! Paul you have to help me forget who I was, you have to help me forget! He leaves. Non WTC Member entering Facility be advised. "CIA agent Titus" The WTC put on their masks and talk to each other by their codenames.

He enters the hospital room. How are you doing Max?

I am going to have Selah and Black Phoenix erased. If That is what you think is best. If I can't have it done, You have to kill me. Titus leaves his room

Bull's Eye Red comes to him and says You can't let him do it. Titus grits his teeth If he does not have the memory erase, I have it on orders from above to terminate him. Bull's Eye Green adds And my guess even when he is out he will have a big target on his head. He knew the risks he was taking when he joined up.

Bull's Eye Red Yells He volunteered! Red and Titus begin fighting it out! Titus yells I am nothing like BENT! He just got to the Toy Store first! He is like a son to me! WAM!

WT yells Stop it right now! Link is here lets get this done. And She comes into his room and lays her hands on my head and begins the process.

And He wakes up in a hospital bed in Chicago.

# Chapter Twenty-Six
## "Choices"

Nineteen Eighty-one I wake up and I am in the 11th grade. Over lunch K. Ray C. says My Cancer tests are still negative. Hey that is great goes all around the lunch table.

Hey Max why are you so quiet?

Oh, I am just thinking of the road I am taking in life. Is it really where I need or want to go? Churchill and Dan are going to be doctors.

Reed is going to be a fireman, Paul is going to join The Air Force and work on the farm and work for Wildtale Comics. Jack and Ruth Leanne are going to get married right out of high school. Adam is going to be a Detective. Steve is going to know it all.

K. Ray C. says I want to be an English teacher. I continue Jason and Jamie is going to teach too. Steve says And you are going to join The Marines. I pause and say I don't know any more if that is right for me.

I wake up and see my clock and fall asleep again.

Nineteen Eighty-one Me and Marcus are sort of speaking to each other. And Mom and Marcus invite the Family home for a family reunion. I have not seen all my family in one place at one time except for my mom's funeral and God willing that won't happen for a long time. I still feel like the odd one in this group. Corry I can talk Cop shop and we get along. The rest I need Connie to reintroduce me to my brothers and sisters. And nieces and nephews.

Connie my Oldest Sister is 36, Marcus jr. my Oldest Brother is 35, Keith is 34, Penelope is 31, Rachel is 29, Webster is 28, Corry Faraday is 27, And I am still 17.

Martha's Foster kids are here too. They are part of me and Mom's family now and mom wanted me and Wendy to do a song "The Rose."

Wendy's voice is something special, my piano ain't half bad either. Dinner is served.

Connie does her best to introduce my nieces and nephews. There is something in the air not said yet can be felt. I get alone by myself crowded by family I feel alone.

Bridge comes to me in a ghost form and says You should go back in there.

I say Why so I can hear Marcus's I am sorry speech? Bridge explains Because getting them here was a little miracle in itself.

Instantly I see tires that could have blown seal up. A tire gone flat on the highway fixed by the kindness of a stranger. Time off given by a nose grinding boss. Schedules that were thought too much to get time off for are reorganized by the miraculous.

I say So, some of them they don't want to be here. Bridge says True.

I see and hear a sister saying a hurtful Mom is taking in Bastards again.

A brother saying He is the reason mom and dad separated I wish he was never born.

Just as I am about to leave Bridge says Max they would not be here if God did not want them here. He drove their hearts here and they came. Now for once go back in there and listen to Marcus and don't give the Devil Victory in this day.

I wonder The Devil victory?

Bridge explains All this pain and suffering in your life was brought on by the Devil Satan The Dragon Lucifer and so many other names that he goes by. All the pain you went through in your life happened with purpose. The people like Marcus are actors in a play. Everyone has a part to play.

In the act of regret and a search for redemption Marcus needs your help. Just go back in there and listen that is all you have to do. Your brothers and sisters even the ones who came here to get a monkey off their back are also looking for redemption. Don't give the devil the victory in this moment by walking away. You want me to Forgive them for being assholes? Bridge pleads They are your blood even blood deserve second chances. If anyone of them could die on the way home Max, the Devil's victory will be worth their soul. I go back in there.

Martha's Foster kids leave, this is a Faraday family moment. Marcus gets up to speak.

Thank you for coming. I have been on a slippery slope of sin a good part of my life and I have myself to blame. I thank God for my marriage to Maxine we had some wonderful years. I let sin enter my life and gave my life away to it and I had a double life.

Some would say I was a good father on the surface and underneath I dragged myself into the pit of hell.

I see a broken man trying to set things right. Tears are falling from my brothers and sisters. The Holy Spirit is doing a work here. Bridge shows me Pastors from different denominations and a Rabbi getting together praying for restoration in my family.

Marcus continues I had to reach the depths of Hell before I could ever think about reaching for the light of Christ.

In Nineteen Sixty three /Sixty four I was drunk a good part of the time and did not care how low I went in my privet Hell that I went to in secret. I played the chameleon the good father who slept around. Your mother my guess could imagine all this and more and wept while I was out on the town. I was unfaithful to her and you as a father.

The one time in her life she had enough and hired a babysitter and went out on the town.

"A few of the kids are remembering that moment in their childhood."

For all the world she and I met at the same bar at the same time. "It is starting to go the first few layers." Strangers never to meet again. Your mom was pregnant, and I blamed her for her unfaithfulness.

"You Bastard"

I was a bastard, I lived in sin, and I blamed everything that was wrong in the world on others. I dragged you with me. After Corry left for college, it only got worse.

Corry looks at me with tears. Nineteen Seventy-five I went too far the hell I put your mother and your precious little brother through my alcoholic hell one too many times and I involved the neighbors. I broke into the Pearson's house practically kicked the door in and Frank Pearson beat me to a pulp, and I look back at it he was the hand of God in that moment. As I was dragged out of the house on a stretcher. I saw Father Michaels and I had the gull to say to him Forgive me Father For I have sinned.

The good Father was too angered to cry and too damn disappointed in me too care and said Marcus instead of saying Forgive me Father for I have sinned. Why don't you just cut to the chase and say Forgive me Father for I have sinned Big Time!

Just get out of my face I don't want to see you anymore and waved me away in disgust.

I had to reach the bottom. Being dragged out on a stretcher and Divorced from my wife was it.

When Christ was offered, I was broken and beaten lost and confused and I am thanking Jesus I am free at last. My sons and daughters don't wait, you don't know how long you have in this life. Make that choice.

Keith and Penelope come forward their hearts are broken they could not see their father for who he was until now. They themselves have been going through their own privet hell and have fallen away and long to come home. Connie and her husband a pastor himself as does Marcus Jr. and mom and a few others. Corry stays in his seat as do I and he reaches out his hand and I reach out mine and we get out of our seats and hold each other as brothers. Tears are shed around the room as if we are I guess a family.

After breaking down and sobbing Marcus tries to compose himself and says I am Max's father, he is my son. Max, will you come here?

So close yet so far away I have just a few steps to walk to him it is what they all want one big happy family right. All is forgiven. Sorry for the hell I put you through and brainwashed your brothers and sisters to hate you and all, so sorry. Come give me a hug.

I walked away.

I can hear Marcus Max please! Mom says Let him go he needs to be alone Marcus.

I come back in a few hours and Marcus has my guess been sobbing the whole time.

I watch from a distance a conversation between them. Mom says to him. It is wonderful about Keith and Penelope giving Max some time Marcus he has so many hurts.

He admits I was a terrible father Maxine one night does not erase all the terrible nights I caused for you and Max. Mom looks around this is just for Marcus. I can read her lips and she whispers. You got that right, why did I ever think I deserved to be your whipping post and your door mat all those years is beyond me, you son of a bitch. Maxine?

You want redemption you want forgiveness it takes time Marcus you spent a great part of his life being an ass! A few months of him knowing of you as a so called Saint is not going to make up for what the hell you put him and me through. Marcus hangs his head and begins to cry again. Mom walks away and I walk by Marcus.

We say our goodbyes and say we will keep in touch and for the life of me I think we will.

I see Marcus leave I see that look in his eye that I have seen in my own.

I take mom home and I say to her mom I need the car. What for? I need to check on someone. And she hands me the keys. I drive to Marcus's and I go to the door and find it unlocked and I walk in. And I yell Put that down now! Marcus has an adult beverage in his hand. Max I. You don't need a drink now anymore than you did the nights you beat me and mom! You forget Marcus I am a 38 year old man trapped in a seventeen year old body. With tears I tell him I may not want to acknowledge you as my father.

When I look at you and I look at myself in the mirror I know I am my father's son.

He drops the bottle in the garbage and we just break down and cry together.

Marcus asks me How did you ever start to drink? I am a Marine it comes with the territory. I drank to celebrate I drank to mourn and I just drank to drink.

I drank so much after a successful black ops mission that I did not even feel it when they gave me my Selah tattoo on my arm. I have been sober for almost. Don't give up now.

You won't even call me father. Give me time Marcus you ripped down the love between a father and a son first. Allow me to see if this is for real or is this double life you are living.

Marcus asks Then why does God let it happen? I put you and your mother through Hell. Why did it take so long for me to get things straight? I thank God I didn't die thanks to my own stupidity and the fact I had the chance to see Keith and Penelope come to Jesus. Why did it have too? With tears Max lowers his head for a moment and says Because he trusts you with the pain. Because you went through it your testimony has helped others who if it did not happen this way would not have been touched.

You have changed Marcus I see that, but don't force me to try and love you. As a father.

As I get ready to leave Marcus. Marcus wipes his eyes and says Maybe this time travel stuff is God's way of saying you should not join The Marines and your other activities.

I admit Don't you think I have thought of that? Maybe this is your chance to change a few things in your life too?

As Max leaves Marcus's He drives home unaware that something is going to happen.

As he takes a back road home he is confronted. Satan comes out and roars like a mighty lion! He stops the car and gets out. And he declares Satan IN THE NAME OF GOD THE FATHER AND THE SON JESUS CHRIST AND THE HOLY SPIRIT I AM GOING TO KICK YOUR ASS!

AND HE DOES!

And Satan keels over in pain!

He then takes the sword of the Spirit and cuts his "Tail" off and he vanishes!

And he roars like a lion!

In shock he is still standing there.

I Bridge ask him So what are you going to do with that? Make a whip out of it?

Max says Hang it from my rear view mirror. Bridge wonders Hang it on your rear view mirror?

Kicking Satan's ass is a testimony. Hanging Satan's Tail on my rearview mirror is a landmark.

Bridge says with glee Oh they are enjoying this in Heaven. Max, Satan would not be allowed to attack you like this if Our Heavenly Father did not already see the victory.

You see Satan in all his power cannot see tomorrow he exists in today and in the right now. He sees you as seventeen year old boy. Big Mistake. Not the total man God created.

We serve a God that is ever there in the past in the present and in the future all in one.

Trust in him to show you the way you should go. You did not give Satan any victory tonight. Don't give him victory tomorrow. Do not trust in man, trust in your Heavenly Father. Bridge leaves me as I go home with a trophy.

I wake up and look at the calendar Saturday Nineteen Eighty-one

"Deer hunting season." I didn't go hunting myself at this time but I would go out with Paul and Jason. Steve went out by himself and anything he put his eye on he could shoot it and kill it. "I guess you could say he was Bull's Eye Red back then"

Jason I remember at this time used to climb trees to get a bird's eye view. Can't shoot the broad side of the barn. The date makes me get out of bed and get dressed. I have the day off so I borrow mom's car and head to the woods where I know Jason likes to miss shooting deer. My training has given me the ability to stalk my prey. I find him Psst! Hey up there. Max what are you doing here? I am keeping you from falling out of a tree.

And Jason sees a deer off in the distance and in his excitement slips and falls out of the tree. Like in slow motion he falls and I get into place and he falls on me. I break his fall catching him I then get my breath and ask Are you OK? Yeah I think so? I roll him over and I grab the gun and I take aim and shoot! One shot is all it took. With my glasses I have close to 20/20. Max wow.

I tell him Save your arm for football.

I go to bed and wake up Two thousand two and go back to sleep.

Nineteen Eighty-one ,Eighty two Senior year Jason and Big Paul are in The Foot Ball Program Big Paul wants to go to school to learn how to do drafting and art work and comic book art. His Dad has plans for the Air Force or Farming.

Jason and the rest of us come over to the Chapel Farm. Paul has been working on the farm and between football and school his grades are falling. Paul mutters What are you doing?

Jason says If we want to go to district you are going to have to be there. We will help tutor you to get your grades back up and help out on the farm so you will have time to study. Paul is about to tear up he has been wondering how he will be able keep his grades up and farm chores and football? I can't say no to you guys.

I go to bed and wake up Two thousand two and go back to sleep.

Nineteen Eighty-one ,Eighty two

The Big Game The Cavanaugh City Cats VS The Lincoln City Loggers. We made it to district Paul has passed all of his classes and has a scout looking at him and Jason's throwing arm. Those two are going places. The final quarter And the home team needs a touchdown. In the huddle Jason says Paul you go long I'll throw it to you. Hey I am a blocker not a catcher. Paul you can catch it I'll throw it to you! You are the last person they will think to get the ball. We break out of the huddle with seconds to spare.

We take our places on the field Jason calls out the play. Hut! Paul goes long While the rest of us protect Jason! And then he lets it fly The boy has an arm I'll give him that.

Paul takes a glance back and sees the ball coming at him he turns at the right moment in time and catches the ball and runs with everything he has in him. We were so concerned about Jason that we left Paul out all by himself.

Kapow! Paul plows through the Loggers leaving splinters on the Gridiron! Touch Down! We win and the crowd goes wild!

Paul and Jason they Air Force Bound.

Everybody wins, right?

I get a well-done son from Marcus, and I say thanks. The fans have gone home, the lights go out. Time to think about my future. As I walk home from the game the reality is Marines are out Black Phoenix & Selah must not be created.

I find I have trouble going to sleep. I can tell myself it is for the best and pray about how much peace there will be in my life without that destructive past. But I don't think God or myself is really buying it. I say my Amen to my long prayer and just lie there in my bed till I fall asleep.

# CHAPTER TWENTY-SEVEN

## "This was your life"

August Saturday 17, 2002 I wake up and I cannot see because I have not put on my glasses? I fumble around and find them? This is not my house? Where is my dog? This is not my house? I look at a photograph on my dresser and see myself with my wife Kate Dent and my kids. And a little baby I know, and then it hits me his name is Joshua. My heart is full of joy I am a father. I am married? From the kitchen I hear Bridge call out Breakfast is served. Bridge what are you doing? I made you breakfast, and this is how you say thank you? What happened? You had a history rewrite Max.

You are married to Kate Dent and you work at the Faraday Cavanaugh City Bank.

You still wear glasses because there is no Selah or Black Phoenix in the world.

I look at a picture whispering I have a little boy named Joshua. Bridge says I am happy for you.

Bridge continues As you can read the paper or watch the news The World is a more unsafe place than you remember. Your Mother, Jamie and his family, and the foster home have moved out of the area. To say the least The Cavanaugh and Carter City P.D. are corrupt. Where is Kate? You have been getting threats on your life from a certain Mystery Man. You suggested she take the kids out of town for a while, call it a vacation.

I ask, "Nobody has done an investigation?" Bridge answers Oh sure The FBI have a few leads. The WTC well the Mystery Man really has not been picked up on their radar to speak of. There a lot more dangers in the world now than you might remember. Cockroach and Blue Bomber were able to disassemble a nuclear bomb in Chicago not too long ago. Looking for The Mystery Man is not exactly top priority right now. Where is Marcus? Your father died when the bank was robbed about a week ago Max. Don't feel so bad you could not save him because you lack skills and knowledge.

Then again Marcus was doing an investigation on his own, and the bank robbery was just a cover for getting his information. In this time around Jamie never called the police to tell them there was a drug smuggler in the area because he does not live in Cavanaugh City. He moved out at the first threat. As Paul would say little pacifist Baptist.

And Jamie did not stick around to get his daughter nearly run over; he never even came back for the class reunion either. Nobody saw the tow truck hauling the smuggler's banged up vehicle. You did, but that was another time and place.

What about Paul? Paul and his family have moved and became a full-time comic book artist. The Dutch own the farmland and put a fifteen hundred cow plus farm on it and are expanding. Reed moved to Nashville his wife has a TV ministry.

And Churchill? He and Candy are back together seems you and him went through The Twelve Step program together and you have not had a serious drink since college.

You teach a Self Defense class and piano after school to the local kids. You even played piano with Counting Tornadoes. My God, "Bridge" Ralph. This means I was not part of their security. "You don't know what you are going to miss till it is gone?

It hit me This is not the first time my memories my were sent back in time.

The First time I was a Marine mechanic I remember now.

I served in World War Three I fell in love with Kate Dent when I was a Marine Mechanic.

I was injured and sent back to the States. It was my heart I needed a transplant.

Kate was my wife-to-be. She had a car accident just as I was on my way back to Colorado where we lived. I had a heart transplant, and it was her heart.

Maverick Robins my God that was Ralph! Kate came to Maverick in the spirit while he was being tortured by the Arabs who were trying to get secrets out of him. Mav was shot down behind enemy lines. Ralph wrote the experience as a song he said it came to him as a dream.

 "My heart is with you"
You were my Knight in shining armor.
My light house when I was on a stormy sea looking for safe harbor.
I was your red haired tomboy beauty.
And you were my blond haired blue eyed cutie.
You were called to fight in the war.
The notion of you dying over there hit me at the core.
You were far across the ocean and All I could do is pray a Hedge of protection.
My mind body and spirit may be in Colorado but my heart is with you.
When you asked me to be your wife and your duty called you to take another's life.
Baby, Jesus said no man hath greater love than to give their own life.
 You gave me a ring and said when I come home I want you to be my wife.
My mind body and spirit may be in Colorado but my heart is with you.
I seen men like you on the news and I am so proud of you and I look at my ring.
Then I remember the fallen and the reason for the yellow ribbons and I feel a sting.
Your mother called and said something happened to you.
I got down on my knees because that is all I can do.
They sent you to Germany to make you stable.
You called me from there and said All I can do is think about you baby, it is my heart. They will be sending me home when I am able.

I am at peace that everything is going to be all right.
As you were flying home to Colorado I had an accident that night.
The doctors didn't think you were going to make it they could not see it in their sight.
Baby don't give up, give it one more fight.
My mind body and spirit is in Heaven but my heart is with you.
When you asked me to be your wife and your duty called you to take another's life.
As a woman I hath no greater love than to give you a piece of my own life.
I give you a second chance at the ring of life it wasn't my turn to be your wife in this life.
My mind body and spirit is in Heaven but my heart is with you.

After World War Three the earth was in bad shape so they froze us veterans in hopes that we would be awakened somewhere down the road. While in Cryogenic sleep we received digital programming we all learned skills and the abilities. I learned to speak different languages and other mechanical skills. While we were asleep Technology advanced and when it did it was added to our programming. A meteor hit the earth and then there was another war. The earth was a waste land when we woke up. Ralph wrote his novel and then a song about his Ice Soldier experience. Wow it is all coming back!

Medical technology advanced to the point doctors were able to repair my heart.

Veterans who lost an arm or leg even an eye were able to get new ones.

The earth was too far gone though. The other planets in our solar system by that time were populated with genetically altered humans from earth. There was a great war between earth and the genetically altered humans from the other planets. Earth lost and they were stripping her bare and taking what they wanted back to the other planets. Stuff like water, fertile soil, and slaves. Maverick and the rest of us did not just wake up after World War Three just to be anyone's slave. Maverick took us to the stars. In the years that passed we rebuilt what we needed from junk in space and mining asteroids. I can't believe Ralph wrote all our life's histories down as science fiction. I got to know a new love and we were married.

My God how many kids did I have with her? My God so many years. Even when we were fighting so many damn enemies we pulled together and did it. Bridge adds Ah a good marriage can make mortal life worth living. And The blessing of children one of God's wonderful gifts. You see Max Marriage is supposed to be wonderful, it was what God designed it to be. The love that is shared between two people helps them get through the hard times. But then man had to screw that up. Then again what man can screw up Our Heavenly father can fix if you allow him too.

Max continues "It was a good life." My health came back to me I wanted to be more active and I went back in action. I active, Drill Instructor just to stay in the Marines. It was my transplanted heart that held me back, and in time it did come back. A hundred years of clean air and regeneration and I wanted to be back in the action again. We were attacked and she died in action. My children moved on and I was alone. My Children Bridge where are they? Yet to be born in the flesh world my child.

Maverick faded from the forefront and went to live on Paul Chapel's agriculture ship The Land of Plenty. He felt others should take on the role of leadership. His wife and him fell out of love. Ruth was unfaithful and Mav up and left. She remarried Richard Smith and started a new family. Maverick Became Ralph Shurlow and went underground.

We were still friends after all those years, and he is so down to earth it is hard to believe this was the guy who took the human race to space? He took me to his lab said He still tinkered around from time to time. I was still a mechanic we got along pretty good.

The Changing of The Guard

Stephen Pearson Steve Pearson's son Became The new blood that took Maverick's place.

A real Future Soldier.

Churchill Smith jr. AKA Cross Hairs became head of Special Forces.

Jason Cooper's son Daniel Cooper Became one of the great chemists of the Ice Soldier Age. We nicknamed him Chef. Owen Jackson, Reed and Deborah's adopted son became a great scientist we called him Mr. Science.

After World War III Maggie Max Chapel Married Daniel Cooper, she became a mechanic in the Marine Core just like me. She and Dan had a bunch of kids.

When Dan Died at the hands of our enemy The Pirates it changed her, She went into Special Ops Training. And She became Sweet Angel of Death.

Bridge comments Your wife died at about the same time by the same enemy.

And through the pain there was Maggie Max.

Danny Cooper died, and we were two broken hearts My God Bridge all that history.

I helped bring her into the world. "We." You filled a need that is what love is meant to do.

In The Final days we ended up finding what was left of The BRAVE. They were about to be defeated by The TRI. When all hope is just about lost Maverick comes out of retirement and turns the tide. The TRI not willing to admit defeat arm a doomsday device to destroy the known universe.

The Elders of The Brave Choose Maverick and David Roth The Infinity and a few others and myself to have our memories sent back in time to our younger selves.

My God that is where I got my ability to speak all those languages, I was an Ice Soldier.

I don't have them here in this time do I? Not in this time period no.

In the Second Time around What Ralph calls The Age of Twilight I was changed in to Black Phoenix and then Selah. I was Max Faraday When The Wild Tail Champions were all killed in Ninety-two and I was never Selah during The Age of Twilight's World War Three was I?

No You were Ralph's Head of Security For Counting Tornadoes and then you went back to the CIA and then joined up with the Marines for WW III until Two Thousand eight when the world blew up.

Twilight and Infinity and the others memories were sent back in time like Maverick's and mine were from Ice Soldiers. They stopped the Eliminators from killing the Wild Tail Champions in Ninety two. Selah carried the memories of the past time periods.

Bridge hangs his head In this alternate present Maverick, Ralph went through all that without you The Ice Soldiers and all? David Roth was there for support. Oh.

Eat up Max your breakfast is getting cold. I think I just lost my appetite. "What have I done?"

After breakfast I find I drive a Volvo. The town is filled with Home Hearth's Bed and Breakfast houses..

I need to make contact with somebody? Steve and Adam Bull's Eye Red and Green.

I walk into The Home Hearth Complex and Steve is there to greet me. Max what brings you here? Steve I need to talk to you. Ok about what? In privet. My office is down the hall. Ok Max what seems to be the problem?

I try to explain Ever wake up and find you are in a world you did not create? Steve hears my story and does his best to comprehend it.

So let me get this straight. You have the ability to go back in time and change things and when you go to bed in the past you wake up in the present? That about sums it up brother.

Max you have been under some stress I can tell.

I did not tell you I know that you are Bull's Eye Red and Adam is Bull's Eye Green.

How do you know that? I guess I used to be someone too. Selah.

I tell Steve my story and he listens. I see you have done a lot in your past Max. It must have been a hard choice to choose another path. I still don't have anything to tell me you are telling me truth. I told you, you are Bull's

Eye Red. And you have no proof that I am. I do because I lived another life that I knew you as Bull's Eye Red damn it.

So you said and there is this Mystery Man who is running drugs and nobody knows about it right? Get Adam in here and I will take you to where the body is. Body?

Yeah The Mystery Man killed a man in my time and my guess Toney buried him in a compost pile on Duke's farm.

That farm still exists in this world, alright lets go and check it out. Max takes them to "Duke's farm" where the body of the driver killed by The Mystery Man is. Max Steve and Adam go to the farm and they ask Ok where is the body? Max starts digging.

Quietly Steve asks Adam did you bring the tranquilizer dart? Adam whispers back he is practically your brother Steve? He knows who we are, I don't know how he just knows?

Maybe he is telling the truth? Oh right an Alternate time line and Max is a one man killing machine he screams at mice for God sakes. Oh shit he found it? No that has to be a dead cow? No that is a human head? Max asks Why don't you get your Gauntlet out and take a cell tissue sample and see if it confirms what I told you. The driver Bob Black has a file with the FBI you can compare it to their files.

This is just too damn Strange I need a drink. Damn the A.A. and Twelve Step program.

Max goes to S&G Ralph is practicing and entertaining The Saturday lunch crowd singing.

"John Conlee's Rose colored Glasses & How high did you go?"

I just break down and cry and put my head on the table and make a fist and pound the table. I don't drink my beer and I can't bring myself to eat a BBQ rib.

My stomach is tied in so many knots. I go to the bank it is Saturday and I am the only one here. I look up the bank records and things just don't add up? Max trips over a computer trip wire. Alerting the Mystery Man. His computer Geek gets an e-mail and he begins yelling "They know about the money laundering!" The Mystery Man and his men and The Cavanaugh City Cops attack The Cavanaugh City / Faraday Savings and loan.

Max says Oh shit I did it now! Pete said they had trip wires and I probably set them off.

I better call Steve. Steve, I have a problem. Steve says You telling me. You were right about that body you found; he matched up like you said. I yell Steve under normal circumstances I would say I told you so, but now I have a problem!

I remember from my timeline Pete said there were computer trip wires in the bank's computer, and I just tripped over them. Steve, I need you to get over here and save my ass! Because somebody is chasing the bank.

Steve assures Max I am coming. The bank's computers crash the virus is taking them down. The bank's security camera's are still working and I recognize a few who they are. Cavanaugh City Cops and Tony. Damn I wish I had a gun right about now! Here take mine. Bull's Eye Red offers me a 45 pistol. Green asks Do we shoot now or when? I say This is my life real or not, I have to defend it! I shoot first Bang!

This is personal That is for kicking in my taillight! The bank is in a shootout now! I can't hit the broadside of a barn! Bull's eye Red is just picking them off one by one and Green shoots an arrow down the barrels of their rifles! When all is said and done, I get up.

And I hear a voice from my past You took my brother from me Bastard! And I am shot!

# CHAPTER TWENTY-EIGHT
## "Reality Check Praise The Lord"

"Nineteen Eighty-two" It is my birthday I am eighteen. I wake up with the reality I am who I am. I was created for a purpose I am not an accident or a victim. I never thought of myself as a victim, it was just the shit I had to go through like most people do. Your love, your dreams, your desires are there for a purpose. God put them there because he knew me before I was even born. I have more than a glimpse of what that is to come and I can hear in my Spirit- My Son I find no fault. I will take this path. I leave behind little Joshua, my little boy. That me and Kate made. Tears flow down my face thinking of the possibilities. The children from the days of the Ice Soldiers Lord you know their souls and you are holding them in your loving arms. Maybe I guess it was not yet to be. I have to live my life and I ask you to help guide me in my directions.

At school Shop class I begin work on Maximum. Me and Paul have been going through junk yards finding parts for the bike today I begin putting her together. Paul and Jack's project is restoring and painting his old pickup. After School I go to The Marine Recruiter on my own. The recruiter says We will be expecting to see you after you graduate.

When I get home Everyone yells Surprise! Uncle Sherman is here to greet me, and I give him a big hug. When It is all said and done I show him the paper.

With pride he says So you are going to be a Marine. Marcus turns away shaking his head I will spare him the details of why this is the right choice. Mom says You will be a fine mechanic.

Mom does not need to know the details either.

# CHAPTER TWENTY-NINE
## "Making the crooked path straight."

August Sunday 18, 2002 Sunday morning I get a call from Ralph Shurlow. Hi wonder if we could talk where are you going to church I'll meet you there? Ralph it has been awhile I think I'll be going to Reed's church. Good I'll meet you There. I have some songs that were sent to me and I wanted to do this in person. As I get ready for church I see my Trans Am in the drive way and I say Thank you Jesus. No more Volvo. When I get to church it is filled and the music is calling down the angels with praise and worship!

I see Deb's son Owen he is worshipping with friends of the family. Missy Chambers and K. Ray C. jr. The Cancer treatment has taken his hair but not his spirit. In a way I can feel for Owen. He may be going through. Deb a teenage girl and whoever the father was an African American a baby to take care of by yourself? Parents say abort. And a Lord God says there is a better way. A nice old couple that always wanted to have kids but couldn't buoyed Deb up and volunteered to raise her son. Dear Jesus help Owen. One day you have a loving family and you know who you are. The Next The parents you called Mom and Dad are dead. And a person you thought of as a friend of the family married a Red Neck Fire fighter and moved to Michigan where is that? Comes back into your life and says Baby I am your real mother.

Ralph comes to visit. He stands out in this crowd. Literally he stands there he does not clap he has no rhythm what so ever, it is only an act of God he can sing is my guess.

We are lifting our hands in praise in worship and he is just standing there?

Reed sees Ralph and yells "Get up here" as he does, he grabs my arm and says You are coming up too! Ralph begins to sing "I can't even walk without you holding my hand" and I get to the piano and play. "He sounds like a real black man." Then he starts to sing Jesus is with me when the storm clouds gather. The sanctuary goes crazy the Spirit has come down big time here! He takes a handkerchief out of his suit and wipes his sweaty face. And declares I have been chased by The Ku Klux Klan and the Black Panthers both at the same time! And next to my wife this man here can ride shotgun with me any time.

I have to laugh out loud and clap my hands because I was driving the car. Ralph's Dodge Viper named Ulysses S. Grant. Oh some day I'll have to tell the story but right now is not the time we are at church. "Ask me later you will pee your pants laughing I guarantee!"

When the author of the song "I have a river of life flowing out of me" wrote the song.

I don't think peeing one's pants is what they had in mind.

And he gets me out of my seat, and I get up and take a bow.
Then I see a sight I and a few others have prayed for. Counting Tornadoes at a Trailer Park and Christ taking apart anger through prayer reunion. Reed begins to sing When bad Christians happen to good people is who I used to be"
When bad Christians happen to good people is who I used to be.
When I look in the mirror it is a sinner saved by grace I see.
I pray repentance that Jesus will have grace on me.
I am the only Bible some people will ever read is reality.
Take the rod out of your own eye.
 Before you take the speck out of another's eye.
Are words I better heed.
When bad Christians happen to good people is who I used to be.
As a child in Christ, I was not as innocent as I should be.

I told off color jokes to my friends that was me.
The light of the world people did not always see.
Hurtful things I said and done because I thought grace was free.
Seeing the same actions in others makes realize the change God has to do begins with me.
 When bad Christians happen to good people is who I used to be.
When I look in the mirror it is a sinner saved by grace I see.
I pray repentance that Jesus will have grace on me.
I am the only Bible some people will ever read is reality.
Take the rod out of your own eye.
Before you take the speck out of another's eye.
Are words I better heed.
When bad Christians happen to good people is who I used to be.
Counting to ten before I might say a swear word is a start.
Asking forgiveness from those I have wronged.
Asking the Good Lord to help me do my part.
The road to redemption begins on my knees asking the Holy Spirit to renew my heart.
Knowing I cannot do this on my own.
My Heavenly Father protects me from the enemy's dart.
When bad Christians happen to good people is who I used to be.
When I look in the mirror it is a sinner saved by grace I see.
I pray repentance that Jesus will have grace on me.
I am the only Bible some people will ever read is reality.
Take the rod out of your own eye.
Before you take the speck out of another's eye.
Are words I better heed.
When bad Christians happen to good people is who I used to be.


Tatyana Shurlow sings Reed's song
"She was born in the Bible belt"
He was the guy she loved in High school.
Listening to him saying he would love her forever she played the fool.
He was the summer lifeguard at the pool.
In his sunglasses he looked cool.
He said if he wore a condom it wouldn't feel right.
 So they did it one night.

It didn't take long and her clothes began to get tight.
She packed her things in a couple bags and she was gone.
She had to get out of there leaving this town has been coming for far too long.
She bought a bus ticket I gotta get out of here.
My Daddy wants to whip me my Mamma wants me to abort.
Dear Lord help me with the fear.
As she passed the county sign she began. to tear.
When the bus went as far as it would go on her dime
She saw a help wanted sign.
She found a job at a Saloon bar and grill cleaning off the grease and the grime.
Her new boss treated her good.
Helped her out like a father should.
When regulars asked about the new girl this is what he would say.
She was born in the Bible belt.
Her father took it off his hip and with liquor on his lip he used it occasionally.
Her mother said how could you?
You know what you are going to have to do.
Abortion was not the solution.
She cursed at her mother for the notion.
She was done crying tears that could fill an ocean.
She was in the family way.
Was asked to go to church one day.
She had hit rock bottom and needed to pray.
Redeemed by the blood of The Lamb.
Cleansed by the healing stream.
The child was born and was given in open adoption.
She knew in her heart this was the Lord's option.
She was lead by a teacher.
Went to seminary and became a preacher.
Counting Tornadoes at a Trailer Park came to town and they liked to rock it.
Christ Taking apart Anger through Prayer came to her church and she was perplexed because they had the Spirit.
She asked How can you serve both God and man?
The leader of the band said If you are half The Prophet you think you are.
You can go right to God to get your answer.

The Lead singer of the band thought the preacher was cute.
He had some questions about God that his friends couldn't answer.
So he asked her on a date and he began to romance her.
They were married not too far down the road.
Together they learned how to carry the heavy load.
She got a call one night the parents of her baby boy born.
They died in a car accident their car was torn.
There was a history she held back from her husband.
She sat him down and told her best friend.
She was born in the Bible belt.
Her father took it off his hip.
With liquor on his lip he used it occasionally.
Her mother said how could you?
You know what you are going to have to do.
Abortion was not the solution.
She cursed at her mother for the notion.
She was done crying tears that could fill an ocean.
She was born in the Bible belt.
Her father took it off his hip.
With liquor on his lip he used it occasionally.


I don't know how Reed can do it because I am tearing up big time and he
sings
"Together we make a family"
I fought fires and had a need to feed my desires.
Singing Country music was one of my dreams.
Fighting fires doing the bars singing for tips was one of my schemes
I hit the top with my team at concerts crazy girls were busting at the seams.
One night I had a woman that knew all the tricks.
I was hers for kicks.
I thought we were hot and heavy in the back of her Chevy.
Through a friend I found out she was pregnant.
I called her asked is there a chance it could be mine?
Baby you were good. I am not the mother type.
I have made my choice don't worry you are off the hook lover.
She hung up left me on the line.
I couldn't take the notion of her getting an abortion.

I cried tears that could fill an ocean.
I kept that part of my life to myself, put it on a shelf
I fell in love with a preacher who became my greatest teacher.
Together we make a family.
A child born.
A child lost and found.
A child waiting in Heaven.
She got a call her baby boy she gave away needed a home.
She sat me down told me there was going to be a new life coming into our home.
I was excited we had a baby girl.
I could not wait to start building an addition to our happy home.
Honey you better sit down I have things to say.
I put my feelings in song.
She was born in the Bible belt amazingly it didn't take long.
She was packed that night she took our baby and she was gone.
A few days later I got the courage to tell her I am so proud of you.
Honey you better sit down I have some things I have to tell you.
She had a past she kept from me.
Now I can share my reality.
Together we make a family.
A child born.
A child lost and found.
A child waiting in Heaven.
The road to repentance begins on your knees.
Asking the Good Lord Please.
Like king David's loss my baby can't come to me.
Someday I know I will see my baby in Eternity.
When two become one we become a family.
The Lord graced us with a baby girl.
Providence has given you back your baby boy.
Together we have a baby waiting for us in eternity.
She had a past that she kept from me.
Now I can share my reality.
Together we make a family.
A child born A child lost and found..
And a child waiting in Heaven.

Pastor Deborah comes before the congregation and says Jesus Christ has paid the price for our sins at The Cross with his own shed blood. There is a sweet spirit of Repentance and Redemption. Come to The Altar. And those who came and I am one of them are ministered too.

After service. Owen comes to Ralph asking Do you know who you are? Ralph asks, "Are we talking past lives or what?"

Owen yells You are Ralph Shurlow I thought Reed was blowing smoke up my-.. Deb over hears and interjects Owen..

Ralph chuckles and comments Reed tells a lot of stories it is hard sometimes to tell what fiction and reality is. And you are? My name is Owen. They shake hands. I am a big fan of Ice Soldiers! Well, if you are a friend of Reed's you might want to visit Ice Works some day here is a pass. They'll give you a good tour, just show this to the guard.

Thanks!

Reed says to Owen, "I told you I knew Ralph Shurlow." Owen replies Yeah but he is cool, and you are a Red Neck. "I can tell from a distance that comment hurt."

Later as we leave Ralph mentions to me in a whisper I would be careful who you are telling you are getting your Selah and Black Phoenix Memories back to. Titus still has orders to eliminate you, if they do come back.

I ask How?

If you need a new identity I am working with Steve to create an off shoot of The WTC called The Bull's Eye Detectives. You could be Bull's Eye Black if you wanted.

I chuckle That sounds great, but right now I am working on finding the Mystery Man.

Ralph adds After that maybe look for the Russian that reestablished Black Phoenix?

I was so busy blaming myself for what happened I never thought about going after whoever it was that sent me out on a killing spree. Ralph quotes "Well you know what they say, Vengeance is a dish best served cold." It is damn cold in Russia Siberia. Tatyana still has connections with The KGB she might be able to help you look. Ralph just stares at my car and asks Is that Satan's Tail hanging from your rearview mirror? I ask You can see it? Well sometimes I can see spiritual things and His Tail hanging from a rearview mirror kind of stands out.

I can't hang dice from my rearview mirror anymore I am a recovering gambler.

Kicking Satan's ass is a Testimony, hanging his "Tail" from my rearview mirror is a landmark.

Ralph shakes his head laughing I want to see that on a T-Shirt! Kicking Satan's ass is a Testimony. Hanging his "Tail" from my rearview mirror is a landmark. Tatyana has the kids you want to go and talk?

We go to S&G. Ralph changes his clothes to blue jeans and a T-Shirt that says Everyone looks shorter when standing next to Achilles and Ajax. Just remember who built The Wooden Horse.

I ask, "So how is Maverick?" Oh! This is good BBQ. Ralph how is Maverick? Oh my alter ego gets around. You and Tatyana doing Ok? Yeah, we are great Ice Soldiers and Ice Works is doing well I get to play in the lab from time to time too. So how are you doing?

Little by little I think it is coming back. There are some gaps, but I am trusting they will be filled. Ralph looks at me with wisdom in his eyes and gives me a Prophetic word.

"Take some brotherly advice. You get another chance Max don't let Kate Dent go.

Two broken hearted people holding each other up can be a good thing."

Hey, if the universe did not blow up in our Ice Soldier Timeline we might still be there.

I tell him You always did look to the bright side, didn't you? Yeah, I am a glass half full type of guy most of the time I guess. You and the band going to get back together again?

Who knows what might happen Max.

After lunch John Henry and Jack go for a ride. Jack says Hey that is Toney's car.

John says Lets tail him. They follow him from a distance and Toney takes them out in the country and he disappears back in the woods. John asks Ok where did he go?

Jack says It has been years since I have been back down this road, but I think there is Oh there it is. Ah I see it wish I had my spotting scope. A whole Warehouse back in the woods. I wonder who owns the place? Well there is a mailbox get the numbers.

Ok let's see what Pete can find out. "Pete has computer will hack." Hi guys, what is going on? John asks, I wonder if you could look up some information. We want to know who owns this address? Sure, come on in. The computer is fired up and lets see what I can find. What am I looking for? Jack says I spotted Toney and me and John followed him to a warehouse out in the boonies. Ok let's get a satellite view. Yeah, that is it.

Ok I just started a title search. Anthony Howard. No news flash, I guess.

John asks, "Should we be doing this without a search warrant?" Pete says Why I am a public citizen with friends in pretty good places.

Here we go Toney Howard. John stunned says Point and click and you know everything.

I mean you have credit cards, criminal records everything. Pete gets a call. Hello? Then he starts speaking in Spanish. And he goes by the name John Doe. And starts punching keys and turning monitors on. A picture of Mexicans out in the middle of a desert of nowhere comes up on the big monitor. John asks Mind telling me what you are doing? Pete says I might be helping this group of Mexicans cross the border into the U.S. The Border Patrol is somewhere in the area, and I have been asked by Pepe to find them. And give directions to help avoid them. I have activated a program that will individually scan them and cross reference them with CIA NSA ISA and other criminal personal files. You see as everyone of them is looking up to see the stars or a passing plane the program will take pictures of their faces and compare it to criminal and terrorist files. How long will it take? Moments actually the monitor starts listing files and names and criminal records. Minor stuff some of them have been caught trying to make it a crossed before. Most of them are just trying to make a better life for themselves.

A red circle comes on one of the group. Pepe I need you to make the man on your far right look up. Why? Because I need to see his face. Pepe walks over to him and points to him. Pete says Yes that is the one? Pepe says to the man There is a search plane up there and points up can you see it? Pete's computer automatically starts its search.

A file pops up Possible Arab Terrorist suspect. Computer gives it a 75 percent possibility.

Jack shakes his head An Arab crossing into America as a Mexican? Pete says Learn enough of the language wear the right clothes ignorant people will think hey they are Latino or Mexicans. A computer can be programmed to tell the difference but people.

John asks, "So what are you going to do? This program is still experimental 75 percent." Damn! The Border Patrol is over there and that is where I'll send Pepe.

Pete goes back to Pepe and gives directions. He hangs up and passes his information to the Border Patrol. He watches as they get arrested.

Pete says Every day we have the possibility of having another 9-11. If that guy is who we think he is we will never know about it on the eleven o'clock news. If I am wrong, I just sent a group of people who are trying to make a better life for themselves a one-way trip back to Mexico. And this is just one case guys. What about the ones they don't catch.

Jack asks, "Can't we close the boarders?" Pete answers No. The only way we can afford to pay for the manpower it takes to patrol what we do have is because of commerce between the countries. And the belief that we will catch these terrorists before they do anything. John asks, "We have caught them, right?" Pete says It is best you forget what you just saw for your own good. Like Ralph says it, "It is kinda hard to get people to buy a new car and invest in the stock market if they are too busy buying shot gun shells and can goods and waving their hands in the air yelling It is all over we haven't got a prayer."

There are some things people just don't need to know about. That is why I am in the business of helping in Keeping the world from blowing up on a daily basis.

John asks What if there was no terrorist among them Pete? Then I guess I would have helped them get crossed the border. I need guinea pigs to test out this system and I guess Pepe volunteered. I can't track them with the system but if I can identify a location, I can pick them out. If Pepe did not call me, he might have made it a crossed and so could the supposed terrorist. But he got nervous and called.

John comments He could turn you in couldn't he? Tell the Border Patrol he had help. Pete shakes his head saying He is going to be slapped on the wrist, but if that guy was a terrorist like the computer says he is. Pepe could be in deep trouble. What if Big Brother or somebody was watching? Well, I have to test my system somehow. What is a handful of Mexicans?

Besides Pepe is my only contact if he is behind bars, I am all done testing my system like this anyway. John ponders aloud Why don't you and Bill Gates just buy Mexico and get it over with? Pete replies He or she who controls the flow of information already owns the world, John. It is just the delusion that the powers that we think they are in control.

It is better they think that then to allow them to know the truth and they would go insane.

At S&G Me and Ralph fill up on BBQ and get caught up on life. One by one they begin to show up Reed & Deborah she is looking hot! Slap my hand and gouge out my eyes she is Reed's wife and a pastor. Tatyana kisses Ralph and takes a lick of his BBQ on his cheek saying I can't take you anywhere. She is wearing her "You can enjoy the view, but you better treat her like your sister." On Front. And on Back "I kicked a many bad man's teeth out and I had to put them back in." T-Shirt. Ralph's comeback is That is why I married you so you can clean me up. Reed has Deb in his lap and yells to Ralph, "I want to laugh my butt off get up there and sing!" The home crowd at S&G have been waiting for a reunion Sam especially! Sam yells, "Come on Ralph!"

Ok we have a couple new songs. The band begins and Ralph sings
"Starved for a little Wahoo"
You call me for dinner with you who!
When you make me watch a sad movie you cry Boo Hoo.
When I hit my thumb with a hammer you kissed my Boo Boo.
I watched you and our daughter dance ballet in your "Tu Tu".
We both agree the boy won't be getting a Tattoo.
At a Touchdown Homerun and goal I yell Yahoo!
Honey I am getting a little starved for a little Wahoo!
I am alone with nobody.
The wife went to her Bible study.
The boy and the girl are off to their after school things.
The door bell rings it is my co-working pair of Ding-a-lings.
They are lonely batches that have only each other to scratch.
Their TV VCR broke down and they had a great idea.
Since my spouse was gone.
They would come over to my house.
They had a Girls Gone Wild video they wanted to see.
Against my better judgment I said Come on in with glee
They popped it in and I saw some way ward mother's child.
Doing a dance and going wild!
My wife heard a Wahoo as she stood at the doorway
I popped the video out and yell at the two jokers!
This is not a World War Two movie about D. Day!
Their eyes popped out of their sockets!
They left like a pair of rockets.
I try to argue a good defense at the time it made some sense.
Honey I am getting a little starved for a little Wahoo.
She said By staring at girls that are old enough to be your daughter!
What am I going to do with you?
Well honey I am a man you need to see the situation from my point of view.
She says That reminds me I need to call the vet to neuter the dog.

Maybe I should do the same with you.
I make my fort on the couch.
I have time to ponder the situation.
I confirm the opinion I am a lousy slouch.
I wake up and I take the day off.
Because if I went to work today I would bite the Ding-a-lings' heads off.
It is time for me to do some Honey Do.
You call me for dinner with you who!
When you make me watch a sad movie you cry Boo Hoo.
When I hit my thumb with a hammer you kissed my Boo Boo.
I watched you and our daughter dance ballet in your "Tu Tu".
We both agree the boy won't be getting a Tattoo.
At a Touchdown Homerun and goal I yell Yahoo!
Honey I am getting a little starved for a little Wahoo.
You sent the kids away for the night.
Baby it is just you and me I say Alright!
The next day I am late to work because I didn't get much sleep last night.
A couple weeks later my wife gets sick?
Goes to the doctors her clothes are getting tight?
When I come home she gave some news that put me in a fright.
Baby I am Forty-five and you are never you mind That Ain't right?
Two kids going to college and Early retirement was just in sight.
You were just starving for Wahoo you can go fly a kite.
My life is flashing before my eyes I think I'll call it a night.
We were scared at our first child.
Not much has much has changed since then.
Situations like this separates the boys from Men.
Serious Situation On a scale of one to Ten.
This is an Eleven!
I kiss my wife in awe and silence and pray my prayer and give my concerns
to Heaven.
And I wake up and thank God for the gift of children.
Nine months later I'm a Papa
When I take the kid in the stroller at the park they call me Grandpa
At Church they call me Father Abraham I just say Ha ha.
You call me for dinner with you who!
When you make me watch a sad movie you cry Boo Hoo.

When I hit my thumb with a hammer you kissed my Boo Boo.
I watched you and our daughter dance ballet in your "Tu Tu".
We both agree the boy won't be getting a Tattoo.
At a Touchdown Homerun and goal I yell Yahoo!
Honey I am getting a little starved for a little Wahoo.

Ralph is addicted to the applause!

"They say I am Square."
I go to bed at Eleven and get up early in the morning.
I grew up farming and now I am making a living writing.
I don't drink coffee and don't need the half and half cream.
Tell you the truth, I think I am living out my dream.
People ask me how did I do my scheme?
All I can say I don't know?
I thank God every day and try my best to grow.
If I have a dime I try to share.
They just shake their heads and think I am Square.
They say I am Square.
If I have to compare, I guess the judgment is fair.
I have a buddy with VD and Hepatitis-C.
 It burns when he has to pee.
I don't want that to be me.
I like my T-shirts and white socks.
My good buddies ask me to get drunk and stay out all night.
I say go fly a kite.
They say I am Square.
I am happily "married."
I have a friend who is in jail for back child support.
They would rather have the money throwing him in jail it is the last resort.
He would send me letters in the mail.
About his misadventures in the jail.
I think he might have a bestselling novel if he ever told his tale.
He says he is too pretty to be in there.
He has a big list of woes to share.
He thinks I am Square.
They say I am Square.

If I have to compare, I guess the judgment is fair.
I have a buddy with VD and Hepatitis-C.
It burns when he has to pee.
I don't want that to be me.
I like my T-shirts and white socks.
My good buddies ask me to get drunk and stay out all night.
I say go fly a kite.
They say I am Square.
My wife loves me even though I am Square.
She calls me her Big Teddy bear.
I pray and ask for wisdom for my children and the load they have to bare.
My daughter likes to wear low rider jeans and thong underwear.
I am concerned for the boys and their thoughts that wander down there.
She says I love you Daddy, can I have a tattoo?
I say on one condition and the boys have an idea of the situation.
The tattoo says, "Daddy's little girl and NRA FOREVER!"
He likes to play his video games, I guess I am to blame.
He grows tired of that and likes to play farmer with his uncle and his grandfather.
Some day he wants to have a farm in the family name.
They say I am Square.
If I have to compare, I guess the judgment is fair.
I have a buddy with VD and Hepatitis-C.
It burns when he has to pee.
I don't want that to be me.
I like my T-shirts and white socks.
My good buddies ask me to get drunk and stay out all night.
I say go fly a kite.
They say I am Square.


Debby yells that's my Baby Ralph! Wahoo!


Reed gets up and sings his song "You can drink a beer for me".
I go to the bar everybody knows my name.
I go there to watch the game.
Beer on tap flows like a river.
That is ok because I am the full-time designated driver.

When I get home there is a drug test waiting for me.
Into a cup I have to pee.
An old buddy of mine offered me a beer.
I hold up a soda pop and he just stare at me and gives me a jeer.
It is not easy being the sober guy here.
I pat my friend on the back and say-
You can drink a beer for me.
 In to a cup I have to pee.
My wife gave me the advice
I had to give up my vice.
In order to keep the peace
The Budweiser had to cease
You can drink a beer for me
With glee he asks What happened to me?
She sent me to a Twelve Step Program so here I am.
They ask for a testimony and everybody is looking at me.
Even if I had to ride a mule.
Getting drunk after the game was the rule.
After waking up in the pool of my own drool.
My kids didn't think I was very cool.
I felt the need to make it to the stool.
Because if I puked over the rug I would feel like a fool.
I was beginning to tear when she poured out my Blue Ribbon Beer.
I was beginning to Shiver!
I was not ill it was my happy liver.
With the help of my one and only lover.
I later became stone cold sober.
She is determined to stretch out my life by feeding me fresh food and fiber.
You can drink a beer for me
In to a cup I have to pee.
 My wife gave me the advice
I had to give up my vice
In order to keep the peace
The Budweiser had to cease
You can drink a beer for me

Connor sings-
-Girl you are messing with my mind
I gotta get in gear.
I am late for my date looking forward to a round of beer.
Leaving right from work with a cheer.
"I am out of there" No need to worry I am here.
 I am hungry for BBQ Buffalo wings and I see my girl kissing another man.
It is time to kick some rear!
Girl you are messing with my mind.
Seeing you kiss that man isn't very kind.
I remember you saying I love you like a video tape I rewind.
Looking up to Heaven You were the closest star I could find.
Girl you are messing with my mind.
I am mad enough to tare up this place!
And I get into their face!
What are you doing here with him?
I could see fear in his eyes then he looked at the girl.
Then summoned up some courage because he held life dear.
Then out of the blue she twisted my ear!
"Ow That hurts" now I see two of my girl Friends?
I am about to tear!
Girl you are messing with my mind!
Seeing you kiss that man isn't very kind.
I remember you saying I love you like a video tape I rewind.
Looking up to Heaven You were the closest star I could find.
Girl you are messing with my mind.
She says Hello you are late!
You were supposed to be here by eight!
I would like to introduce you to my "Twin" sister Kate.
I say Oh Baby I am sorry can I ever make it up to you?
You never told me there were two of you.
I feel hot I am sweating like my butt is in a stew.
She asks me What am I going to do with you?
Girl you are messing with my mind
Seeing you kiss that man isn't very kind
I remember you saying I love you like a video tape I rewind
Looking up to Heaven You were the closest star I could find
Girl you are messing with my mind!

The Crowd Yells COUNTING TORNADOES!
COUNTING TORNADOES!
COUNTING TORNADOES!
COUNTING TORNADOES!
COUNTING TORNADOES!

# CHAPTER THIRTY
## "Nineteen Eighty-two" Jack purposes to Ruth Leann"

Lunch time!

It is a beautiful spring day. Jack comes to each of us as his close friends and asks us to come outside. He has an announcement. He comes to Ruth Lee Anne and gets down on one knee. Offers not his class ring but a real wedding ring. She just about faints in pure joy. Yes she declares yes! I will marry you! Kathy looks at Steve and asks, "Where is my ring?" Baby I had to buy my Corvette. She lets her nose get out of joint and pouts Go marry your Corvette. I am happy for Jack and Ruth Lee Anne, it just makes me tear for what will happen and wonder why would God allow Ruth to die of cancer?

How can Mom Wendy Jimmy and Marcus live and Ruth Lee Anne die? And Jack who has come from his life and experiences? To be treated like, I don't know?

Lord sometimes you just don't make sense.

August Monday 19, 2002 I get up and go to work and me and John Henry are on patrol.

Elsewhere Reed has Owen for the day. Reed says Deb come on?

Debbie replies Listen Reed I have things to do today you can show Owen around. He is going to live here. You have the day off, use it and show him around.

Half-heartedly Reed says Hey Owen lets go I'll show you around.

Owen replies sarcastically I can hardly contain my enthusiasm. Owen follows Reed to the garage, and he takes a gander at Reed's fire truck! Hey, that is a cool painting job!

Reed states proudly Yeah Paul Chapel did it. Shocked Owen asks Wait you know Paul Chapel. Yeah? Owen knows Paul by reputation. He has done Selah and Ice Soldiers and a bunch of other comics.

Proudly Reed declares Son stick with me we will go places. As Reed and Owen exit the driveway Reed sees a friend, beeps his horn that plays Dixie!

Owen comments You are such a Red Neck. Are you going to your K.K.K. meeting today or something?

Reed turns off his truck and counts to ten saying You better take that back. A bit startled Owen murmurs Hey I am sorry I just don't like being ripped from my home and stuck in Red Neck central. Just then a white teenager drives by playing Rap music loud and proud.

They both say at the same time "That is so sad, man that is so sad."

Reed smiles and adds Excuse me but white boys listening to Black Rap music is not Red Neck central. As for being ripped out of your home. Deb and me are trying to do our best here. We are walking on eggshells. Can you try living with us awhile before you judge us? Owen I am sorry for the life, the way things happened to you. I would like to be your friend if you will let me?

Owen tears up They were my real Mom and Dad. Deb was like my Big sister, and you took her from me? Reed tears up Knowing the choice Deb was given saying I am thankful she chose life. Because I have a little boy or girl waiting for me in Heaven.

I wouldn't want anyone to go through what I felt. So, I give it to God and ask for his forgiveness. Right now, any and all kids that make it out of the womb are a blessing.

You are a blessing Owen a gift from God. With his help Me and Deb are going to do the best we can to help you grow up to be the man He wants you to be. The miracle is he chose two people who were screwed up as kids and made mistakes along the way. From our mess Jesus can make something beautiful out of it. So, you want to stick around and see what The Good Lord has in store? Owen nods his head.

Reed starts his truck and tells his story As for K.K.K. Back when Counting Tornadoes were touring Ralph's wife Tatyana or as we like to call her TNT bought a Blue and white striped Dodge Viper and written on the sides in Big letters was "Ulysses S. Grant".

We were below the Mason Dixon line to do the math.

TNT unveils the car to us! Ta Da! As for me and the band, we were in shock. Ralph cries, "Oh my Baby has given me a car!" TNT continues the surprise That is not all look Ralph.

Oh my Baby has given me a picture of herself in a Bikini laying on top of my car!

Enjoy the picture Ralph, I won't have this figure for long I am having your baby.

Ralph is in happy shock saying Oh my Baby is having my Baby. Ralph hugs and kisses his wife. Reba McEntire is there also, she is like Ralph's big sister in Country Music. She sees The Ulysses S. Grant car and says Good Lord! Then sees TNT's picture with TNT in a Bikini on Ulysses S. Grant. Good Lord. Ralph asks, "Do you think we can get this picture on the cover of a Country Music Magazine?" Reba and TNT both say Shania Twain gets on the cover enough.

They both get a good laugh.

Ralph comments Nothing says love like my wife having my baby and giving me a brand-new Hot car and giving me a picture of her laying on top of my Hot new car in a Bikini.

Julia Dent Grant never gave Ulysses S. Grant a horse and a picture of her in a Bikini.

Reba McEntire comments under her breath Julia had shame. Ralph counters with Oh Reba everyone had shame it was the eighteen hundreds. The Victorian era. Besides Julia didn't need to wear a bikini to get Ulysses' attention. Reba asks She didn't?

Ralph explains No, she wrote Ulysses the nicest coxing letter.

Reba smiles Ok kid you are back on my good side. When are we going to do our duet?

Well, if TNT is pregnant you want to star in my music video?

"I LIKE MY RHINESTONE BELLY BUTTONED COWGIRL."

TNT spouts Ralph I am not even showing yet and you have Reba doing a music video!

Oh, honey don't be so touchy. TNT pouts I am going to be fat big as a barn!

Oh, honey I know how you feel. Reba and TNT tag team Ralph OH Really!

Yeah, when I was a little kid mean girls used to say stuff like When does the baby do?

And what is your bra size? Holding back their laughter Reba and TNT say Oh Ralph.

Ralph continues And you just got to take all that hurt and pain and file it in the back of your head and forget about it, and move on. File it right next to "Kindergarten babies wash their face in gravy. We'll rap them up in bubble gum and send them to Navy." Mean First Graders.

I hated public school. Reba and TNT laugh Big baby!

Ralph waves the women away Man I can't wait to drive this baby! Max is drooling over the car Ralph you can't drive this; you drive automatics this is a stick shift. Hey, I drive Big Bertha! This is a finely tuned instrument it takes finesse to drive this. OK you can drive it. But you will teach me how to drive a stick shift sooner or later. Deal.

This car has GPS and everything! Max beeps the horn. The Horn plays CHARGE! Oh Ralph, I love this car!

Reed continues telling the story As the girls go off to do whatever they do. I say Ralph you can't take that car out of here.

Ralph asks, "Why?" We are below the Mason Dixon Line son Do the math! There are people down here who are still fighting the Civil War! Ralph stares at me stating Then we have something in common. I wouldn't be so worried Reed. The public school system is so bad down here they probably don't even know who Ulysses S. Grant is anyway.

He is just the guy on the fifty-dollar bill.

It was late, we had just finished a show and was packing up to go. Max and Ralph take Ulysses out to cruise the streets. Just driving around the country looking for a Barbeque joint. Those two love their BBQ, I do too to be honest. They found the joint and loaded it up to go because the rest of us were hungry waiting for their return. They take a side road and end up at a K.K.K. meeting. Men wearing white sheets burning cross and everything.

As the story was told to me Max asks Ralph what do you want to do? Ralph says You are asking me? You are driving because you say I can't drive a stick shift. What do you want to do?

Can you drive on dirt roads? Hell yeah. I can drive on anything. Are you comfortable behind the wheel? Fits like a glove. Well go down there and ask them how to get back on the highway. And remember you scratch the paint Paul is going to kick your ass.

Max pulls up to them and Ralph I am told rolls the window down and asks Have any of you people seen The General Lee? We are looking for The

General Lee! It's a Sixty-nine orange Dodge Charger with a Zero-one on the doors and a Confederate Flag on Top?

Max revved the engine and starts doing donuts kicking up dust and stones! Yelling We just had to take a shortcut Ralph! Hey Max you are the one who says I can't drive a stick shift! And they take off like a Bat out of Hell! Remember Max you scratch the paint Paul is going to kick your ass! Yeah, yeah, yeah!

"Chase scene music"
Looking For The General Lee
My Virtuous wife gave me a car she is as shiny as she can be.
Super charged blue with white stripes Dodge Viper she is a sight to see!
It's name is in BIG bold letters ULYSSES S. GRANT
The horn plays "Charge" and we are living large!
Now we are looking for a car named The General Lee!
Looking for The General
Looking for The General
Looking for The General Lee
Looking for The General
Looking for The General
Looking for The General Lee
I grew up watching Dukes of Hazard when I was a kid.
Daisy was the cutest thing I ever seen!
My Daddy has a Confederate flag that he never hid.
It has a picture of Hank Williams jr. and the words
"If The South would have won we'd have it made."
He would sing along as the song played.
I am not white trash.
I may live like a Red Neck.
I have a rebel heart, but Dixie ain't my song.
I am a fast paced Country boy.
I can write my own stories and music.
 If you want to you can sing along.
Looking for The General
Looking for The General
Looking for The General Lee
Looking for The General

Looking for The General
Looking for The General Lee
Boys from below the Mason Dixon Line think they are the only ones who
live and breathe Country Music.
I am not saying it is not true.
Give me a chance, and lets see what I can do!
Come on and lets pick up the pace I am ready to race!
Did you hear me I said I am ready to race!
 Looking for the General Lee!
Looking for The General
Looking for The General
Looking for The General Lee
Looking for The General
Looking for The General
Looking for The General Lee

Following close behind our anti Red Neck Heroes was over thirty KKK
driving pickups in hot pursuit! I got a call on my cell its Ralph. When are
you bringing The Barbeque!?

Stop yelling, I can't understand you! You did what? I told you driving a car
with Ulysses S. Grant written on the sides down here was a bad idea but no!
You had to find a bunch of K.K.K. burning a cross and ask them, "Do you
know where The General Lee is?"

Joe! Get Big Bertha loaded up we got to pick up The Yankees on the fly!

Those two were driving up and down back roads trying to lose The K.K.K.
Convoy!

Max gets an idea He called an old buddy who lived in the area! Rufus Hi
this is Max Faraday! Son what are you doing calling me up after Midnight!
Rufus are you still a cop? Yeah I just got off duty! Mind if we bring over a
few friends over who are following us that you might want to meet! We get
called and Ralph lets us in on his plan and we are packed and ready to pick
up the two carpetbaggers. Joe drives The Big Bertha right in front of them
and lowers the ramp! I get out my new rifle with laser sights and point it in

the direction of the K.K.K. TNT does likewise that girl is the poster woman for the NRA!

K.K.K. Following in hot pursuit! BANG! Me and TNT shoot a couple times and they start turning left and right going into ditches and into front lawns of subdivisions because we just entered a neighborhood filled with African Americans! Once Ulysses S. Grant was on board Joe turned out the lights and hit the stealth button and we were gone!

Nice thing about those K.K.K.'s white sheets in a pinch they make really good bandages.

Man that was some of the best BBQ I ever ate! Next to the stuff I get at S&G's of course.

We had to ship U.S. Grant back to Michigan man that was a great tour.

Owen adds, "You miss that life, don't you?" Yeah, I do, but the lives I have had a hand in saving Thank God I am still a fireman.

Max While on patrol John says After lunch yesterday me and Jack found and tailed Toney. I ask, "Were you followed?" John replies No we kept our distance there is an abandoned warehouse. Pete looked into it for us, you know Pete, little guy with computers.

Makes me want to get rid of my credit cards checking and bank accounts and go to cash only. You have some high-powered friend's boy. What did he find out?

The place is owned by The Howards it is under Toney's Dad's name actually.

We pull over to look with a high-powered spotting scope. I recognize at least two Cavanaugh City cops. John leans over to look through the scope. John says Yeah, I concur looks like a car stripping set up too. Steal cars in the city and bring them here to take them apart.

My guess is the equipment was purchased through one of their secret accounts that The Faraday Saving and Loan bank didn't know about and didn't show on the books.

And most likely repair damaged cars here too. If Toney just kept the car here, we would never have found it at the junk yard. John quotes "Thank God for stupid crooks."

Max asks Tonight you want to do a little recon on the place. John asks, "Do I get to wear one of those night seeing goggles?" Max shows him saying I happen to have an extra pair.

"Marcus Faraday and Steve Pearson finish their Monopoly game."

Marcus Seventy-eight years old has been given another chance at life. "Don't screw it up." Setting his house in order he makes an appointment with Steve Pearson. He walks into Steve's office with a cane. Dr. Steve Pearson does not offer a handshake and sits at his desk asking Well Markus what brings you here? Markus glances around at the diploma's books written by Dr. Steve Pearson and comes to the point stating I would like to get my affairs in order Steve. Right some wrongs I have done in my life. Take some time and smell the roses along the way if you will. Steve asks, "Are you ill?" No Dr. Sam tells me I am doing pretty good for seventy-eight. I would like to ask forgiveness for what I did to you and your family so many years ago. That man died shortly after that night and for some reason the Good Lord has seen fit to breathe new life into me. Steve comments I am glad, and it seems you and Max are patching things up? Marcus adds It seems that I may get a second chance with him The Lord willing. Steve gets out of his seat and walks over to Marcus and sees the husk of a man that slapped him and knocked him down the stairs.

He opens his arms and tears flow down their faces. Moments pass and Marcus says I almost forgot the other reason I came here. I have been looking up your Home Hearth operations and I am quite pleased with what you have done. The complement coming from Markus pleases Steve and he says Thanks. Marcus continues I am getting too old for this. I have tried with The Lord's help to be a good steward of what he has given me.

The problem is "Lucrative Options Key Investments or Loki International Bank" has been trying to buy my bank franchise out. Steve's eyes go big when he hears the name "Loki" The mythical Norse god of mischief is not so mythical to Bull's Eye Red or The Wild Tail Champions. Steve scans the documents for himself and asks, "Why have you brought this to me?

Marcus answers If I was still the man you beat playing Monopoly, I would have given them what they wanted a long time ago. Steve proudly chuckles.

Marcus states I am too old to fight for the farmers the store owners the kid starting a savings account. I would rather sell Faraday Savings and loan to you and watch you fight them. For some reason they want the land in this area for what my contacts say Loki Corporation is tight lipped about. From what I hear about you is you were a former FBI trainer and teacher maybe you could find something I can't.

I can't let my bank go for chicken feed, but I think you and your people can make me an offer.

At lunch Max and John H. are back at our usual spot. My mom sees us on her walk's waves saying I'll get some lunch and be with you in a sec. She orders a Coney dog and a diet pop. Max, you look so impressive in your police uniform. But not near as impressive as you were in your Marine dress uniform you wore when you graduated. John agrees Yes Mam he turns a few heads at roll call. "Max's mother asks When are you going to get married?" Mom! Well little Busy Bee calls me Grandma, He is the cutest kid.

Mom, everyone calls you Grandma. Well Max I am just trying to help you; don't know how much longer I will be around. Mom, are you sick? No, then again Hattie died last week, and the doctor gave her a clean bill of health. You just never know. John says My Mom wants another grandchild. Said I should get one of those refrigerated underwear thingies. Maxine comments Oh they don't work, Corry tried that and all he got was-. Mom! I get up and take care of my trash.

Elsewhere Reed drops Owen off with Deb. Fireman Reed Jackson receives the address of the fire on his cell phone and runs to his fire truck. He is The Captain of Cavanaugh City Fire Dept. Truth is he is always on call. Being a fireman is what Reed is meant to be. Besides his wife and daughter his other love is music and at times he misses being on the road with The Counting Tornadoes. When he made the choice to leave the band, he felt like a tied-up dog that wanted to run the countryside. The good citizens are thankful his wife put the leash on him and kept him home. "That boy knows how to put out fires."

He is a hero in his own right he teaches First Aid and Boy Scouts classes after school.

His siren screams get out of my way fireman coming through and if that isn't enough, he beeps his horn that plays Dixie! Redneck with a fire badge you gotta love him.

On the wrong side of the tracks in Cavanaugh City is The Jones' rental houses.

Welfare and working poor mostly live here. White trash and all colors of the rainbow people that have fell through the cracks and hit bottom. At the rental house things are quiet could this be another false alarm? Reed arrives ahead of everybody and scrambles getting his gear on so they can put out the fire before the situation burns out of control. Then again what fire? He is Pondering the stupid jackass who built the houses so damn close together Isn't there a chapter or verse in the Bible saying, "Woe unto you who build house unto house" The houses are too close together if there were a fire they would have to get the fire out fast before it starts another house on fire. The Cavanaugh Fire Dept. has begun to arrive. The front door is locked so Reed has his partners Dave and Joey bash it down. Reed is the first in he finds Missy Chambers overcome cover come by gas fumes.

She momentarily gasps air from Joey's respirator Dave picks her up and carries her when she gets outside, she then realizes and says Save my son Karl!

Oh my God Reed in an instant he remembers picking him up for church with the church bus. He runs back into the house The Fumes ignite causing an explosion! Reed hears Karl screaming coming from upstairs! Reed takes to the stairs as Dave and Joey are turned back from the flames! Just then a "secondary" explosion in the basement takes out the downstairs and for Reed there is no turning back! He makes it to the top of the stairs Reed opens the door and the screaming kids panic as he enters. Where's my Mom Where is my mom? Is she Ok!? Reed yells Get back! And he breaks out his axe and starts hacking at the window the only escape left to them! Over the radio Dave hears I have to chop out the window! Hurry Reed the house is going fast! Outside They wonder Where is he? Just then Smash through the glass!

Reed hands Karl to Dave and Joey and he makes it out onto the ladder just as the roof collapses under him.

The rest of the Cavanaugh City Fire Dept is here, and the fire is put out. Reed does not have to brag Dave and Joey do it for him. Me & John Henry arrive on the scene I ask Reed What happened? Reed explains There was a gas leak Missy was overcome by the fumes. She and Karl are taken by ambulance. The fire is finally out and Reed searches through the ashes. I ask what are you looking for? Reed answers Missy is a schoolteacher she and Jamie and Ellen and Jason Cooper and his wife became close when her husband Karl died with cancer. "K. Ray C." They used to take turns babysitting and take the kids on vacations with them. They have been helping each other out. Let's see I was standing over there and the fire started there. The gas started the explosion and the fire but what caused the spark that caused the gas to ignite? John said, "There had to be a spark."

Reed answers Yeah, I have been at enough gas leaks to know if you are very blessed you can let a house air out and be no worse for wear. Missy didn't make the 911 call I checked. The voice was changed and there was no telephone number to trace where the call came from? So that leaves the possibility that someone caused the accident.

Bingo. What? Reed holds up what is the charred remains of a little black box. Reed looks at me and says, "You look like you have seen a ghost Max?"

Max says an uneasy I have, a ghost from my past.

John H. adds Someone wanted Missy dead? They could have wanted Reed dead too and she was just part of the bait to set a trap. Why?

Later I find Jack with Missy at the hospital, she is weeping over the loss of her home. It may have been a rental, but it was home to her and her son. Reed comes into her room and asks, "Can we talk for a minute?" Jason, who also has been by their side in leaving says Missy you and the kids can stay with us tonight my wife insists. Oh, thank you Jason Thank you.

Max says Missy Me and John Henry are working on an investigation. She Adds Yeah Jamie and Ellen and their kids had to leave town because of it right? Jack enters the room.

Jack leaves the room and I run after him because I am angry enough to join him. I grab his shoulder at the parking lot he yells Max don't stop me I am going to kill him! Who?

Toney he might not be The Mystery Man, but he is close enough!

Max yells, "I won't let you destroy everything that we have done in this investigation!" Who is going to stop me! John Henry says I will, and you will calm down, or I will calm you down. Get out of here Max I'll take care of him.

Max ponders I am angry with Righteous Indignation. Someone tried to use Missy as bait for Reed and I want to know why?

Steve is still a little bit stunned at what has transpired in these past few hours.

Adam has come into his office at Home Hearth and Steve finds him. Steve comments You know Adam together we have brought down a lot of S.O.B.'s. Adam ponders what Bull's Eye Red has said and agrees We do pretty good for a couple Normals. Steve continues We fought Cain The Tri The "T" but if you were going to ask me who was the worst villain before today you know who I would have said it was? Adam ponders in silence? Steve answers Marcus Faraday. I have never had closure a defeated enemy to chalk up a victory.

Adam asks Come again?

Steve asks Ever hear the expression Busy as a one legged man in an ass kicking contest? Adam smiles I think I have heard Paul use the phrase. Steve continues That was my Dad beating the crap out of Marcus.

I never got to finish our Monopoly game until today, and I won. Adam asks, "Were you The Top hat the car or the thimble or what?" Marcus actually sold Faraday Savings and loan sold me, sold it to Home Hearth. Adam asks Wow how did Kathy take it?

Steve smiles stating I think she laughed so hard she peed her pants. Her and Wendy both I think I'll call them The Puddle Sisters.

Loki is up to something? His "Lucrative Options Key Investments or Loki International Bank" has been trying to buy Faraday Savings and Loan out. We may have a fight on our hands. Adam adds He is the last god on earth. He is small "g" but how? I mean after their home galaxy was taken over by The TRI and Xeddren Loki has stayed on earth under an asylum. He is still a god of mischief; how do you bring a god to justice? Steve remembers a Sunday school lesson and replies, "The Armor of God is meant to get dirty from time to time and dings and scratches are badges of honor."

After Missy and Karl have settled in and have rest at Jason Cooper's. It is dark out me and John are collecting evidence against Cavanaugh City P.D. John asks Just to remind me why are we here? Max says to confirm that they are smuggling drugs and parts. John asks, "And why haven't we told Chief Tom what we are doing?"

Because if we get caught, he could get in trouble and be fired because he did not get proper authorization for this mission. Why didn't we get proper authorization? Because The So-called Mystery Man has connections with the local cops and we do not know how far it goes Cavanaugh City, Carter City or who knows even county police. I can do this by myself.

John says No you are my partner, I am here to watch your back. We are loaded for bear, and we start walking. From a distance we can see it is like a convention here. Cars are parked along the driveway.

We get passed the sleeping guards and are thankful and make it to the garage and start taking video pictures of the inventory. The chop shop as good as I have seen anywhere, and I see where I can get a new steering wheel for my Trans Am. We move out slowly and find a store house of drugs. John whispers is this it? The Mystery Man's Stash? No, maybe a failsafe if one of their drivers can't make a delivery somebody from here might be able to complete an order or something? They are all inside talking, you think we should call it good and head back to the car before we are spotted. That would be smart. John whispers, "But if we were smart, we would not be here. Let's go."

As we leave someone takes a shot at me. It was close but I was a better shot and I shoot back with a silenced weapon. The other guy has his trigger on full auto and pulls it as he falls to the ground dead. Make for the car! Lights come on this abandoned warehouse is not so abandoned! It is like old times I shoot to kill; it all comes back to me. John is slow to come around. Then when a bullet flies by your head it is go time!

The people inside started running out shouting "I thought you said this place was safe?" Toney yells back I told you we should've moved to another location!

John We are being hunted this was recon not war in the woods! All I have are pistols, I need rifles! Me and John find cover while they are looking for us. John asks, "How are you for clips? Down to two?" John yells Damn boy at least what you shoot at is hit, I can't hit the broad side of a barn tonight. I smartly say The first step is to admit it, the second is to get help.

John asks Where did you learn to shoot?

I tell him Uncle Sherman is a Marine and Father Michaels he used to be a sniper among other things in Vietnam. Let's go we can make to the warehouse we can get closer to the car.

John yells Yeah, we can't stay here too many damn rednecks shooting at anything that moves!

They make a run for it! Max and John are pinned down at an abandoned warehouse!

John says I am out Max! Max sees a shovel and says You have to knock me out! Now hit me! John says Oh I don't want to hit you. Punch me Damn it!

WAM!

"Nineteen Eighty-two"

I wake up at 4 a.m. and I have to get help but who would believe me? I get on my scooter I can't wait till Maximum is finished and running and I head to Father Michaels.

I pound on his door, and he awakens asking What is it child? I yell Me and John Henry are pinned down we have to get rifles now and bury them.

Father Michaels yells Now hold on Max calm down what happened? I tell him what happened, and He says Ok let's start here in my closet.

A Browning Automatic Rifle. A sub machine gun. I ask, "What do you do in your spare time take over small countries?"

Father Michaels asks Where is it you say you are held up at?

An abandoned warehouse out of town. Well, it is not abandoned here at this time Marcus may know who owns the place. We go to the bank and Marcus says Come in Max, Father, what can I do for you?

I will tell the story. Marcus is in shock You and John Henry did what? Yeah, I know who owns the place.

I tell Marcus to get Pete to get the information August 19, 2002. The place is owned by The Howard's buy it from Toney's father and call the Carter County Police or Chief Tom about 11:30 that night tell them somebody is on your land it will make what we are doing nice and legal. Marcus asks, "And what you are doing isn't?"

I explain "We found a chop shop and drugs while doing a search, do you have any other ideas to do it without tipping off The Mystery Man?" Who has cops in Cavanaugh City on his payroll?

Ok Max I can do that I guess, what are you going to do?

Say a prayer Hope those Science fiction shows I watched as a kid were true and say another prayer. Max takes them to the spot. Ok this is it. The Father says I'll have a footlocker with the guns and ammo, it should be ok for twenty years, I'll pack it right.

Marcus adds, "The owner of this place is a friend of mine. He'll let me and Father Michaels bury what we need. The Howards won't buy the place for a few years if I remember right."

But won't it tip them off we are on to them if I buy it?

I answer Mr. Howard has so much junk and storage places in the surrounding counties and Toney and his brothers are cooking the books so much He probably does not know what all is going on.

Marcus pats my shoulder saying Max you are always playing chess so many moves ahead.

That is how you taught me Dad. "Silence."

You called me Dad. Yeah, I guess I did. Father Michaels says, "Well this is a start."

At school Shop Class Maximum is Done. I get an A++

Paul's truck is done. The engine is a work of art and so is the Pickup.

Paul painted Wildtale Comic book covers all over the truck of first and key issues of Wild Tail Infinity Twilight the WTC and other characters.

Lunch time the guys talk about the prom tonight. Paul says Marcy is ready to dance tonight. Steve says Kathy's Dad is going to drive us in his new Cadillac. Dan adds Burney is even coming home for this, he is taking his girlfriend. K. Ray C. adds Hey even I got a date for tonight. Reed Jackson adds Inflatable or imaginary? The guys Chuckle.

I am silent. Jason opens his big mouth asking Max who are you going with?

I mumble Nobody asked me. Steve says You are supposed to ask the girl man!

Ok I just didn't want to get turned down happy! Jason whispers Chill Max ok.

Paul adds, "Hey Pete is coming home for a visit. Let's see if we can get him a date."

K. Ray C. reacts A thirteen-year-old at a Senior High Prom? Paul states A Thirteen-year-old who will graduate from MIT in about a year. Jamie says You miss the little guy, don't you?

Paul smiles saying Yeah, I miss him, he is my little buddy. The way I see it.-

"The way I see it" is what we call The Gospel according to Paul."

-when you look at history wherever there is a revolution there are fat kids and geeks.

American Revolution John Adams Thomas Jefferson they were Geeks by modern standards. Paul Revere and John Hancock were fat kids And Ben Franklin well he was a little of both. Oh, sure George Washington was a jock, but it took the fat and the geek kids to start the Revolution. Churchill asks, "And you passed American history how?"

What I am saying is wherever there is a fat kid and a geek, or a nerd look out there will be a revolution.

Steve asks me Max why are you here? I say Because I usually eat with you and the other guys. Max, I love you like a brother, but you need help. Now! Get ready for the prom. Why don't you go over and talk to the girls, you know girls. Steve takes me by the shoulder and takes me over to the girl's table. Ladies, I would like to introduce Max Faraday.

The Girls go along with Steve's gag and say Hi Max. Steve explains He needs help getting ready for the prom tonight. Kathy says Kinda late Max? Ruth Leann says I'll take you shopping after school. "Oh, this will be fun."

After school When I get home, I just fall into the couch. Ruth Leanne knocks at the door Max are you ready to go shopping? We have to ready for the Prom! Oh, the Prom I forgot! Graduation Prom. With the contact lenses that my mom gave me as a graduation gift and the fact I look good in a Tux The girls are stunned at the transformation. I am not because I look good. It is just Ruth Leann dressed me, and I just can't help but think Jack and her are going to get married right after graduation. And that is a good thing and all.

They will have less then seventeen years. How can I be comfortable saying I wish you the best when I know what will happen? Pete takes one of Paul's sisters by the arm and walks her to the dance floor. Wendy says I hope you saved all your dances for me.

From a distance I watch Jack and Ruth Leann slow dance. And I sit the dance out.

Pete tries to drag Paul's sister back and. Wendy says Come on Max dance with me.

After the dance I asked Pete to go get me a cold drink. And get some for the other guys they are drooling over Wendy and Kathy, and they need to get cooled off. As boy genius and hormones leaves

I hear a voice from the past. Ruth Leann whispers, "You know we were a cute couple." And I whispered back "Yeah you were." Don't feel bad, I loved him for as long as I could no regrets Max.

Ruth Leann, I wish I could-. I am happy you can't Max it is Ok. You don't get the full picture down here because you are not supposed to. You are supposed to listen to God and make your way through it trusting on him not on your own understanding.

You know Jesus is what makes Heaven, Heaven for me and you don't get that here on earth. You get a little glimpse with good love from friends and family, but nothing could ever be imagined for the whole. I know I leave Jack and the kids in good hands.

But the way you died and what Jack did.

Ruth Leann states How I died is what you call a "mystery." I fought the good fight and God called me home. What Jack did, he is forgiven and through his sorrow he has helped others, and he will continue helping others. As you say, The Lord trusts us with the pain. Life will go on Max as it always does, we are born we live we die. Some die sooner than others. And I look over to K. The dancing fool Ray C. And some live longer than others. Very few live to be immortals. And Ruth Leann leaves me with more questions. "Immortal."

Wendy says Come on Max let's dance!

# CHAPTER THIRTY-ONE
## "The Long Night"

August Monday 19 /Tuesday 20, 2002 I wake up to hear Max I am sorry I hit you. I grab a nearby shovel and dig because my life depends on something being there! One of the armed drug smuggling Rednecks says Hey it is quiet, I think they are out of ammo. John Henry picks up The Browning and says Oh this is what I am talking about. And takes aim and fires mowing the grass before them! Oh Shit!

John yells, "You are under arrest!" Off in the distance I hear police sirens of The Carter County Police. In a scramble they run for their cars. As they do I find Toney and I run after him knocking him down he punches me I am not out, but I am still a little dazed and woozy from John's hit I guess. John shoots up the ground and says Boy don't make me shoot you for punching my partner! I get up and slap cuffs on him and say Let's get him out of here we can't question him here and we can't let Chief Tom or The FBI have him just yet either. So, what are you saying? Let's take him to Paul's.

We drag Toney out through the woods and put him in the car. He yells, "You can't do this I have friends they will take care of me!" I say Just like they took care of "Bob Black."

Toney goes white You know. John says Oh snow flake you would be surprised what we in the hood know you dig.

When we get to Paul's he comes out to greet us. Damn It took you long enough to get here who do you got? John asks, "How?" Paul says Police band scanner. Ah little Toney and his big brother son of a bitch sold me a used truck and would not repair the transmission two days later after I bought it, it fell apart. Bring him in.

John asks Max, "Do you mind telling me what Paul has to do with getting information out of Toney?" I look at Paul and smile and wink saying He has a way of getting answers.

Paul Jr. asks, "What do you want to do with him Pa?" Paul grits his teeth saying Go get me the calves that have just been weaned. And bring them to the shop. If we don't get the answers, we want, we will get them one way or another. Marcy says to me Max you look tired why don't you get some rest I'll set you a place on the couch for old times' sake.

I get up and look at my calendar "Nineteen Eighty two" Graduation day!

I wait in line to get in the shower. Steve yells "Come on Wendy me and Max are graduating today too!" After a shower I put on my clothes and head to school to help decorate.

Out in the driveway Maximum glistens and shines because I paid one of my little brothers a dollar to wash it. I made this bike, she is mine.

Steve on the other hand saved his lawn care and other money and bought an Eighty-two Corvette. He did a little gambling on the side too, but we have held each other accountable, and we have not rolled dice or played evil cards for three months.

Of course, four months ago we raised some cash to pay for repair work on the foster home by a secret benefactor. We help in the finishing touches and then we are called to get ready in the cap and gown.

The school gym, basketball court and bleachers are filled as we walk down.

Steve Pearson Valor Victorian Steve talks forever it is like background noise to me and I kinda zone out and look at the crowd of family and friends. Uncle Sherman wore his uniform for me as I look at him, he solutes. Steve ends by saying, "And that is why you are the class of Nineteen Eighty-Two!" We Stand up and applause and I really don't know what I am applauding for.

Mr. Cooper Keynote speaker I know you have chosen me to speak because after Steve you know I will keep it short. Laughter. When I started teaching again, I had a lot more hair, and it wasn't this gray. Pause for laughter. Oh, you can laugh now son, but I have one word for your heredity. More laughter. For the past few years, I have watched this class grow up. Through laughter and tragedy, you have shown yourselves to be great overcomers. Class of Nineteen Eighty-two stand up and take a bow!

Let me ask you, where are you going? Some are going into the military Semper Fi.

Some education Hopefully I'll be out of a job. Some careers and industry.

Few are going into agriculture so how are we going to eat? One of you is turning eighteen and I get my den back. We begin Patting Jason on the back. I began teaching again because I was let go of what I thought was my dream job. It helped me raise a couple wonderful kids and help put my wife through law school who got me fired from my job.

The God Lord works in mysterious ways. So, I started a little factory and made some doll houses and little by little a seed of faith grew. Along the way I was offered a teaching job.

I thought I would do this till something better came along. And it did I found out I loved to teach. There is this rumor going around that I might be retiring. Not quite so.

I think I will stick around and watch my little girl graduate if you will let me.

"Applause."

You are the class of Nineteen Eighty-two Now go take on the world!

After hugs and goodbyes, I head for home and have dinner with the family.

Mom's original family and me and our extended foster family. Uncle Sherman shakes his head at Maximum and says You are going to drive that Quantico?

Afterwards Going for a ride on Maximum makes me think this is as good as it gets, and it is pretty good. I park at the diner and put the kick stand down and put my feet on the handlebars and lay back and watch the stars come out.

Born in the U.S.A. comes over the speakers. Paul and the guys are all loaded up in his pickup. Churchill is puking as he stumbles out onto the parking lot. K. Ray C. helps him up. This moment is so right. K. yells out, "You going to give us rides on that thing or what?"

And I do even drunk Churchill and when it is all said and done the guys give me hugs and the girls give me kisses. Soon I'll be leaving for Quantico and God only knows.

I wake up after midnight and it is still Tuesday August 20, 2002. John Henry has been talking to Toney laying evidence before him. He still won't cooperate. Tom comes by and says The Sheriff of Cavanaugh City has been arrested. Your FBI agent is looking for you.

I ask Tom, "Has any of them talked? He shakes his head No my guess they are scared of retribution from the Mystery Man."

Then maybe I should have a go at Toney. Tom asks, "What can you do?"

We string Toney up on the crane and Paul jr. pours milk over him and he comes to- Yelling What are you doing!? I start asking Toney questions and for the ones he lies to us on Max the dog barks and growls on and we lower him into the pen of just weaned calves that are going through milk withdrawals. They are now sucking on his toes and have begun to draw blood. They have teeth and Toney is the other white meat.

We get to Who is The Mystery Man? I won't tell you he will kill me! Pete lowers him a little more. The calves are biting his knees & calf muscles, and he is screaming. This is insane you can't do this! Who is The Mystery Man? Toney is kicking and screaming, and he is lowered, and a calf head bumps him! Jason and his Dad Mr. Cooper have just arrived, and they say Ow that had to smart!

I ask again Who is The Mystery Man? I can't tell you he will kill me! OW they are eating me alive! I ask, "Who is his CIA contact that got him the explosives and equipment?"

Badger! I think his name is Badger! I push the button and Toney goes up in the air.

Oh, thank you thank you! Can I come down now?

I screamed, but Badger tried setting me up to tell him about my investigation into the drug smuggling! And he blamed the FBI! And I almost Damn! I ask Toney Who is The Mystery Man?!

Toney cries He will kill me! I lower him down and look into his eyes and say I will kill you if you don't tell me Who is The Mystery Man?! And Toney falls to the floor!

The calves stomp all over him and bite and suck on him. Paul says Max just calm down and give me the controls. Toney Screams OUT JAKE HAMMER!!!

Jack takes control from my limp hands. As I whisper Oh you gotta be kidding.

Jack raises Toney up and asks Where does he store his drugs?! Toney has had enough and gives the location. Paul murmurs, "Son get my Trebuchet." I say, "Tom just gives us a few minutes head start." Tom says, "Hell, I am going with you The FBI can come and get Toney after we are gone." We get Toney off the crane and wash the calf milk and drool off and put a blanket over him with Marcy holding a gun on him.

Paul jr. hitches up the Trebuchet to Big Bertha's flatbed trailer and me and Pete are in the back seat. I look at the Trebuchet and ask Paul what are you going to do with a catapult?

Paul says It is not a catapult it is a Trebuchet. There is a big difference.

I am going to fling dead cows to Jake's warehouse. Pete has a computer program, all we have to do is factor in the weight of the wind and distance and we can fling just about anything and hit a target. Pete says I have a Satellite picture of the layout looks like they are still packing. Paul jr. says Ok Dad let's go!

The FBI arrive just as we are leaving. Where do you think you are going? I yell out Jake Hammer is The Mystery Man! Who? That is it! CIA Badger must have erased him from the records that is the CIA Connection! You didn't tell anyone you came here?

No, I am not taking any chances. The rest of my team is back at Cavanaugh City I kept radio silence getting here. We have the location to their hideout if you want to arrest them follow us Lets GO!

Paul looks back at me and says Max you don't look so good; you should get some rest.

So, I nod off.

As we drove through Cavanaugh City the FBI get rounded up and speed out of town.

The FBI are in such a hurry, and they pass us as we head out on the highway.

"Deer Crossing Alley Valley Highway" Peddle to the floor they hit deer and one by one they end up in the ditches and all we can do is shake our heads and one by one we have to pick them up and they have to ride in the back of the pickups. Jason Cooper yells "You idiots! This is Deer Crossing Alley Valley Highway! You can't go over Forty-five!"

Oh, shut up Cooper! Reed Yells Hey Cooper They ran over The Cow that thinks she is a deer! Cooper Yells First they hit The Midnight Stealth Jogger! Now they run over the Cow That thinks she is a deer! Come on, son let's go! "Music Charley Daniels Simple Man"

# CHAPTER THIRTY-TWO
## Nineteen Ninety-Three

I got the call from Cavanaugh City Hospital. Paul says Max it won't be long now K. will be going home soon. I say over the phone I am already there.

I then say to Ralph I will have a death in the family I gotta go. Ralph replies, "Hey you and Reed go I'll be home in a couple days." You know Counting Tornadoes / Christ Taking apart anger Through Prayer could play at the funeral. I hug Ralph for his friendship and support. Before I know it me and Reed are packed and on a plane for home. Marcy picks us up at the airport and takes us to the hospital. The cancer has ravaged K.Ray C.'s body.

His wife Missy says It is so good to meet you. This is the woman that Jack was dancing and kissing with. A part of me thought I knew her she is K. Ray C.'s wife. "K. got married?"

He awakes Hi Max it is good to see you. I held his withered hand. He is so pale I can tell it won't be long. Paul and the others begin to fill the room and his wife gets up to leave.

He whispers I am so blessed to see all of you again. Life is too short live it for me will you. Paul, I have to ask you, why was I put on this earth? Paul with tears says to teach us too love sometimes the unlovable. To put actions, our words and deeds are too good use.

To remind us we are only given a short amount of time to make a difference and impact on the world around us. To include others in the fold so our world does not grow stagnant. To put a smile on others faces when they are down. To teach us to be grateful for the little things like your health and tomorrow is more than just another day it is a gift from God. K. takes a labored breath, saying I did all that? With tears Paul chokes and says, "You sure did."

Gee all I thought all I did was make colorful commentary.

Jason adds Hey you became an English teacher You introduced kids to Shakespeare George Orwell and the written word. My son loved your John Bunyan's Pilgrim's Progress book reading you did through the summer. K. Coughs To be or not to be that is the question? I guess in a few hours I will fall into the Not to be category.

Steve says Ah never Not to be. The answer is always To Be K. We have an eternal soul next step is Heaven, and the real To Be begins and who knows after that.

Jamie says, "We will take good care of your wife when you are gone." K whispers, "You will make sure she remarries, I don't want her to be alone for long." Reed adds Hey we will put up flyers and start looking tomorrow. Karl replies No don't rush it, let her greave a bit and then let her get on with her life. Churchill consoles You fought it all the way K. The doctors have learned so much about cancer since you began fighting it. They will be able to be that much closer to a cure for-. K. struggles with saying My son, God I hope they get a cure for him. "K. has a son?"

One by one we take our turns with him alone and when it is my turn. Thanks for telling the guys I had cancer Max. And he begins to fade. At The Funeral Reed sings Death Ain't No Big Deal.

# CHAPTER THIRTY-THREE
## "WE ARE STILL HERE"

August Tuesday 20, 2002 still in early morning's twilight I wake up on the ride.

The Mystery Man has the drugs at a warehouse.

Pete gets the location on satellite. Cars are starting to move they are packing up and getting ready to move out. Paul calls up a friend on his cell phone. Yeah, Indy I need you to put on your Blue Bomber union suit and do some hit and run for us. Oh, we found the Mystery Man guess who it is.

Jake Hammer. Jack is taking it hard. Pete is sending you the location to your Gauntlet.

You know slash tires set off explosions stuff like that, slow them down we are on the way there, it will be a few. Thanks buddy I owe yah.

Max takes another cat nap on the ride there.. Blue Bomber Mag transports to the warehouse. With his skills he can silently move through the night. His scenes adapted he is a shadow the boogie man the bump in the night all rolled into one. He sets off an explosion! The sound waves energize him, and he runs like lightning with a knife in hand he slashes tires! Throws grenades and then Explosion another energy boost! The guards can't get a bead on him one second, he is there the next? The Mystery Man calls out What is happening out there? Talk to me!

"October Two Thousand One" I wake up in Chicago and it goes through my mind.

Mrs. Horton's voice You have burdens of your own Max. It was The Devil that told those Bad men to put that girl in the trunk of the car The Devil himself. Yeah, but it was I who pulled the trigger that killed the driver, and the bullet went through the driver's head and through the backseat and through the hostage. Next time shoot the engine first let the car roll and shoot the driver from behind the car. It will stop before it comes to anyone's danger. I got a call on my phone. Max our Hostage case just got hot again!

The day unfolds just like I lived it. When asked Are you up to this Faraday?

I say I am the only one who can do this right Chief. We found them at a rundown apartment building. We all hear the engine revving up! I pick up my rifle and say I can't make the shot from here and I run and yell back This is my shot nobody takes it but me!

I get into a new location in front of the car as it charges! This time I shot the engine first! The car rolls right by me, and I shoot the driver from behind the car! And just like Mrs. Horton said It will stop before it comes to anyone's danger. I yell "The Hostage she is in the trunk!" The Chief comes by me as they get the girl out of the car. Max if you shot from up there you could've? I know Chief I know. How? Divine intervention.

I got off duty and I look for Kate Dent at The University of Chicago. She was an English lit teacher and still is as far as I know. I find her from across the campus. It has been so long since I have seen her when we last spoke in Ninety-eight. I walk up to her, and she stares at me with longing tearful eyes. I ask, "Any chance you and me could go somewhere and talk." She swallows down a lump in her throat and says I have no real plans for dinner. She asks, "How have you been doing you look great?"

I tell her Oh I guess I can say I have had my moments. Right now, I am on The Chicago P.D. and you? She says Back and forth between here and Colorado. The university agrees with me, but my heart is still in Colorado.

I remind her "You used to say to me My heart is with you." She whispers I used to say a lot of things Max.

"That sounded cold." We go to a nice restaurant and sit down near a TV and the news comes on about the kidnapping and the hero marksman who took out the kidnapper. "Officer Max Faraday" Kate stares at me and says I have been praying for that little girl and you saved her.

I say Yeah Thank God I was at the right place at the right time.

Kate cries a bit and says "When you were shot I gave you an ultimatum, you either quit the force or the engagement is off." Yeah, I remember.

If you had done what I asked that little girl and how many others could be dead now.

I whisper That is a strong possibility. Thank you for. She tears up and I hold her hand and I say, "You are welcome." After dinner we talk, and I feel the urge to sit down at the piano and I play-

"Say you need me"
I've been alone and put up on a shelf.
Wondered if you've been with someone else.
I've been living on just a vague memory.
So please.
Say you need some company.
Say you need a friend and together we can set each other free.
Say you need shelter from the storm.
 Say you need to be kept safe and warm.
Say you need say you need me.
 I've been burdened with responsibilities.
Filling shoes that weren't meant for me.
Wondering if I took right path for the wrong.
For the future I cannot see.
So please
Say you need some company.
Say you need a friend and together we can set each other free.

Say you need shelter from the storm.
 Say you need to be kept safe and warm.
Say you need say you need me.
I've learned through fiction and reality.
The future is written in pencil and the past is written ink you see.
I don't know if this song makes any sense.
Maybe it will remind you of me.
So please.
Say you need some company.
Say you need a friend and together we can set each other free.
Say you need shelter from the storm.
 Say you need to be kept safe and warm.
Say you need say you need me.

She whispers tenderly, "You have not talked to me since you were shot?" I kinda thought you needed some space and if you wanted to talk, you could make some contact with me. I may have moved but I always left a forwarding address and phone number.

She says I needed the time to be alone I guess Max. So why did you come look me up?

I guess if I can get almost run down and shot at, I guess I can risk you telling me to go to Hell or I still think about you from time to time at worst you could say let's be friends.

Would just being friends be the worst? Shoot me now and get it over with.

She smiles saying I still think about you from time to time. I say I think there is a heartbeat.

We talked a little more and she handed me a picture of a boy about two years old.

So, you already have someone? She says My son. His name is Max.

My heart stops. After you were shot, and we did not talk, I found out I was pregnant.

In shock I stammer You could have told me Kate. Would you quit the force? I was not given a choice. Would you have quit your so-called secret life?

Silence.

She continues, "Well at the time I could not just wait by the phone and receive the message 'We regret to inform you, your husband is dead.' So, with the help of my parents, I raised Max by myself."

I ask, "So how is Father Fruit and Mother Nuts doing? Max that is just it you hate my parents."

Hate is such a strong word Kate, loath is a bit more like it. She gets up and walks away.

Damn I really let my tongue fly.

Bridge sits down and says, "Well she will be back she just needed to cool off."

I ask How could she keep that kind of information from me? Bridge asks, "And you did not keep information from her? Remember Max in The Age of The Ice Soldiers you were injured and as fate had it, she gave you, her heart.

But she wouldn't remember that?

A whisper of alternate futures memory can be gleaned from mortal man or woman.

They can come as a dream, a sensation of simple clarity. You think you are just limited sight taste touch smell and sound. You have a spirit and a soul they have scenes too.

Your two souls fulfill each other Max she is a bit more order and you are a bit more chaos. In another time and place You shared a heart for God's sake.

Is it right for me to ask her to risk her heart again?

Bridge gives a fatherly smile and says She did what she did because at the time it was for the best. Anyone who says different has not lived in her or your shoes. Or have not been asked to endure what you have been asked to endure.

A fresh start. Yes, Max, a fresh start from here on out use what you have been given to influence your future.

Ask God to guide you. He knows the end result. He would like to share with you some wisdom to help you along the way. Because if you don't, he will let you go your own way.

That is why it is called free will.

I bow my head to consider what Bridge has told me. And it does not take long, and she returns.

She cried her tears and said "As opposite as we are Max, I always knew where you stood."

I tell her "A bullet can scare people a bit, I didn't even tell my mom that I have been shot at." She asks Max if we grow back together what kind of life do you think we would have?

I pause then I reply I don't know Kate. I would rather do it with you. Then go on and do it without you. And she smiles I don't know Max. I would rather do it with you.

Then go on and do it without you. We talk late into the night till they close the restaurant.

I come back to my apartment early Saturday morning and I feel the need to write myself a message on the wall with red ink. Mafia crimes and connections. Locations of hide outs stuff I found out after the crimes were committed. With my photographic mind I have a lot of details. I don't know when or if I'll have my memories sent back in time again. With Kate I felt the need to say what I needed to say and thank God I did. I have a son and I pray we just might have a chance to set things right again. This message on my wall is another thing I feel I need to do. I'll go to bed here and I don't know what my path will be when I wake up. This Writing on the wall may set myself in the right direction.

On Saturday morning I am still writing. I order in Pizza and hot coffee I have to stay awake a little longer. I am exhausted it is Sunday morning The sun is about to rise, and I go to bed.

# CHAPTER THIRTY-FOUR
## "SHOCK AND AWE"

August 20, 2002, Morning comes.

"When Fat kids and Geeks or nerds get together there will be a Revolution."

As we arrive, we see on the satellite The tires are slashed explosions are going off! They Ain't going nowhere. We arrived at the convoy of cars and motorcycles and pickups and a dead stock semi, begin circling the warehouse. Paul and Paul jr. and Pete set up The Trebuchet. I say, "Me and Steve, Adam John Henry will go in first picking targets and taking prisoners..." The FBI agents say We are coming. Jack demands He is my brother I am going in too! You are in no condition! He tried to kill Missy and threatened my friends! I shook my head and Steve handed him a gun.

Paul Jr. loads The Trebuchet with a skid steer loader. Jason asks Ah Paul this cow is dead and all right? Paul replies Yeah. How come there is steam coming from its nose?

Worms or maggots or something crawling around inside? Paul replies, "You may be dead, but if you lay in the sun a few days you can take on a life of your own."

Reed says Oh Paul that thing is about to bloat and explode! Paul just chuckles.

With GPS Pete factors in estimated weight and distance for the first target and has the weights adjusted accordingly. The FBI agent says You can't do that you will disturb evidence!

Paul replies Let's see Evidence a CIA agent screwed with everyone's files to erase a man from existing. Evidence that you let the ball drop and let drug smugglers run the countryside. Evidence that a small-town bank was money laundering millions of dollars under your nose. Evidence......

Fine, do whatever you want.

Paul gets on his cell phone. Hello Mystery Man or should I say Jake guess who this is?

Jake wonders How did you get my number? Well, you are running out of trusted friends who give a damn about your sorry ass.

Who is this?

As Paul talks to the Mystery Man, we start bringing in the so-called guards / deserters with hand cuffs. "They have been shaken up thanks to Blue Bomber and did not give us a fight."

Paul Chapel the guy who knocked your sorry ass down a flight of stairs remember.

Oh, I just got to tell you your guards tried to make a run for it, and they are tied up at the moment. You would be wise to give up now.

Jake yells Well come on in Paul I am going to enjoy kicking your ass!

Paul gives the signal, and they launch the first dead cow! First cow strikes terror at the front door. Splatter! And the carcass goes through what is left of the door!

The FBI nods. Paul murmurs I am going Medieval on his ass.

They all take turns looking at it through the night seeing scope. The warehouse comes to life with sirens and spotlights! Gunfire! Jason Yells Paul, I think you got their attention!

Reed yells Get down they are shooting at us! The Second cow goes over the warehouse and takes out the power poll! Sparks go off and the sizzle of dead cow flesh can be smelt in the warehouse because the wind is right. Everything goes dark! No backup generator.

The FBI agent says Oh that is destruction of property! Paul shows him the printout of the local power company stating this complex is off the grid. My guess somebody paid a bribe, and they hooked them up. Me and Steve have night vision high powered rifles and start picking off their gunmen. Wounding them not shooting to kill who are shooting randomly from the warehouse.

Third cow goes through the skylight and lands on the drugs and money pile!

The FBI points a finger and Paul says Hey that was my last cow. You don't say anything, and I won't say nothing.

The sun comes up. I contacted Paul by cell phone I said everything is quiet. Ok we are going in. When all the clear flares go off then Churchill and Dan and Mr. Copper can come in for first aid. John Henry Watson, Chief Tom, Steve, Adam, Jack, Reed, Mr. Cooper, Jason, Rabbi Burney, Plus militia. As we walk in, we have people surrendering left and right. Handing over weapons and laying down before us. Some are going to need a bath, blood splattered from dead cows and the shock of it all. "I will never eat dairy again."

A few take pot shots at us too at this point nobody is worrying about wounding it is up close and personal. A gun fight begins! Everyone finds shelter quickly! Steve takes a shot and hits a gunman up on a catwalk! Everyone takes turns at shooting each other but tactics pay for themselves. The sun comes up through the clouds and blinds them in that moment we shoot and don't hold back! In the silence The FBI yelled "Get on the ground now! You are under arrest! Reed is out in the open and I see someone about to shoot."

I grit my teeth and say Put it down Badger I am so tempted to pull the trigger.

His Bravado says, "You don't know who you are dealing with Max. I say Titus and Graves are on their way." He drops his gun.

A voice from my past yells You took my brother away from me! He points his gun at me Jake Hammer The Mystery Man. I reply I did not take your brother away from you. You threw him to the wolves every chance you got!

Jake yells, "I took care of my brother!!" Bang!

Jack fired his gun. I have had enough of your lies! You left me long, long ago to waste in the wind. Jake yells with a dying breath He got me arrested He! Bang Shut up! He was a friend when I had none! He gave friendship when I had none! Paul Steve Churchill Dan Jamie Jason and Adam are my brothers you are nothing to me Jake.

Jake has nothing to lose so he points his gun at me and pulls the trigger. Click.

Jack fires at the same time and shoots his brother.

I yell Churchill Dan Get IN HERE!

The others and the FBI round up The smugglers. First Aid is all they needed.

But Jake. Lay dying on the floor. Jack comes to his side and says to me Jake was going to kill you Max. I picked up Jake's gun and removed the empty clip from the gun. Jake didn't know his gun was empty, but I did. Jake says in his dying words Jack I am sorry I am sorry..........

It does not take long, and Titus and Graves show up. Jake's body is not even cold, and they are arguing who has jurisdiction over the case FBI or CIA? Let them fight it out, I don't care. Jack is sedated killing your own brother has hit him to the core. I am just tired.

# CHAPTER THIRTY-FIVE

## "Here we go again"

Here we go again Friday July 12, 2002 I awaken at my Mother's and Dale Chapel's Home. Mom asks Max are you all right? I look at the calendar Friday July 12, 2002.

I see the pictures of my children and Kate. Yeah mom I just had the strangest dream. "But was it a dream?" I look outside and there is my old Chicago patrol car.

Well get dressed and I'll have breakfast ready for you. As I go to the bathroom I look at the mirror and my scar on my arm is gone? I eat my breakfast and mom and I talk mother and son stuff. She knows about Kate and the kids in witness protection, and she says We will get through this.

I give her a hug and I go out and I stop at a pay phone. I get on the phone and call my FBI friend in Chicago. I am a concerned citizen. You have a safe deposit box "1865G" with some information in it, you need to get it now. Who is this?

I then go for a drive in the country. I come to what I called the safe house or Paul's deer hunting shack. And I come to a wall in the basement and I find the hidden switch to the "Safe house" is "Selah H.Q." As I enter it is all coming back to me. Max Faraday Black Phoenix and Selah are finally one mind. I pick up my Gauntlet and turn it on and it scans me. How may I be of Service Max? Call Paul we have to talk. It does not take Paul long to come to the safe house. There are no words that need to be spoken he is one of my best friends and we are back together again. We open arms and give each other a hug.

Paul with tears says I knew you were too good to forget who you were. I say I could not have done it without you. You know more about this contraption than I do.

I need to see if the FBI found my evidence. Paul wonders Evidence?

Yeah I have been having a secret investigation into the Mafia. A concerned citizen slips them evidence under the table and it keeps me and Kate in the clear. I want to see if they jumped on it yet. And Paul tunes in the Magnetic N-space monitor. This device allows us to monitor anywhere in the world via a 3-D picture. If you have bugs or listening devices you can have sound too. Me and Paul watch as the FBI storm the Mafia complex. I say to Paul with clinched teeth There is a part of me that would love to take them down personally as Selah. Paul reminds me Yeah you do that and Titus will hunt you down and The WTC might have a war on our hands to defend you. I shake my head saying He still has an order on me if Selah or Black Phoenix returns so what now? One step at a time Max, One step at a time.

We catch Churchill leaving the hospital for lunch. Big Paul yells from my car Max is home THE ANTI BULLY IS BACK! Come on Churchill you don't have anything to do, you can come with me and Big Paul. He asks with a stunned look on his face What are you two doing? Trying to solve a mystery. last night I went out to play Basket ball at the park as I walked from Mom's to the park I saw a tow truck leave Howard's Garage it went east and about an hour later it came back through town with a car with a smashed up front end. So? The tow truck did not have it's emergency lights on. And did not stop at the garage. Paul adds Howard's junk yard? Possible. As I was driving into town, I noticed a dead dear along the side of the road. Churchill adds Yeah, they are an eye soar aren't they.

How much you wanna bet the dear the driver hit could still be alongside the road.

Churchill scratches his chin whispering Or human? I just heard somebody hit the Midnight Stealth Jogger, Jason is taking pretty hard. In that case it could be murder.

Churchill reluctantly gets in the back. We go east of town and take it easy going down the highway and then north on Deer Crossing Alley Valley Highway until we see a dead deer and piece of earth carved out of a ditch. Paul opens his mouth Well that's a Dead dear that's what we are looking for. I open the trunk to put on rubber gloves and say Don't touch anything until you put on the gloves. This is a crime scene here treat it as such.

Snap goes on Paul's glove he says Cool. The good doctor says Crime scene don't you mean disturbing a crime scene? Before I have a chance to explain, Big Paul says. "Max does not trust the Cavanaugh City Cops because if they were doing their duty they should have pulled The Tow truck over for not having their emergency lights on. But they didn't so they are in on it right Max." I say, "You have been paying attention." Hey, I might look dumb, but I am not. I never. Paul winks at me with a smile, and I don't have to explain.

So, you think the city cops are in on it, what about Carter County Police? I shrug my shoulders saying Don't know yet. Doctor, I need a tissue sample of the deer. Give me an educated guess about how long it's been dead. Churchill also takes pictures of the scene.

Big Paul yells Hey I found a bloody Bandanna! I walk over to see it yeah it is a bandanna. Churchill takes a picture. Bag it is or could be the drivers. Big Paul mutters Or what is left of him. I look at Paul? Hey, I listen to Tom Clancy and Dean Kuntz and other mystery books on tape in The Tractor and when I am painting there are ways to get rid of a body.

I smile because I should know.

Get the glass and paint chips we will need them to compare when we find the car.

Big Paul mutters Ah that had to be a ten point or at least a twelve-point buck!

Churchill declares You are crying because there is a dead dear?

Paul yells back Well if The Midnight Stealth Jogger that wears nothing but a black sweat suit you would say he was stupid son of a-. The good doctor stops him by saying Only if I was drinking, I try not to swear when I am sober.

I begin to make a plaster cast of the tire tread left on the ground alongside the road.

Churchill adds guessing This car had to be going seventy-five ninety or even a hundred to do this kind of damage to a dear and the car? What kind of hurry was this guy in?

Big Paul mutters Late for his own funeral my guess. Meaning?

Big Paul explains Jamie has been on an anti-drug mission with the kids when that junior high school boy overdosed. Churchill adds Yeah, he got a list from The FBI's Most Wanted of possible people to look for and he spotted one. It was a driver, I think.

Big Paul Yeah it happened a few months ago Jamie spotted the guy in the diner.

The guy was eating at the diner, he calls the cops, and a Cavanaugh City rookie arrests him. The Drug runner is sent to prison Jamie is the local hero. Drug runner gets killed in prison Jamie is silent. I ask "And the arresting officer?" Moves out of the area never to be heard from again.

We are going to need to cut that bloody bandanna up I have a couple places we can send it to. Maybe the driver was a sex offender, and they might have his DNA on file.

Big Paul yells Hey I found a hubcap must of come off from when the car hit with the deer!

I ran over to look at it and I saw fingerprints and double check to make sure Paul still has his gloves on. In the excitement I hugged him. This could be a big key to this mystery.

Churchill says Hey here is a cigarette pack. Bag it we will keep and dust it for prints.

Churchill asks, "Where are you staying?" I guess I am staying with my mom. Churchill adds I know you can stay in my guest room. I can use the company. As Big Paul searches the ground for broken glass and paint chips I say to Churchill and you and me we can find out where when the Alcoholics A. meet. You and me need to make an appointment.

We leave the crime scene and come back to town, I drive past The Hospital and Churchill.

Churchill looks at me. I say Dan can take care of the hospital Selah needs you.

Churchill's eyes goes big whispering You remember? Yeah, I remember, and a few other things. Do me a favor and Call Steve and Adam and Jason, Pete and Reed tell them we will meet them at Duke's farm. Churchill asks, "And why are we going there?"

I say, "To find the body of course." Paul asks, "What body? The body of the driver."

Churchill and Paul get on their cell phones. I call Father Michaels and Marcus my Dad.

We all converge at The Compost pile. Duke gets off the bike and Paul says You gotta see this. And what we see it is a human body half buried in the compost pile..

I open the trunk getting out the kit and put on the gloves the body is fresh and had not a chance to decompose, I tell them my guess is this is our missing man.

Paul whispers Ah Max you think this is who I think it is? I get tweezers pulling a piece of bandanna out of his nose and I say I think we have a match.

Churchill asks Duke what is this? Duke says Compost, I put my dead cows and old feed when it goes bad out here. Ah Duke there are dead cows in here? Hate to see them die, but they make good compost. Jokingly Jason asks, "You didn't put this guy in here did you?"

Duke says No this is three-year-old shit, this poor son of a bitch is too fresh. If I was to bury him I would have put him over there, where the fresh shit is. Paul asks me, "Who do we call on this? I mean if this got out, we would stir up something." Yeah, I would like to keep the Mystery Man thinking we are just spinning our wheels if we can?

I'll make a call to The FBI I have a contact in the Michigan office. Duke asks What is going on? We give Duke the long and short of it. After explaining the situation Duke says Damn.

"Well, Somebody should do something, they leave dead deer all over on the highway."

Duke leaves us.

And Paul says Max you act like you have been here before what gives?

I am living what is called A Second Time Around. In an alternate past or future Wendy Jimmy my mom and Marcus were not alive. And somebody tried to threaten Jamie by almost killing his little girl. I rescued her and I was hit by a car and I was in a coma.

I awoke in Seventy-eight my adult mind my experiences were in my fourteen year old body. Steve says That can't be?

Father Michaels says Believe it son I was there.

Marcus adds Max saved my life when the bank was robbed.

I explain By the grace of God During that time I changed some things for the better. When I went to sleep in the past I would wake up in the present. For me it was the present to the past after I recovered from the coma I became a Cavanaugh County Police Officer and began an investigation into the drug smuggling. I guess tonight after the reunion they are going to attack Jamie again. I intend to be there. Churchill adds I'll go back to the hospital if anyone asks, I'll say I took an early lunch break. Then it is agreed none of us says a thing about the body.

What are you going to do Max?

I'll call the FBI and The CIA and then I am going to see a Rabbi about some money.

Starting over again Since I pretty much lost everything thanks to my Mafia investigation. I have been doing everything on a cash basis. Kate and the kids have been living on family charity thanks to Uncle Sherman and her parents. The Mafia got involved when I was working on an underground gambling network in Chicago. I had a solid case and then they destroyed my name and reputation trying to get me to back off. I was told by my old partner to drop it now Max. I didn't drop it besides my gambling debt that I was just recovering from, they destroyed my name and reputation. In the end We shut down the Mafia's racket for a while. I still have a bullet with my name on it and my picture on a dart board. All I can say is get in line. "I have a family now?" Things change.

Do not put all your eggs in one basket. A phrase I have used over the years. Religiously I have been sending money to "Abba" Rabbi Hyman It started with The Rainy-day fund and the found money in the lawnmower and when Grant retired from the bank Abba was given the account. Kate is a college English teacher and has her own money. And I just live in her house or apartment. She likes the independence. "It is all coming back to me."

I am not the money miser Marcus was. Just give me my Pizza and pop money and pay my payments and tithe and what is leftover send to Abba. I don't want my friends in Chicago to send money to John Doe via Western Union in Cavanaugh City. That is right just say Max Faraday and red flags go up and it is What money where did it go? Please somebody give me a terrorist to shoot. That I can handle, finances internet commerce telephone identity fraud I am screwed.

I come to Hyman, Hyman and Hyman. Burney greets me Max hi! Burney is Abba here?

Burney asks, "What is the problem?"

I tell him I am tired of dealing with this on my own, I need to talk to Abba.

Burney says to his secretary Hold my calls or take messages. I am taken back to the Study of Rabbi Hyman. Max! How is The Christian son I always wanted? I could be better.

Tell Abba and I will make it better. I tell the whole sorted details. So, you started gambling again and these Mafia destroyed your finances? Everything but what you have kept for me here.

Abba mutters, "We had a hacker try to break in about that time. Almost crashed what Burney calls a firewall?" Oh no. I called a few favors, and it was taken care of no need to worry your money is safe with us my child. Would you like to see it? Sure, it has been a while. Burney says I'll print it up. As he leaves Abba reaches out his hand and says in Hebrew "You are one of my sons and nobody messes with one of my boys."

"Abba these people are dangerous" "The danger is to let them win and go unchallenged an eye for an eye." I know what you did in Israel I have friends they tell me things.

We have a few options. "Now you know where I got that We have a few options."

I have a few favors I can use let me call them in and we can clear your name.

Burney comes back saying Whoa here you go. And I look at it I am rich. How? Don't tell me I am not a money manager it will just go over my head. You had better talk to Rachel, she can help you find a nice home, somewhere in the country perhaps. For you Kate and the kids. I have been looking at The Trans Am over at Howard's. But that will take cash.

Abba says I'll get you cash. And we will get you a phone, a cell phone at least and a mailing address, a P.O. Box now and they will not bother you because you are one of my children. And you will spend the next Sabbath with us. I can't say no to that.

I call Kate at Uncle Sherman's Camp. Hello Kate? She is ecstatic Max it is incredible The FBI just gave us the good news! I tell her, "Honey, I want to start off fresh I want you and the kids to come home with me to Cavanaugh City."

Speechless she says Max I don't know what to say?

I plead, "Please I want to give our family a fresh start. Is there any chance you could get the kids and be here tonight. I want to show you off at my reunion." Kate thinks about it Well if I leave right now. Uncle Sherman has been wanting to see you; I'll ask him and let you know by calling your mom.

I stopped at Howard's Car Sales and Garage. I get out of my cruiser and go over to the Trans AM and look at the price. I can afford it thanks to The Hymans. But I also know how to deal with it too. I walk into the Garage, and I see a Mechanic under a car and ask Jack is that you?

Jack asks Yeah who wants to know? It is me, Max. I just wanted to-. He rolls from underneath the car and says Max it is so good to see you. I say I hope you can come to the reunion.

Jack replies No you don't, I haven't been myself since.

I tell him Yeah, I can imagine I miss Ruth Leanne, it does not help to say things happen.

Jack dusts himself off saying "So what can I do for you? I want to know a little about the Trans Am." Oh I can help you there she is just waiting to run wild if somebody can give her a good home that is. I ask, "Did you do work on it?" Yeah, some fiberglass but hey she is all there.

Mr. Howard comes out of his office. Jack, aren't you supposed to be doing a Transmission? Yes Mr. Howard I was just talking to my good friend Max Faraday because the Trans Am is such a great deal. Mr. Howard says Well get back to the Garage. Max, it is a surprise to see you around.

I tell him I would like to buy the Trans Am, but I feel it is a bit much. I take out a pad and write out my amount and show it to Mr. Howard. Come on Max did you bang your head on something? And he writes an amount. What about the extras, what can you give me? Well, you are a friend, and this car has been sitting here waiting for you to come along if you can get the money today I can throw in under coating and that three oil changes.

I will write a new amount and say how about this amount. He bites his lip saying if you can get me the money today "I mean cash" we have a deal. And I shake his hand it is cold and clammy.

I get back in my cruiser and head to The Hymans. Abba says Max I need to talk to you, and he motions me back to his office. What did you do to piss off the Mafia?

I did not give up in my investigation. What happened? I tell the story and Burney says Nobody messes with my little brother. Burney is just a couple months older than me but ever since Abba has called me one of his sons, he has never been jealous.

Ever since we started getting your name cleared things have been happening.

We have been attacked by someone on the net, so I called in some help.

Burney waves me back to the computer room and Pete is going at it like a nerd possessed.

Pete looks up and says Max you have some people who don't like you very much.

"Sometimes you are better judged by your enemies than your friends."

Pete replies, "Well a number of them have computers, they don't like you. Abba adds If they want a fight we will give them a fight." Pete smiles saying Oh I can give them a fight, the nice thing about technology it can be the great equalizer. "The digital battle ground." I have just about all of them running for the hills. Amazed at what all Pete can do I say Pete have you given them a good scare? Oh yeah! Pete, tell them to back off and leave me alone. Just restore what is mine. I want justice not vengeance. Mess with me again and I will have vengeance.. Can you do that. Sure Max.

He almost looked sad. I think he really wanted to bite someone's head off. Thanks Pete.

Oh, by the way could you stop over at Faraday Savings and Loan my Dad needs you to look into something. Pete winks at me and asks, "Is this part of your new investigation?"

FBI Agent Anderson will be here in a few. Abba asks, "So what are you going to do now?"

I am going to be a pillar in the community. And go to Gambling A. & Alcoholics A.

I guess if you can get my finances straightened out, I'll call my chief in Chicago and tell him I am staying. Oh, that reminds me I was at Howard's and I got a great price on the Trans Am. I handed over the memo pad to Abba. Abba says Ah I can get a better deal let me make some calls.

I tell Abba No Howard's is a part of my investigation this gives me an excuse to snoop around. Burney adds, "You know he has built that new show room and expanded the garage. Where does he get money when we are in a bit of recession?"

The Trans AM "MAXIMUM II" Mr. Howard takes the money and asks no questions?

I walked around the garage there is a map of the counties that the garage serves. Jack comes by and says You are getting the Trans Am? I say Yeah. He bends his head down and shakes his head as if he is ashamed of me? What is the matter? You are a cop right. Right? Where would an honest cop get money to buy a Trans Am? I have invested wisely. It has added up over the years. With a smile Jack says You got a cool car boy. He high fives me! Damn Howard thinks you are into drugs. I wink whispering Let him think that if he wants. Tell me about this map. Jack explains Oh that is our map of crashes that we have towed cars into the garage. Deer accidents? Yeah. Not too many around Deer Crossing Alley Valley Highway? Only a jackass would hit a deer around here, everyone knows you don't go fast through there. I mention But you don't have a listing for July 11 last night is there? No why? Mr. Howard comes by and brings me paperwork and smiles from ear to ear.

I say to Jack you and me we gotta talk. Howard asks, "What do you want us to do with your piece of crap there?" Oh, I'll take it with me. Really so you are staying?

Yeah, I am thinking about joining the Carter County Police Force. Mr. Howard replies, "Well I feel safer already."

By the way Jack you need a date for tonight. A date tonight? Yeah the 1982 20th High School reunion. Why don't you ask Missy Chambers. Jack asks, "How did you know I was seeing her? My Mom gets all the gossip." I don't know? Come on Jack. Ok but you are going to have to pick us up I can't drive any more.

I say that is cool My wife should be coming home and be here tonight we will double date.

Later I find Reed's wife at the church. It takes a moment for her to recognize me.

Ah Max, it is good to see you. If you are looking for Reed, he is still on duty.

I told her I came here to see you. She asks, "What about?" I tell her I don't know how this prophetic stuff works. At this moment there is no thus sayeth The Lord. All I can say is you have been holding back information on Reed about your first child, your son you put up for adoption.

I think you should invite the family up or you should go there and introduce Reed to him.

The boy has some issues, and you at least need to be a big sister to him. Reed, he loves you and he will love you through it. She asks, "How? I hand her the song that Reed had written and say It is my handwriting but Reed wrote it." "She was born in the Bible belt."

Debby tears up Prophesying You have come full circle. This is a day of new beginnings Max. For all of us. The rest of the time I spent with her is privet.

Kate arrives with the kids. I pick them up and I can hardly contain my joy. I don't know if this separation has been harder on me or the kids. Kate says Can I get in on the hug.

I look off in the distance and mom and Uncle Sherman watch us from a distance and then I see Marcus's limo drive up and he gets out. I motion them to join in the love fest.

CLASS OF 1982 The First to greet me is Churchill Smith Dr. MD. How you doing Max?

I look at my wife and say Good can't complain, and you? Churchill asks Hey Jack how you doing? Good Doctor. And the kids? Jack says I wish I could have them at my home but someday. Churchill puts his drink down my guess looking at Jack and knowing what all he has gone through it sobers him up. Jack is quiet he may feel out of place, I want him here, he belongs here.

Churchill says The Hospital is growing under my tutelage; we are going to have five new specialties. For the public. The Hospital in Carter City is barely even basic. Don't even deliver babies anymore. I ask How come the Hospitals never merged Carter City is a bigger town than Cavanaugh City? "The room goes silent in a Hush."

Churchill looks me in the eye, and says Because They Are Carter City we Are Cavanaugh City there is a big difference you would be well to remember that. I can hear Big Paul in the Background saying Damn right.

Hey Max! Big Paul & Marcy! How are you doing? Paul starts off with Farming has its ups and downs, but life is a Roller Coaster. I ask How many kids are you two up too? Paul says Last time I was here it was nine? Well, you have been gone a while we are up to ten. Our oldest is getting ready for The Air Force. I look at Marcy she is four feet five if that, and Big Paul is well Big Paul, and the word How? Just comes out. Paul replies, "Well Dr. Churchill is working on a Zipper, so we don't need a C Section again."

"I ponder Again?" I look at Kate and say You and me we gotta get busy if we want to catch up. She slugs me in the ribs.

Paul says See yah Max I gotta talk to Reed about some Organic smoked Pork he wanted to buy.

I see Candy Churchill's separated-wife I ask So what have you been doing? She says If you can believe it, I am a School Teacher 8th Grade English. Kate says Oh I teach college English.

Candy says Well you and me we have to talk. Kate has found a friend.

Candy sees Missy and mentions I have been doing my best to live up to K. Ray C. in a way he has left a legacy here. And they hug.

I see Dan Cottager. How are you doing? Dan explains Churchill is keeping us busy at the hospital.

He is bringing in Specialists. We are becoming our own little Mayo Clinic. Good old Churchill. Good to see you Max.

From across the room, I see Jason. You see Mr. Hyman Rabbi Hyman threw a Bar Mitzvah party for his son Burney. It was a Swimming Party. And Jason was not allowed to go, because it was an overnight party, and he did not keep his grades up, or something. So, he decided to take his chances, and went anyway. Figuring I'll get grounded for a month tops. His parents put two and two together and figured out what he did.

They even called the Hotel to call Mr. Hyman and make sure he was not in a ditch somewhere dead or something. He was there at the party alright and So was I, but I had permission, and I was on the Honor Roll for a change.

While he was gone His Father took down all the posters in his room and painted the walls white. Then with a black marker marked off every day till his eighteenth birthday in July "sometimes" I think. When He got home his father said Son when you turn eighteen you are out of the house. He was pale white for over a week. I have to say it shook him up in a good way. Jason, How are you doing? Great Max! You look wonderful then a Hug.

Jason asked, "I hear you beat some kids out of Thirty bucks." Guilty as charged.

One of those kids was my kid Danny, thanks now I have to hear "Dad I gotta have Thirty bucks." Laughter! What are you doing? I Got tired with The computer game business so I sold it to Ice Works and that kind of stuff is a hobby now. Last couple years I did what my dad did and now I am a Gym Teacher can't you tell? Jason is a bit thick and has a receding hairline. No, I can't.

Connie Mack Former High School and College Basketball Star Modeling Now Gym Teacher. Just Laughs! Jason says That is not funny Connie!

Burney Hyman comes over opens his arms and gives me a big hug. Good to see you!

What are you doing Hyman? He hands me his card Burney Hyman Rabbi and Tax Management. Hey there is Candy I gotta talk to her about her Cottage Industry.

I saw Reed Jackson and asked how you doing? He says Not bad you Wild Man!

I remind him Watch it Reed I am packing heat. I showed him my gun.

You and me have to get together and talk about the old days!

Nice talking to you.

Jason comes by and says For a Fire Fighter he starts more fires than he puts out. Poke to the ribs Chuckle.

I see Wendy and she waves to me. Wendy is Jimmy Thomson's wife. Jimmy Thomson is like a brother. And runs the home schools and the home for foster kids. Wendy is a high school counselor and helps at her Mother's Foster Care.

I see that Joe and his wife Rhonda are here too. They are at the other side of the room and I salute Joe. Me and Joe went to Marine Boot camp together. He drives Semi trucks now for Shurlow Trucking.

Steve Pearson & Kathy Pearson They were the happy couple. High school sweethearts Married shortly after college. When his Psychology practice took off and his self-help books became bestsellers His son was born something happened to Steve. Home Hearth, his own creation started taking more of his time. He was helping people by the hundreds and then by the thousands in seminars, books were selling he did the talk shows and then a radio show of his own. Kathy was his wife and manager and she could see all the good he was doing. And after years of being the silent wife and partner. She gave him a way out to leave their marriage and Steve took it. Kathy came home to Cavanaugh City to raise their son and then she started going to school to school to become a lawyer. Now she is district Attorney for Carter County, and she plans for Commissioner of Carter County.

As for Steve, Home Hearth as before mentioned has become a bit of an empire and Steve is still playing Monopoly. Steve sees me and puts out his hands and we walk towards each other and then run and give each other a hug! I missed you Max! And he whispers into my ear and I miss Selah too. Applause fills the room!

Then Adam comes in room and the room goes Silent. Adam was a detective in Seattle Washington who was sent to prison for a crime he did not commit. He was the marathon runner and long-distance jumper in high school. He was one of us, one of the guys?

But most of our small town believed the hype and no one has fully trusted him, a bad cop on the take reputation can do that. In our small-town prejudices exist. Steve asked him to come home to Cavanaugh City and help decorate his Home Hearth Homes. And as far as I know he is his main decorator and carpenter. Oh, here comes Reed Jackson, what is he going to say now?

Reed says Hey Cupid how you doing? And pats him on the back.

Adam sits down at a table and no one sits with him. Reed goes over and asks Is this seat taken? And then Steve and Kathy sit down with them. I see a chair waiting for me with Jamie, but I think I'll sit with Steve. The dinner was Ok. And I am amazed Reed did not say or tell a stupid dirty joke about pigs bad cops or anything? I ask Adam How did you get the name Cupid? Reed jumps to the answer He does the damnedest stunt with the bow and arrow. He can shoot a dime or even an Aspirin. Adam smiles in modesty. He is one Hell of a decorator. Adam smiles in modesty. Oh it is what I do. Steve adds He has designed and remodeled all The Home Hearth Homes.

I ponder the missing that are not here, and I ask without thinking to get an answer. Why does it take death to wake us up? Silence comes to our table and then. Reed says I think it is because until you have a dead body it is hard to get the point sometimes. I mean Jesus Died on the Cross and that got people's attention. And then he rose again and that really got people's attention.

A Silent pause in thought.

But maiming is good too. My Dad was a Son of a Bitch when he made that crack about homosexuals at a biker bar. Who knew? It is Amazing he is still alive. I mean he was paralyzed from the neck down when he woke up from the coma. He has his right arm, and he can get around in that electric chair now, and he is going places.

Kathy comments It was so good of her to take you in when your father- she pauses.

Reed says Bit off more than he could chew. She died shortly after I graduated from The Fireman Academy. Steve asks Show her the picture. Reed asks, "Of what?" Steve states of Your Grandma? Ok. Reed shows the picture.

Kathy whispers She looks like Elton John. Reed says Well she was British. A lot of those British women look like men when you get right down to it. Just look at that Dame Edna.

Kathy asks, "Where is your wife?"

Reed says She would have come tonight, but she had a revival meeting she was leading at the church. Adam adds, "My wife is doing the praise and worship music there too."

I ask, "Do you have any pictures?" Reed says Yeah and I have a new one of her and my baby three-year-old girl. Reed pulls out his wallet to show pictures.

I can just smile when I think about Reed and his wife and say When "Christ Taking Apart Anger Through Prayer" did the revival concert you two hit it off.

Reed adds Yeah, she has been knocking me upside the head ever since then, and I thank God every day. Yep, and she is Pentecostal and has the same hair problem as Jan Crouch.

Although I don't think it is a problem, I just think that when the fire of The Holy Spirit touches her, it gets her hair singed. As my good friend Ralph Shurlow says it You know there are some things, they really didn't teach us in Sunday school.

As the night goes on I think about the "Missing"

Karl Ray Chambers Memorial High school library.

I see the plaque with the date clearly now I guess there is no need for a blurry mystery.

A voice says I like the library I wish they had it built before I died. K?

Hi Max thanks for holding out till the end. We all have to go at some time and well it was my time.

I see his ghost I say you look good.

Karl continues Well this is an image that you can recognize, and I do look good too if I do say so myself. Life is funny and all we fight to live and to make a statement so that people might remember us. And when we die, they talk about legacy and all. When you are here eternity gives you the shock of a lifetime. How we are just a vapor and God is Eternal but the real answer to it all is we are eternal too we just don't know it or remember it. So, Heaven is a refresher course. Max, you are going to be a great father. Then again you were a mean tough mother to us all, Thank You. We'll have a good life.

I cry tears of joy and Ellen walks by and calmly says It is time to go. They are locking the doors as we speak. So, Kate takes her flower off her dress and sets it by the memorial.

And Ellen does like wise and others who have not gone home yet do so.

Welcome home Max they say as they walk by.

The parking lot is lit up and I see a sight and say Wow! It is Reed Jackson's Fire Captain's pickup! The door depicts a fire fighter twirling an axe above his head with one hand and with the other holding the fire hose and putting out the blazing painted flames at the front and hood of the truck. That is so cool! Reed says Yeah Big Paul did it the city is going to use the design on all our fire trucks. Big Paul adds I'll be doing it in my spare time this winter. Detailing cars is a good side job for me. Since Selah is in Hiatus. And Paul Winks at me.

We say our goodbyes and call it a night. I take Jack to his place and leave him there and drop Kate home with mom, I have places of my own I have to be.

Elsewhere

Jamie says I almost forgot we have to pick up the kids at The Babysitters.

And The Kids half asleep crawl in into the backseat and are strapped in. When they get back to Jamie's and his little girl gets out. And she bounces her ball up and down up and down until it slips from her grasps and rolls out the drive and into the street Jamie sees it in the mirror as he is just getting out of the seat. A car pulls out as the little girl goes from the driveway to the street to get her ball. The car steps on the gas! I spring into action And run after her! Jamie and Ellen are both fighting with their seatbelts! Damn you let me out of here!

Everything is in slow motion. I have her I pick her up and I jump into the air with her in my arms and do a flip with the car going fast beneath me. I gently land and say to her Go to your parents and stay down. The FBI arrive in full force and the car stops. Before Jamie and Ellen can see me I am gone.

I miss this life and going from place to place in the blink of an eye. The Warehouse.

There are no Trebuchet just FBI and CIA Agents. They receive word of the car being successfully stopped and guns and drugs were in the car. They begin to go in silently.

With my "Gauntlet" I calculate the structure and I go in first via transporter to watch from the inside. Badger is not here just Jake and his crew. I pull a pin on a smoke bomb with knockout gas, and they begin to fall. I am however immune to the gas and watch them fall one by one. As they bash the door down, I say You can put your guns down they are all out.

The agents ask Who are you? Take care of this one he is the Mystery Man and here are his original files. You will find he does not exist because CIA Agent Badger erased him from the records.

And I vanished.

Badger has been a bad boy. Titus and Graves are here to clean up the fine mess he made.

Wetworks is not Titus's specialty but sometimes he needs to get out of the office.

Bang!

I come home and I go to bed and kiss my wife goodnight. I say my prayers and I have an uneventful dream where I am walking up and down the halls of my old school in my underwear and I can't find my locker and I wake up.

To be continued in THE GENERATION GAP